ALSO BY ADAM LANGER

My Father's Bonus March

Ellington Boulevard

The Washington Story

Crossing California

The Thieves *of* Manhattan

The

Thieves

of

Manhattan

a ~~memoir~~ *novel*

Adam Langer

SPIEGEL & GRAU TRADE PAPERBACKS
New York • 2010

A Spiegel & Grau Trade Paperback Original

Published in the United States by Spiegel & Grau, an imprint of The Random House Publishing Group, a division of Random House, Inc., New York.

SPIEGEL & GRAU and Design is a registered trademark of Random House, Inc.

Library of Congress Cataloging-in-Publication Data
Langer, Adam.
The thieves of Manhattan: a novel / by Adam Langer.
p.   cm.
ISBN 978-1-4000-6891-3
eBook ISBN 978-1-5883-6957-4
1. Authors—Fiction.   2. Manuscripts—Fiction.   3. Theft—Fiction.
4. Swindlers and swindling—Fiction.   5. Publishers and publishing—Fiction.
6. Manhattan (New York, N.Y.)—Fiction.   I. Title.
PS3612.A57T47 2010
813'.6—dc22 2009040011

Printed in the United States of America

www.spiegelandgrau.com

2 4 6 8 9 7 5 3

Book design by Susan Turner

This book is dedicated to J.
(for reasons that should become somewhat
clearer sometime after page 195).
And also to Nora and Solveig
(for reasons that precede page 1).

He walked toward the sheets of flame. They did not bite his flesh, they caressed him and flooded him without heat or combustion. With relief, with humiliation, with terror, he understood that he also was an illusion, that someone else was dreaming him.

Jorge Luis Borges, "The Circular Ruins"

I ~~fact~~ uP

Girl, you know it's true. . . .

MILLI VANILLI

THE CONFIDENT MAN

To tell you the truth, I'd have noticed the guy even if Faye hadn't pointed him out to me. He was slicker than the usual Morningside Coffee crowd—off-white linen suit, black silk shirt buttoned to the throat, Jonathan Franzen–style designer glasses—but what made me stop wiping tables and look just a bit longer was the fact that he was reading a copy of *Blade by Blade*. That autumn, it seemed as though Blade Markham's book was everywhere—every subway station corridor had posters with that canary yellow book cover on them; every bookstore window displayed a cardboard cutout of a glowering Blade sporting a nine o'clock shadow; half the suckers who sat next to me on the bus were reading that so-called memoir.

Faye, strands of red hair dangling past her olive green eyes from under her Morningside Coffee visor, was humming "Dust in the Wind" and absentmindedly drawing a sketch of the guy on her notepad. She'd written "Confident Man" underneath it. That's how the name stuck with me. Meanwhile, bitter, gossipy

Joseph, all 315 pounds of him, hunched over the counter, going over lines for an audition, vainly hoping that some casting director wanted a guy his size with white-boy dreadlocks, flip-flops, and a goatee. It had been another slow night, and now the Confident Man was the only customer left in the shop.

"Too bad his taste in books doesn't match his taste in clothes," Faye said to me. She smiled and returned to her sketch.

Faye Curry was probably already trying to flirt with me then, but I had a girl, Anya Petrescu. Just about everything Faye said tended to go right past me anyway. Artsy and bookish guys always lurked at the counter and chatted her up because she had a droll wit and liked to be distracted when she was working, but she was way too subtle for me. She had the looks and smarts I tended to notice only after the fact, usually after the woman in question had gotten engaged to someone else or had already left town or had decided she was done with men. Back then, with her torn jeans, baseball caps, vintage concert shirts, and paint-spattered boots, I wasn't sure if she was into guys anyway. So that night I wasn't focusing on the fact that she was grinning at me instead of scowling, that she was wearing perfume or maybe using new shampoo. That night, I was more interested in the book the Confident Man was reading.

"Bogus pile of crap," I muttered. I didn't realize I'd said it out loud. But Joseph shot me a glance and Faye smiled at me again as if both of them had heard. I looked back down and went on wiping the tables, putting the chairs up, trying to stop thinking about that book and Blade Markham.

Just the night before, during yet another bout of writer's block and insomnia, I'd been flipping channels when I stumbled on Markham blowing hard on a rebroadcast of Pam Layne's daytime talk show. There the guy was, hawking his memoir on the biggest book show going, yammering about his heroin addiction and the time he spent with the Crips and the month he went AWOL during the first Gulf War and his conversion to Buddhism and whatever else he'd made up and sold to Merrill Books—a half million bucks for the North American rights alone. I didn't believe a word of it, but Layne's studio audience couldn't get enough, gasping and clapping and laughing as Markham spouted one lie after another. All the while, Pam Layne kept up her credulous questions, using street slang that must have been written on cue cards by whichever one of her assistants had actually read the book:

"Don't you worry that some of these men you mention in your book, some of these *hustlas,* might try to *put a cap in yo' ass?*" she asked Blade. "That they might try to *take yo' ass out?*"

"Naw, that ain't too likely," Blade told Pam. "You know, *sistuh,* the punks I wrote about in my book, they all dead, yo."

Up there on that TV talk show set, Blade was acting like some old-school hip-hopper, throwing his arms out, crossing them over his chest, flashing made-up gang signs, ending all his sentences with "yo," even though he was probably just some rich boy from Maplewood, New Jersey, whose real name was Blaine Markowitz—that's what Anya and I used to joke anyway. Everything about Blade Markham seemed like some kind of lie—his words, his shabby outfit that he'd probably planned out a week in advance, even the cross he wore around his neck.

"It ain't a cross for Christ; it's a T for Truth, yo," he told Pam Layne. That's when I flipped off the TV, went back to bed in my clothes, and tried in vain to think of a story to write, tried in vain to get some sleep.

Now here in the coffee shop was the Confident Man, one more Blade Markham fan than I could stand. So when I went over to his table and told him we were closing and that he had to scram, I might have sounded harsher than I intended. Faye bust out laughing, and Joseph, who seemed always to be looking for just the right time to can me, flashed a "one more outburst and you're gone" glare.

The Confident Man dog-eared a page of his book, put on his black cashmere gogol, belted it, went over to the tip jar, and stuffed in a twenty-dollar bill, which just about doubled our tips for the night. He walked out onto Broadway without saying a word.

"Think that guy craves you," Faye said, raising one eyebrow. Joseph snickered—jokes at my expense always cracked him up. I finished cleaning, collected my share of the tips from Joseph, said *sayonara* to Faye, and headed down to the KGB Bar to meet Anya. By the time I got there, I was still stewing about *Blade by Blade,* but I had all but forgotten the Confident Man.

THE ROMANIAN

In every bar, in every city, in every country, on every continent since the beginning of time, there has always been and will always be some sullen mope who walks in with a beautiful, charming woman on his arm, and everyone in the place stops and looks and wonders how that woman wound up with that mope. For a time, I was that mope. And Anya Petrescu was that woman.

Anya had the kind of beauty that was not subject to debate—it was just a fact. She had a devilish laugh, eyes so blue that people assumed she wore tinted contacts, and then there was that charming Eastern European accent.

But even when Anya was telling me how much she *luffed* me, even when we were kissing in subway cars or making mad, passionate chinaski on my lumpy pull-out couch, or skinny-dipping at dawn beneath the Morningside Park waterfall, even when she was discussing how much she *weeshed* she could *tekk* me home to Bucharest to meet her *femmilee* but that was *eem-posseebull* now, spending time with her had begun to depress me. I knew that our relationship would never last, that one day, her infatuation with me—something I often attributed to a cultural misunderstanding—would end. And then I would be alone and miserable, just the way I had felt before I had seen her scribbling away in Morningside Coffee, sat down at her table, asked what she was writing, then babbled for an hour about my naïve and undoubtedly ridiculous theories of honest writing and narrative authenticity and whatever else I thought I believed back then. Anya never pointed out that she was a better story-teller than I would ever be. Later, she would often say that she fell in love with me because deep down I was just an "old-*feshioned, romenteek Meedwestern* boy" who fell in love with her stories; looking back, I guess that was true.

That night, I was meeting Anya at KGB's "Literal Stimulation," a weekly showcase of emerging writers curated by Miri Lippman, editor and publisher of *The Stimulator,* a bimonthly literary review that wielded an influence far beyond its 2,500 paid subscribers, largely because Lippman had impeccable taste and a knack for identifying young scribes with "stimulating potential." Just about every up-and-coming author published in *The New Yorker* or *The Atlantic,* every first-time novelist with a two-book deal at Random House or Scribner, had appeared on Miri's program. Four out of the last five authors that Pam Layne had chosen for her TV book club had read at Lit-Stim. The only one who hadn't was Blade Markham, and even though I hated the way Miri Lippman looked through me every time she saw me, resented the fact that I was introduced to her for the first time on six separate occasions, I had to respect her for snubbing Blade.

As always, KGB on Lit-Stim night was filled with a posse of authors, most of whom had published stories in magazines and journals that were still sending me form-letter rejections; agents, all of whom had sent my story manuscripts back to me in the self-addressed stamped envelopes I had provided; editors and publishers, all looking for the new Zadie Smith or Nick Hornby, all completely uninterested in Ian Minot. I couldn't blame them; at that point, I was pretty bored with myself too.

After my dad finally died of the cancer that had been slowly gnawing away at him, and I moved from Indiana to New York with my pitifully small inheritance, I went to Lit-Stim every Monday night. Now, a little over five years later, with my bank balance sinking into the mid four figures, I never did. The only reason I was here instead of back in my West Harlem garret, staring at a blank computer monitor or lying on my lumpy proust, watching TV, was that it was Anya's turn to appear at Miri's podium. Three other writers were on the bill, and Anya was the only one without a book contract; I figured that would change before the week was out. When Anya had treated me to dinner at Londell's to celebrate our six-month anniversary and told me that Miri had chosen her for Lit-Stim, I could already feel her slipping away from me, could feel myself becoming the "old boyfriend" she'd soon discuss with her rich, talented new beau—*yes, but I vas yunk and fooleesh den, end eeven though he hedd no tellent, he vass allvays switt,* she would tell Malcolm Gladwell or Gary Shteyngart or whichever writer would next succumb to her charms.

"You are *lett* again as always, but I *forgeef* you, *Ee-yen*," Anya said as she patted the barstool she had saved for me—even now, I still love the way she used to say my name.

I took the stool beside her, guiltily eyeing the Manhattan that she had already ordered for me. I could barely afford to buy the next round, but I knew that Anya would never expect me to buy her anything, not even a beer. Strangely, money never seemed to be an issue for this twenty-six-year-old woman who had left Romania with barely a *leu* to her name; Anya usually had cash and a nice, furnished place to stay—someone was always loaning her the keys to his or her apartment or summerhouse, hiring her for odd secretarial jobs with flexible hours, inviting her to this or that swanky party. When we first met, I obsessed about what she might be doing to win so many favors, but after a while I stopped worrying—Anya was the kind of woman you wanted to help without even considering what you might get in return.

At the bar, I sipped my Manhattan, hoping to make it last, while I pointed out to Anya all the agents in the crowd—Eric Simonoff and Bill Clegg of the William Morris Agency sipping club sodas; Faye Bender and Christy Fletcher talking shop; Joe Regal of Regal Literary handing out a business card; Geoff Olden from the Olden Literary Agency nursing a cocktail. I recognized all of them from writing seminars I'd attended or from when I had served them drinks at private parties in Sonny Mehta's or Nan Talese's apartments, back in my naïve days when I thought that getting close to publishers would bring me closer to getting my stories published.

Sitting beside Anya, I caught only snatches of their conversations, but every phrase filled me with envy—*exclusive contract with Vanity Fair; boxed review in PW; a "significant" six-figure deal; optioned by Scott Rudin; adapted by Ron Bass; profiled by Chip McGrath; interviewed by Terry Gross; selected by Pam Layne; short-listed for the Booker; headlining at the 92nd Street Y; bidding war for the paperback rights; got a free box lunch at Yaddo.* I kept suggesting to Anya that she get up and introduce herself to somebody, but she said she thought everyone there was a *fekk.* She didn't want to meet anyone, just to sit with me and make fun of them—I was the only person with whom she could ever really be herself.

·"Good evening everybody, and welcome to another *stimulating* event," Miri Lippman said from the podium, her monotone reverberating like a tuning fork held too close to my ear as she introduced the evening's writers.

Anya would be last to read. The second round of Manhattans, which I bought for Anya and myself with the night's tips from Morningside Coffee, helped get me through the first three readers, but only barely. If I hadn't been waiting for Anya to take her turn, all the Manhattans in Manhattan wouldn't have kept me at the bar. I wasn't nearly drunk enough to tolerate listening to Avi Kamner, a weedy Jewish memoirist who read an essay from *Cold Cuts,* an anthology of purportedly humorous circumcision stories he had edited; or to Rupa Ganguly, author

of *Immigrant Song,* a collection of contemporary fiction about
South Asians struggling to survive in America, loosely based on
the struggles of her own brave parents, she said. Very loosely
based—her grandparents had immigrated to the States in the
1950s, and her Connecticut-born mother and father were respectively chairs of the radiology and orthopedic surgery de-
partments at Mount Sinai.

Worst of all was Jens Von Bretzel, a slim, unkempt guy with
an army jacket, a luxuriant chabon of black hair, and a "to hell
with this crap" demeanor that he barely concealed as he read
from *The Counter Life,* his debut novel about a barista with a
girlfriend who was too good for him, a future that was drifting
toward oblivion, and a lousy attitude that kept getting him into
trouble. The novel was based on the decade Von Bretzel had
spent working at a Starbucks in Williamsburg. Von Bretzel's
work was so much like the stories I was writing that I half suspected he had hacked into my computer and plagiarized my life.
Except that Von Bretzel's work was more confident than mine,
as if he considered his life worthy of committing to print, while
to me, just about every aspect of my own existence seemed
wholly unliterary—how often had agents told me that my protagonists never did anything, that they always waited for things
to happen to them?

"I'm so jazzed we got an audience; weather's been so bad
lately. You ready to do this, Anya?"

I was staring at a giant atwood of auburn frizz, the back of
Miri Lippman's head. Miri had positioned herself between
Anya and me. I didn't even bother introducing myself, just kept
my eyes focused on the ever-dwindling fluid in my glass while
Miri fawned over Anya's stories—how she envied the life Anya

had lived as an orphan on the streets of Bucharest, such *won-drous* material.

"*Weesh* me *lokk,*" Anya said to me. I kissed Anya as if she were about to take a journey far longer than the three yards between the barstool and the KGB podium. But I didn't *weesh* her *lokk;* she didn't need it.

The story that Anya chose to read was like every one I had listened to her whisper while she snuggled next to me on my proust. It was the title selection from *We Never Talked About Ceaușescu,* the collection of stories she'd been working on ever since I'd met her, and this story, in which a Romanian girl on the cusp of becoming both an adult and an orphan attempts to cope with her father's terminal illness, was heartbreaking and beautiful and self-effacing and charming and hilarious and, most of all, true. Even though the whole story took place in a country thousands of miles away from the tiny Indiana town in which I'd grown up, Anya's tale resonated with me, reminding me of the late nights I'd spent at my father's bedside, reading him stories, helping him to bring his teacup to his lips, turning out his light when he had finally fallen asleep. I couldn't help but feel jealous that the raptors and poseurs at the KGB were being invited to experience these moments that had felt so personal when Anya had first read the story to me, that night when I had told her it was perfect, and she had called me a liar and told me to *shot* my *trepp.*

But what was most amazing and moving about the story as I heard it tonight was how Anya read it. In a mere ten minutes, she transformed from a nervous beginner to a confident professional, much like the heroine of her own story. At first, Anya leaned in too close to the microphone, giggled when she realized her pages were in the wrong order. Her hands shook while she read her opening sentence ("When I was *leetle, eff'ryone* who *shoult heff luffed* me left me"); after she finished page one, they were still.

"*Luff* is *nussink* but a lie," she read. "In my house, we *neffer* talked about *eet.*" Two people in the audience gasped. Anya was like the pool shark who muffs her first game, gets everyone to put their money on the table, then runs every ball.

Once Anya was done reading and applause thundered through the bar, her endearing neuroses returned. She laughed too loudly, apologized too much, clunked the microphone when she returned it to its holder, tripped over its cord as she walked back to take her place beside me at the bar. But it didn't matter anymore. For a second, I looked down into my drink to see if anything was left; by the time I looked up again, Geoff Olden was there.

"Suntory?" he asked, jutting his chin toward Anya's glass.

That night, Geoff Olden wouldn't be the only agent who would swoop down upon Anya, offer to buy her drinks, then hand her business cards. But he was the first, and for me, his was the presence that rankled most. Yes, he was Blade Markham's agent, but Olden was also the man whose literary agency had sent me the most perfunctory, condescending, and offensive rejection letter I had ever received.

"Good luck placing this and all your future submissions elsewhere," the letter's author wrote, thus shutting the mailbox door on any story I might ever write in my life.

"*Señor?*"

Olden was holding a twenty in one hand as he rapped his fingers against the bar—who knew why he was speaking Spanish to the poor bartender, who was no more Spanish than Geoff Olden was. But everything about Olden seemed calculated to draw distinction between himself and whomever he happened to be speaking with—the round yellow frames of his eckleburgs, his white turtleneck, his cuffed blue jeans, his black velvet jacket, the watches he wore, one on each wrist. Olden's brushed-back hair had the fullness and the shade of premature silver-gray that I recall only ever seeing in Park Avenue apartments when I'd worked for a caterer during my first summer in New York.

But Geoff Olden wasn't merely a confident man; no, he was imperious, unctuous, and snide—even when he laughed his loud, self-possessed, metrosexual cackle, you were always aware of whom he was laughing with and whom he was laughing at. And when he held up two fingers and bought a round of fitzgeralds for Anya and me—*"Dos, por favor"*—I was thoroughly aware of the category in which Olden had placed me. The moment after he handed me my fitzgerald, I became invisible. Drinking too fast and thinking about how I might wreak revenge upon Olden, if only I had the opportunity, helped to pass some time before I was once again staring at random points in space and contemplating stories I might try to write, before deciding that Jens Von Bretzel had probably already written them.

"Exquisite work, truly. *Mucho mucho bueno.*" Geoff handed Anya two of his business cards. He said he always gave two— "keep the other in case you meet someone else with a great story to tell."

The evening proceeded with more compliments from editors, publishers, and agents; more of Anya's inscrutable smiles; more fitzgeralds—lots more fitzgeralds. Before Anya had read her story, I was her boyfriend; afterward, I became her roadie. The only thing that prevented me from bolting for the door was the fact that Anya kept making fun of all the people who approached her. She rolled her eyes at me, made yakkety-yak gestures with her hands, mouthed the sycophantic words she was enduring.

"What a *bonch* of *kripps*," Anya said when we finally emerged from the KGB and started walking quickly along Fourth Street. She was taking the business cards she had received, ripping them into quarters and eighths, flinging the scraps of paper behind her.

"You know who that guy represents?" I asked Anya when I saw her starting to rip Geoff Olden's business card, but she kept ripping it.

"Who he represent? A *bonch* of *kripps*," Anya said. She started running south toward the subway station, laughing all the way as I tried to keep up.

Some of the happiest memories of my time with Anya come from those brief hours just after we started running to the subway but before we fell asleep—even now, I still recall those hours as one unbroken journey of laughter and giddiness and love. But after I'd been sleeping for some time, I dreamed that someone I knew was walled up in a prison, trying to claw and scratch her way out. The more I listened to the scratching, though, the more I realized that I wasn't dreaming those sounds. When I opened my eyes, I saw Anya beside me, writing furiously in a journal, her pen clawing and scratching the paper. As I watched her, I wished I could have her sense of purpose, her drive, that feeling that everything was at stake. And as I opened my eyes just a bit wider, I wished too that I hadn't seen the second business card that Geoff Olden had given Anya marking a page in her book.

RETURN OF THE CONFIDENT MAN

I was getting ready to finish my shift and head out to meet Anya in front of Morningside Coffee when the Confident Man walked into the café, slipped off his cashmere gogol, and hung it on the rack by the door.

"Your buddy's here again," Faye said with a wink, but this time I didn't make much of the guy's presence until he approached the counter, where he ordered his usual hot tea. I had become pretty good about not paying him any mind when he came in with his copy of *Blade by Blade*—after all, he was the biggest tipper we had. I tried to ignore the book just as I usually did, but this time, Faye wouldn't let me.

"Good read?" Faye asked the man, then flashed me a grin— she and I had been discussing the book, and I'd told her what I thought of it, but she was in one of her wise-ass moods tonight. She liked needling people, seeing what it took to make them burst. Usually, she left me alone and concentrated on Joseph. They kept up an ongoing repartee—"Sold any paintings?" he'd ask. "Hell, no," she would reply; had Joseph been cast in any shows? "Hell, no," Joseph would say. When I first started working at the café, they included me in their game ("Sell any stories, Minot?"), but since my answer was "hell, no" every single time, while for Joseph and Faye it was only 90 percent, they stopped. Tonight, though, Joseph had just gotten a call from his agent, who said she was dumping him as a client unless he lost weight. Whenever he got bad news, he ate more, so he was in a foul mood; he had already told Faye that he didn't want to hear any of her jokes tonight, so I became the beneficiary of Faye's wit.

"Have you in fact read the book?" the Confident Man asked Faye. It was the first time I'd heard him speak a full sentence, and his voice was as smooth and deep as that of a late-night DJ.

"Twice," she said. "Ooh, it's a real page-turner. Ian here digs it too."

"Does he?" asked the man.

"Let it go," I told Faye. I was feeling stressed out. Anya had told me that she'd have a *"fonny sooprise"* for me when we went out later, but I wasn't in the mood for *sooprises*. Lately, I seemed to be getting more rejection slips in the mail than ever; the adjunct creative-writing lectureship positions I had applied for weren't panning out; neither the New York Foundation for the Arts nor the NEA was going to give me a grant. Anya had recently been named one of *American Review*'s "31 Most Promising Writers Under 31"; this year, I was too old to qualify. Sure, I could survive for another few months on my meager savings and the few hundred bucks a week I was making at the café, but I needed another plan fast. And the fact that the only tangible plan I had involved secretly hoping Anya would sell her book already so she could buy an apartment and I could move in with her showed how desperate and pathetic I was becoming.

"Didn't you know? Ian is Blade Markham's biggest fan," Faye told the Confident Man. He smiled patronizingly in my direction as if he thought I was the moron for liking Blade Markham, even though he was the one reading Blade's book. Still, the man didn't say anything else. He just slipped a twenty into the tip jar, the way he always did, went back to his table, and cracked open his book.

"Told you that guy craves ya," Faye said, cocking her head in the direction of the new twenty-dollar bill atop the loose change in our jar. She raised an eyebrow. "Bet he's gonna ask you out," she said.

"Jesus Christ, Faye." I was about to finally let her really have it, ask why she didn't do some work instead of just busting my balls, doodling, working on her laptop, and using Joseph's printer to make flyers and postcards for her gallery opening— Joseph always let Faye get away with shit he would have fired me for on the spot. But then I heard someone rap on the front window: Anya.

"Ee-yen!"

My elation at seeing Anya was followed closely by a sense of impending doom as I noted her snappy, black Holly Golightly cocktail dress. I didn't know where she and I might be going, but I was sure that wherever it was, I would be underdressed.

"Your Ukrainian's here for ya," Faye said and smiled—she always acted as if she thought Anya was a pain in her ass. It never occurred to me that she might have been jealous.

"Romanian," I corrected. I took off my Morningside Coffee smock and visor, hung them up in back, and started to head out.

"Have it your way," said Faye, but then she reached into the tip jar, pulled out the twenty that the Confident Man had put there, and handed it to me.

"Shouldn't we split it three ways?" I asked.

"Nah, take it, you earned it tonight," said Faye. I feared she was mocking me, but then I realized she was telling the truth—

she'd come in late and had been working on her computer ever since she'd arrived, while Joseph had been binge-eating and moping. I'd been the only one doing any work, and besides, wherever Anya was taking me tonight, I was sure I could use at least a twenty.

I thanked Faye, and told her that was probably the nicest thing anyone had ever done for me at a job. She smiled at me and said, *"Sayonara, tomodachi,"* as I walked outside onto Broadway where Anya was waiting, a guilty Cheshire-cat grin on her face.

"Where're we going?" I asked, and when she didn't answer immediately, I asked if I might hate her after we were done with whatever we would be doing.

"Only for *leetle* while," Anya said.

BLADE BY BLADE

The Blade Markham reading and Q and A at Big Box Books's flagship Upper West Side store had been moved to Symphony Space to accommodate the overflow crowd, and you needed a pink wristband to get in. Anya and I were fifteen minutes late, and I felt a surge of hope when I saw the NO MORE TICKETS AVAILABLE sign in the box office window, but Anya already had two wristbands in her shoulder bag, and by the time I had completely processed where we were and what I was about to endure, she had already affixed one around my wrist. As I looked at all the posters of Blade Markham, all the stacks of his books, all the people here to buy them for Blade to sign, I kept thinking of that scene in *Taxi Driver,* when Robert De Niro takes Cybill Shepherd on a date to a skin flick.

"It *weel* be *fon,*" Anya said. "Let's *seet.*"

But there was no place to *seet.* The chairs were filled with Blade fans—scruffy, denim or khaki-clad bankers and traders, all of whom looked like they wanted to be Blade; women in black who looked like they wanted to screw Blade, at least for a night before they'd return to their boyfriends or husbands, all of whom I assumed were employed by Lehman Brothers, Citigroup, or Goldman-Sachs. The talk was moderated by a host from the public radio station WNYC who sported a three-day growth of salt-and-pepper ginsberg. "Any advice for a writer just starting out, Blade?" the moderator asked. "Yeah, carry a gauge, a shiv, and a gat, and all you fellas, you stay away from those hoodrats, and make sure all y'all got a mad sexy shorty to roll with too, yo," Blade replied. Applause and whoops of laughter from the crowd.

I kept puzzling over why Anya had asked me to come here. She told me that she just found Blade *fonny,* but I wondered if maybe she really did want to get me to hate her so I would end our relationship, thus saving her the trouble of doing it herself. Looking back, I think she might just have wanted my company, but at the time I was sure there was something more to it, and when I saw Geoff Olden approaching us with two fitzgeralds in plastic cups, I figured I was right.

"*Bienvenida,*" he said, and this time, Anya didn't roll her eyes or mouth his Spanish BS back to me when he wasn't looking.

Up on stage, Blade was discussing his craft. He told the moderator he approached writing as if he were a DJ—he didn't "write words down on paper"; he "laid down mad beats." As for the accusation from one spectator that Blade had plagiarized a prison conversion scene from *The Autobiography of Malcolm X,* Blade said he didn't believe plagiarism existed. "I just like to call it a remix, yo," he said.

Geoff Olden peered at Anya through his eckleburgs and his voice went lower as he said something to her about an email exchange the two had had on the subject of "representation."

"Comprendes?" he whispered.

I excused myself to go to the john, and then left it when I saw some beefy trader at one of the sinks with the words BLADE BY BLADE tattooed in script on his arm. When I returned to the auditorium, Olden was gone, and Blade was standing in front of a microphone, taking questions from the audience and answering them in his falsely humble mode ("That's a righteous point yer makin', *sistuh*"; "I truly appreciate you askin' me that question, *brutha*"). Anya was holding a slip of paper that she was tucking into a zippered pocket of her shoulder bag. The paper had an address on West Twenty-first Street scribbled on it.

"Olden invite you to some after-party?" I asked.

Anya smiled, a little embarrassed, it seemed, but she quickly recovered.

"You *vant* we should *tekk kebb* or *sobway*?" she asked.

I wanted to ask her "whatcha mean *we?*" then walk out and head home, tell her I'd meet her back at my place whenever she was done being wooed. But after I'd groused in the lobby for a moment or two, I lost heart. I couldn't say no to her.

"*Kebb* or *sobway,*" she asked again.

"*Sobway,*" I said gloomily.

THE BASH AT OLDEN'S

Anya said we'd stay at Geoff Olden's apartment only for ten minutes, and after that we could do anything my *leetle* heart desired, but I wasn't surprised when that ten minutes stretched past an hour. Actually, apartment isn't the right word to describe the Chelsea townhouse where Geoff Olden hosted his *Blade by Blade* bash. His was the sort of New York dwelling I only ever saw in movies. On screen, it would have served as an embassy, a ballroom for some costume drama starring Daniel Day-Lewis, or maybe as Woody Allen's apartment. There was a spiral staircase, an enormous, built-in library with books alphabetized and organized by subject, a kitchen that was bigger than my apartment, three bathrooms, a billiard table, a back deck with a hot tub. That was only the first floor, and Olden owned all three. Mind you, none of this had been purchased with the money he made as a literary agent; that career paid for the summer home in Rhinebeck, the wardrobe, and the eckleburgs. This Chelsea place had been in the Olden family since 1909, when Henry Olden made his first million in textiles. I liked to think that Geoff was sole heir to a jockstrap fortune, but I have no idea what was manufactured in the Olden Textile Mills, only that whatever it was must have generated lots of dough.

Save for the waiters, the bartenders, the coat checkers, and me, the Blade Markham party was an anybody-who's-anybody sort of affair—there was Henry Louis Gates, Jr., toting a walking stick and wearing a tuxedo, having just returned from *The Rake's Progress* at the Met. There was a trio of drunk writers, all named Jonathan, each of whom was complaining that the *Times* critic Michiko Kakutani had written that she'd liked their earlier books better. The publisher James Merrill, Jr., was popping a grape into his mouth; Pam Layne was in a corner with one of her assistants, Mabel Foy, both trying far too hard to keep a low profile; the writer Francine Prose smiled at me and waved, then frowned when she realized that she had me confused with someone else.

Anya stuck to my side during our first half hour at the party, when she said she didn't recognize anybody, and spent all that time joking with me, squeezing my ass, and pushing me to the dining room to score appetizers that she claimed she was too shy to snag for herself. We had fun laughing at the whole scene. It was like a swingers' party for celibates, I said—everyone checking one another out, leading one another into private rooms, whipping out their contracts and client lists to measure whose was bigger.

But after Olden showed up with Blade Markham and his posse of droogs and cornered Anya, I barely saw her at all. Instead, I drifted from room to room, getting free drinks and eavesdropping. Publicity, marketing, and editorial assistants were in full effect, but I didn't recognize many of them—they were a transient lot, all waiting to score their first book contract, after which they would give their bosses two weeks' notice. A pair of these overeager types was chatting up Blade Markham's moist, officious editor, Rowell Templen of Merrill Books, and I didn't know what irritated me more—their sense of desperation or mine of abject futility.

I kept drinking and drifting, feeling more and more aimless as time wore on. If this were really a swingers' party, I would have been the one creepy humbert who couldn't have gotten laid even here. I tried starting conversations but never knew how to finish them. Elsewhere, when people asked what I did, I said I was a writer. Saying it in a room full of authors, agents, and editors seemed ridiculous, but saying I worked in a café and wrote stories without finishing them wasn't much of an icebreaker either. I contemplated inventing an autobiography, but I wasn't good at lying. I finally decided to say I was living in New York on my inheritance; this had the advantage of being easy to remember because it was true—no one needed to know that barely four thousand dollars remained of the money my father had left me—but by the time I settled on this story, I couldn't find anyone who seemed interested in hearing it.

Anya was in the main ballroom, her back framed by a cathedral window that gave out onto Twenty-first Street. She was smiling at Geoff Olden, who was letting loose with his nasal cackles as he introduced her to his assistants and underlings, all dolled up in their black golightlys, all depressingly plain beside Anya.

The library seemed to be the only unoccupied room on Geoff's first floor, so I passed some time there, browsing through all the books he had represented. I flipped through first editions by his famous friends and acquaintances, who had written loving dedications—*"To a heavyweight of literature, with much love, Muhammad Ali"; "To Geoff, Thanks for all the correc-*

tions, Jon Franzen." The only qualified remark came from one Phil Roth—*"To Geoffrey, a true human stain."* I wondered how much I could sell the books for on eBay if I absconded with an armful.

In the library, on a small, antique mahogany table between two black leather armchairs illuminated by a Tiffany lamp, was a stack of copies of *Blade by Blade*. Stacks like this were scattered throughout the apartment, and as I inspected the book's canary yellow cover, I realized that I had never actually tried to read Blade Markham's book, had based my opinions about it mostly on reviews I had read, appearances Blade had made on talk shows, and remarks Faye had made about the book at work. Maybe I hadn't given it a chance. As loathsome as Blade seemed on subway posters or on *The Pam Layne Show*, it seemed harder to despise him when he was in the same apartment with me, life-size—I have always been too suspicious of people in theory, too trusting of them in practice. The more time I spend with people, the more I find myself liking them.

But after I cracked open the book, I almost burst out laughing at the dedication—*"To All My Homies Still Livin' Under the Gun Right Here in Amerikkka. You Know Who You Are. Keep Runnin', Keep Gunnin'."* I turned to a random page. No, the book was ludicrous, the grammar and punctuation awful, no sentence lasted longer than ten words and half of them ended with *yo,* as if Blade had dictated the book, not written it. I picked another page; on it, Blade opined about the merits of prison sex—"There's worse things than playin' catcher upriver in Rikers, yo." I couldn't help myself. This time, I actually laughed out loud. But when I sensed someone else's presence, I stopped.

"What you chortlin' 'bout, bro?"

Blade was standing in the library doorway, holding a half-full martini glass and wearing scuffed black boots, a white Stanley Kowalski undershirt under a black suit jacket, a lot of bling, too. Around his neck was that gold cross—*it ain't a cross for Christ; it's a T for Tool, yo,* I felt like saying. Blade ripped the book out of my hands, looked to see if I'd done anything to it, then placed it back neatly on the pile.

"Ain't no browsin' privileges here, bro," he told me. "Y'all gotta *pay* some shit if y'all wanna *read* my shit, *compadre.*" On paper, his hip-hop patois might have seemed laughable; in person, it was scary as hell. I thought all Blade's prison stories were made up, sure, but I didn't doubt that he'd gotten into some scuffles in his life. I pushed my way past Blade and walked toward the main ballroom, not looking back to see if he was following.

Anya was in the same place where I had last seen her, standing with her back to the windows, hypnotizing Geoff and everyone around her with some sad story about the life she had left behind in Bucharest—*"neffer* confuse my life *weeth* my *feection; feection* is not nearly so *tredjic."* The spell she was casting on all the junior agents and editors was a mirror image of the one Blade had cast on his audience at Symphony Space. Here, all the women seemed to want to be Anya; all the men seemed to want to screw her. Save for Geoff—he didn't want to screw or be anyone else in his apartment, just to represent them and screw over everybody else.

"Anya?" I had to say it three times loudly before anyone noticed, and Geoff appeared to hear me before Anya did. He regarded me through his eckleburgs as if I were some stain on his tie that he wanted to rub out fast. I stepped between him and my girlfriend, who smiled and told me that she had been *lookink* for me all night—*vhere* had I *bean?* I leaned in to tell her I was going to *spleet,* but I was interrupted by a low, spiteful "Yo."

Blade, still holding his martini, was walking fast toward me. But when he saw that I was standing beside his agent and our host, he relented, even flashed a cocky smile of surrender, like a movie cop who stops running when he sees a thief jump onto a train, realizing he can't catch him this time. Blade looked past me, clapped Geoff on the shoulder, called him "Bruthafucka," and when Geoff introduced him to Anya, Blade started acting even more polite, as if he were the son of some Sunday school preacher—"a pleasure to meet you, ma'am." He offered to fetch Anya a drink, opining that "G-Dub's martinis" were "off the hook." I smirked, mouthed "off the hook" at Anya. She didn't notice, but Blade did. And now when he looked at me, his unspoken, momentary offer of détente had apparently been nullified; his nostrils flared, his cheeks flushed.

"Hey," he said, "don't you need a plugger to get in here, bro?"

"A plugger?"

"An invite," Blade explained. "Didn't anyone ever tell you y'all need an *invite* to get into this bash?"

I could have kept my mouth shut, but now I hated this guy so much that I didn't care whose apartment we were in, whose guest I was, or whose book deal I might be sabotaging.

"Yo," I said, staring right back at Blade, "didn't anyone ever tell you y'all need to try telling the truth and not making up a bunch of jive if y'all are gonna call your book a 'memoir,' bro?"

For a moment, Blade said nothing. And when he did speak, his voice, though fierce, was soft, clear, and composed.

"Then, I'll ask *you* something, *compadre*," Blade said. "Which window?"

My heartbeat was getting stronger, faster, but I didn't move and I tried not to blink.

"Window?"

"Do you want me to throw you out of, bro?" And now Blade was done being quiet; he was throwing off his jacket, tugging twice at the bulge of his portnoy. His truth cross thumped against his chest as he backed me up against the windows, grabbed me by the shirt collar, then held my throat.

"Which window, dickweed?"

"Easy," I said, struggling to get his hands off me.

"Which motherfucking window?" he demanded. "You wanna *tussle*? You wanna *throw*? 'Cause I'll *throw* right now, you disrespectful motherfucker."

I was looking for a friend, a way out, wondering should I throw the first punch, let him do it, where to throw it, face, chest, solar plexus?

"Disrespectin' *me*?" Blade was shouting in my face, but the only people actually paying attention seemed to find my predicament extremely entertaining. For I was nobody and Blade was just being Blade; he probably did this at every party: *Oh, there's Blade again, throwin' another chump out the window.* Norman Mailer was gone; someone had to take his place, had to start fights at book parties; someone had to wield hammers, bite off ears, or defenestrate disrespectful gate-crashers.

"Anya!" I yelled; she looked over to me and Blade, then erupted into laughter. I didn't know if she was laughing because she wanted to break the moment and save me, because she was drunk, or because the image of Blade, fist raised, profanity spewing from his lips as he pinned me against a window of one of the most beautiful apartments in Chelsea, was truly funny. But Blade heard Anya's laughter, and he let me go. "Yeah, you can kick my ass if you want, but you're still a fake," I muttered as I shoved past him.

"Let's roll, Anya," I said, but when I got to the front door and turned around, I saw she wasn't coming with me.

THE GREAT CRACK-UP

I figured I wouldn't have to wait long for Anya to emerge from Geoff Olden's building and join me, if only to say that I should head home by myself. But after twenty minutes of pacing back and forth along the sidewalk, I gave up. I got a Coke and a bag of M&M's from a corner deli, and drank and ate them fast. I had planned to walk back toward Olden's apartment to keep waiting for Anya, but I walked straight to the subway.

I spent the ride on the uptown train unspooling a film of the future in my mind, one in which Anya kept rising while I kept falling. As my train rumbled along, in my mind I could hear our uncomfortable silences—me bitter about Anya's success; Anya embarrassed by my failures. I could imagine the arguments— Anya telling me to snap out of it already; me saying that maybe if I were a beautiful Romanian orphan, I'd write better fiction too. I could see the guilt on Anya's face as she contemplated telling me to leave our new apartment she'd bought with the zillion-dollar frazier she'd surely get for *We Never Talked About Ceaușescu.* I saw us agreeing to split the apartment down the middle, putting a divider between her proust and mine. I could hear her having wild chinaski in the next room with all of her new boyfriends, madly scrawling in her notebook, furiously typing on her laptop, while I sat alone with my hand on my portnoy. I could see myself finally with new inspiration: a story of a man thwarted by his successful ex-girlfriend, who lives in the very next room. And then I imagined what people would say about it—they'd call my hero cynical and unlikable, a reactor not an actor. "Good luck placing this elsewhere, sucka," the rejection letters would read. One day, I'd walk into the 3B bookstore on Broadway, and discover that Jens Von Bretzel had written a story just like mine, only better.

I maintained a small hope that Anya would be out in front of my building after I'd emerged from the subway at 135th Street, but all that awaited was a mailbox with two rejection letters in it, my credit card bill, a copy of *Writer's Digest,* and a summons for jury duty, the best piece of mail I'd gotten in weeks—I found myself hoping I would be impaneled for a long, difficult case, one that would provide me with forty-dollar-a-day compensation and inspire me to write some blockbuster legal thriller.

At home, I contemplated vacuuming my apartment, washing my dishes, making coffee, or getting some writing done. But I just flipped channels. Pam Layne was on TV again, a rebroadcast of the morning's show, on which she'd interviewed an author who'd written a raunchy memoir about minor league baseball; its title was *Balls Out.* I flipped off Pam's show, then watched the last half of a documentary about the Sex Pistols.

Johnny Rotten was on the stage of the Winter Garden, asking his audience, "Ever feel like you've been cheated?" That sounded just about right.

It was near dawn when Anya finally tiptoed into my apartment, and I still hadn't accomplished anything or gotten any sleep. In the innumerable imaginary conversations I'd had with Anya over the course of the night, I had prepared myself for nearly any exchange. If she were angry, I'd defend myself; if she apologized, I'd accept. But the pitying glance and the "Ohhhh, *Ee-yen*" she emitted shortly after entering surprised me. Apparently, I looked worse than I imagined; I felt like a drunk who had been discovered by his AA partner on a curb after a bender.

"Well, should we do this now?" I asked Anya as she sat beside me on the couch and put an arm around me. She'd been drinking martinis and smoking vonneguts all night, and yet she still smelled beautiful to me.

In the conversation I was now imagining, Anya would ask what I meant by "should we do this now?" and I would selflessly explain that we had to end our relationship when we still loved each other, before our divergent career paths led us apart. But Anya didn't need my explanation. Yes, she seemed to be thinking as she regarded me with pitying eyes, yes, we should break up now. She started to cry those cathartic tears you shed before you leave something behind and move on to the next, more exciting phase of your life: small-town Indiana for Manhattan; Bucharest for Broadway; *Ee-yen* for *Ennybody* Else. We kissed for a half minute or so, both of us probably feeling that it would be the last time this would ever happen.

"*Ve* should *heff* met earlier, *Ee-yen,*" Anya said as she held me close. "*Vhen ve* both *vere* different *pipples.*"

Then she got up and gathered all of her belongings that were still in my apartment—a couple of golightlys, some pens, books, a journal, and a necklace—put them into her gym bag, and walked to the door. I probably should have gone downstairs with her and waited for a cab, but I couldn't muster the energy or the chivalry. In my mind, like Anya, I had already started moving on to the next phase of my life. But I was certain I was heading in the opposite direction.

THE CONFIDENT MAN STRIKES AGAIN

I still hadn't slept, and as I tried to concentrate on my work behind the counter of Morningside Coffee, my head was thrumming with what I probably would have diagnosed as a migraine had I ever experienced one before. Faye, on the other hand, was in particularly cheerful form; her gallery opening was only a few weeks away, and, while Joseph, seemingly more depressed than ever, was downstairs dealing with inventory and letting the two of us run the place, Faye was trading jokes with customers, bopping from table to table, placing flyers for her show on every one. Her postcards were stacked near the register.

Faye's upcoming exhibit at the Van Meegeren Gallery was called *Forged in Ink*. The title didn't really fit her art, she said, but then again, she wasn't to blame; I was. "You're a writer; you're good with titles, aren't ya?" she'd asked on one particularly slow evening. After she'd described her work—copies of old master paintings paired with crude ink drawings—I'd proposed the title, but hadn't given it any more thought. I didn't take her career as an artist very seriously; she didn't seem to give her work any more respect than I gave mine.

"Check out my exhibit," she'd tell a customer after handing him a flyer. "Might be good, might suck, ya never know."

"Come on, pops, you'll check it out, won't you?" she'd asked the Confident Man a few days earlier. "At least the refreshments will be free."

Faye was always cheerful in her self-deprecating remarks; mine usually sounded bitter and nasty, even though they seemed to amuse Faye. She always pressed for more details whenever I told a story—"You're one of those messed-up dudes who's more fun to hang with when he's depressed," she once told me—and tonight I was ranting more than usual.

"Everything out of that guy's mouth, it's all a bunch of jive," I said as I recounted for her the previous night's debacle at Geoff Olden's, and she cracked up at every Blade Markham line I delivered, laughed so hard she snorted when I told her about Blade grabbing me and demanding I choose a window.

I already missed Anya desperately, had begun dialing her number more than a dozen times over the course of the evening before shutting off my phone so I wouldn't feel tempted to try again; still, having Faye listen to and laugh at my stories felt good. The fact that Faye was American and came from Manhattan meant that she could relate more easily than Anya to my Blade stories. Faye knew all the pop culture trivia that eluded Anya; she knew all about music and movies, all about slang, could pinpoint the exact year when "off the hook" entered common usage and identify why Blade was saying it wrong.

I told Faye the grim story of my last few minutes with Anya—"So, what happened with you and your Hungarian?"

Faye had asked—and I felt surprisingly comfortable doing so. Faye's laughter and caustic remarks made me feel far better than any commiseration or pity probably would have. She made me feel as though my stories were worth hearing, and that I might actually wind up better off without Anya. I could feel my headache beginning to lift, and I was starting to look forward to attending Faye's gallery opening, it being the only solid item on my schedule save for jury duty. I was even considering asking Faye if she wanted to grab a beer at the 106 Bar tonight after we'd closed up the café.

But then I heard the front door swing open, saw Faye roll her eyes and smirk. I turned around, and there was the Confident Man, book in hand. Some wire inside of me sparked, and I exploded.

"Motherfucker," I heard myself say as I darted toward the man.

I have no idea if he smiled or gaped, I wasn't focusing on his face. I felt a chilly but overpowering sense of purpose as I reached for the man's book, grabbed it from him, threw open the door to the café, whipped the book as hard as I could down the street, then got right up in the man's face. I could see my breath fog up the lenses of his franzens as I warned him to never, no, *never* come into our café again, and if I ever saw him with that book again, I'd "burn the thing to cinders."

Only when the Confident Man left the café did I notice that everyone inside was staring at me, even Joseph, who had hauled himself up the steps just in time to see me hurl *Blade by Blade* half a block down Broadway.

Joseph didn't need to say anything; I knew that I was done at Morningside Coffee. Faye had talked him out of firing me half a dozen times before, but I knew she couldn't do it now. I ripped off my smock and visor and threw them onto the floor. Then I went straight for the tip jar, poured its contents out on the counter, tallied them up, took my third, and stuffed the money in my pocket before blasting out the door.

MEETING THE CONFIDENT MAN

I headed down Broadway, not really knowing where I was going, just that wherever it was, I wanted to get there fast. I could feel my pulse just about everywhere in my body; it beat against my temples as I began making my usual quick transition from exhilarated "I can't believe I did that!" to panicked "What the hell did I just do?" Then I saw the Confident Man, his newly scuffed copy of *Blade by Blade* in one hand as he stood under a streetlamp at 115th Street. He was staring straight at me.

"Buy you a beer," he said.

"No, thanks," I said. I walked faster, but he kept pace.

"It wasn't a question," he said.

I stopped, but my heartbeat quickened.

"Look," I said, "nothing personal, all right?"

"Of course it's personal," the Confident Man said. "You spend your life trying to tell stories that are true, and you get nothing to show for it. Then you see some con artist getting rich writing a memoir full of lies. How can you not take it personally?"

There was something uncanny about how accurately he had read my thoughts, almost as if he were not simply a man trying to engage me in conversation but a conjurer showing me some parlor trick he had mastered.

"Buy you a beer, Ian?" he asked.

I could feel his hypnotic gaze pulling me in.

"You know my name?" I asked.

"And your work, too," he said.

"My stories?"

He nodded. "I've even read some of them. They're smart, well-turned, but the fact is, they're just too quiet and small. Nothing ever really happens in them; nothing much is at stake.

"Beer?" he asked again.

We stood silently on Broadway for nearly a minute, neither of us moving aside for pedestrians. We stared at each other as I tried to figure out who he was, what his game might be.

"Just tell me what you want," I finally said.

"I want you to listen to a story," he said. "It won't cost you anything."

Okay, I said, I'd let him buy me a beer.

THE CONFIDENT MAN'S STORY, PART I

At the 106 Bar on Amsterdam Avenue, I chose a window table as close to as many other customers as possible. I let the Confident Man buy the beers but insisted that he give me the money so I could go up to the bar and order them just in case he'd been planning to slip anything into mine. I was tempted by his offer to let me keep the change from his twenty, but when I came back from the bar with the beers, I gave him the money—if he wanted to buy me another beer, maybe, but I wouldn't take anything from him, at least not until I knew who he was, and how he knew my name and my work. Even then, I wouldn't have compromised my principles for a lousy four bucks.

After I'd had a few sips of my Guinness and we'd chatted a bit, just small talk and pleasantries about some stories I'd written and he'd apparently read, I began to relax. My headache began to recede too. Something felt reassuring about the Confident Man's presence, his nonchalance, his ability to anticipate anything I might say, the way he seemed to know me as well as I knew myself. His demeanor seemed as smooth as his Jay Gatsby jacket and slacks, his manner of speaking as clear as the lenses in those black-framed franzens.

His name was Jed Roth, he told me as he leaned back in his chair, and until recently, he'd worked as an editor for Merrill Books. I had, in fact, sent some of my stories there—supposedly, the publisher didn't accept unagented submissions, but all it cost me to try was the stamps and the paper, and who knew, maybe if I wrote REQUESTED MANUSCRIPT in big block letters on my envelope, I would catch the attention of some panza going through the slush pile. The Requested Manuscript gambit never worked for me. Once, I tried submitting a story to Miri Lippman's *The Stimulator* magazine and wrote REQUESTED MANUSCRIPT on it in marker; when the story was returned to me, someone, probably Miri herself, had scrawled NOT in front of REQUESTED.

For a moment, I thought that Roth might be offering to publish my work, but he said he didn't work for Merrill anymore, hadn't in more than a year, wasn't working as an editor anywhere now.

"What happened?" I asked. Roth held up his copy of *Blade by Blade,* showing me the spine with the Merrill Books logo on it.

"This happened," he said.

I chuckled when he showed me the book. I still hated it, sure, but said I doubted that it had much to do with why Roth was no longer working for James Merrill, Jr.

"Are you sure about that?" asked Roth.

"No." I shrugged.

"Well, then maybe you should hear the story now," Roth said.

I told him to go ahead.

THE CONFIDENT MAN'S STORY, PART II

Jed Roth said his story was probably fairly similar to mine, but other than the facts that we both loved books and had spent our early adulthoods in New York trying to write them, that didn't really seem to be true. He was the son of a privileged family; his ancestors had come over on the Mayflower. I had grown up in a small town that nobody had ever heard of midway between Indianapolis and Terre Haute, Indiana, the son of a law student and a university librarian. Roth had been educated in literature and writing at some of the finest East Coast schools; twenty years after my mom died, I had dropped out of grad school to take care of my dad and had never completed my degree.

A little more than a decade earlier, when he was about my age, Roth intended to devote his life to books—writing them, reading them, selling them. He worked at bookstores, took internships at publishers. When he wasn't working, he was reading in libraries, writing in cafés, submitting stories to journals and magazines, reading those stories aloud at open-mike nights. This part sounded fairly familiar to me, but even here, our life stories weren't as similar as Roth seemed to think—I was always more interested in character than plot; Roth said he didn't care much about developing characters, what was important to him was telling a good tale.

Roth had tried to work as much as possible in places that would inspire him to write, the older and more atmospheric the better—the Society Library, the Mercantile, the reading room of the main branch of the New York Public Library. At these and other locations, Roth read classic yarns, swashbuckling high-seas adventures, hard-boiled detective stories, Western shoot-'em-ups, stories of prospectors digging for gold. He read Robert Louis Stevenson, Joseph Conrad, B. Traven, G. K. Chesterton, and Arthur Conan Doyle. He liked chase scenes, confrontations aboard tall ships or fast-moving trains. When he first started trying to write seriously, he imitated the stories he was reading, wrote penny dreadfuls, fast-paced thrillers, tales that whipped by so fast the pages practically turned themselves. He gave his stories mysterious, evocative titles—"A Desolate Field, Beneath a Golden Cross"; "It's Always Darkest Just Before the Kill." In every one of his stories there were treasure maps, plot twists, and clues; his chapters were short, and every one ended on a suspenseful scheherazade. He said he was a fast writer; he figured he could make a living cranking out one story after another.

But after he'd begun submitting the stories to prominent literary agents and publishers, he received just about the opposite responses that I tended to receive regarding mine—there was too much going on in his work. Sure, the stories were entertaining and suspenseful, but they didn't speak to contemporary society or the human condition. Given all there was to write about in the modern world, who still wanted to read about buried treasure or prospectors digging for gold? Roth needed to draw on his own experiences and observations.

Roth said he had never thought of writing from his own experience; to him, writing a story was supposed to be about making something up. He had never considered reading to understand more about the human condition; reading was all about escaping it.

Disheartened, Roth spent hours when he wasn't working wandering the streets of Manhattan searching for modern stories, adventures with contemporary settings. He felt hopelessly out of date; maybe he had been born in the wrong era. The stories he read in newspapers concerned property crimes, home invasions, bribery scandals, and all that was too dull, depressing, and real. He truly wanted to write swashbucklers and Westerns, but there were no pirates doing battle on the East River, no cowboys riding horseback on the Central Park bridle paths, no treasure maps in Riverside Park. Nowhere could he detect any glint of buried gold. He placed a few stories in obscure journals and men's magazines, published some in anthologies with titles such as *Fantastic Yarns* and *Unknown Tales,* but the most he ever made from his writing was fifty bucks.

The Blom Library on Lexington Avenue and East Thirty-third Street had once been the property of Chester Blom, an early-twentieth-century railroad magnate and collector of manuscripts and East Asian art. The dusty and mildewed reading room of the Blom Library was filled with seemingly priceless curiosities—Shakespeare folios, letters the Bard wrote to Anne Hathaway, obscure Gospels written on parchment, codexes of the Comte de Graal, original letters written by Cicero, Rousseau, Goethe, and Voltaire. The Blom's most prominently displayed possession was a rare and precious bound copy of Murasaki Shikibu's *The Tale of Genji,* an eleventh-century illustrated version of the classic book that had been used by professional readers who performed Murasaki's tale before wealthy spectators, many of whom were unable to read. *Genji* was a thousand-page epic concerning the loves and travails of the eponymous son of a Japanese emperor. It was considered by many to be the world's first novel and the foundation of modern fiction, and this manuscript was its earliest-known surviving exemplar. The book, with its stained leather cover, adorned with gold filigree, and opened to its exquisite, first illustrated page, which depicted Genji's birth, was displayed in a glass case in the reading room. The character of Genji was nicknamed the "Shining Lord" for his beauty, and the shimmering gold leaf on this book's cover inspired its own nickname—the "Shining Lord Manuscript."

Chester Blom's widow, Cecille, had willed the library and its collection to a private foundation that was run by her heirs, to be used solely for the study of its contents. The library and its reading room were open to members of the Blom family and to scholars and writers who successfully completed a detailed application and paid a five-hundred-dollar annual membership fee. One evening, while walking south on Lexington toward the bookstore where he was working at the time, Roth looked through the library's windows, saw the reading room's green desk lamps and its sagging bookshelves, and, immediately after entering, applied to become a member.

"An odd place, that Blom Library," Roth told me as he sipped his beer, clearly relishing his memory of the place. The Blom collection was bizarre not only for its contents, Roth said, but for the way the library was run. It was too dark and musty to allow anyone to seriously read or study for any great length of time. Manuscripts that were available on certain days became unavailable on others. Well-qualified applicants who truly needed to see a copy of a specific manuscript for their scholarly work often found their research proposals rejected; people like Roth, who just wanted to browse, read, or write, were accepted. Unlike Roth's other favorite libraries, which kept conventional workday hours, the Blom had an idiosyncratic schedule that actually suited Roth well—before he was due to open mail at Merrill Books or after he was done with a bookstore shift, he would hole up in the library. He'd sign out one rare manuscript or another, put on thin white cotton gloves to read for the first half of his library session, then brainstorm stories for the second half.

The Blom's front desk was manned by a gruff, bald, and muscular goon who seemed to have little affection for literature. He smoked unfiltered vonneguts in the reading room and flicked ashes onto his desk. He spoke little and when he did, mangled the English language—"Wot you said?" he'd ask whenever Roth asked to see a volume. He'd demand Roth's ID, study it, then ask, "Wot useta be your name is?" Even though the man never seemed to do much other than work crossword puzzles, he would often tell Roth not to bother him, to sit back down and return later—"How's that soun' like a good idea?" he'd add. Roth began to refer to him as the "Hooligan Librarian."

Most of the regulars at the Blom were academics, writers, or well-heeled senior citizens, who Roth thought might be descendants of Chester and Cecille Blom. Most were men, but one day, a young woman caught his eye. He never learned her name, even now still referred to her only as the "Girl in the Library," and said he just remembered the color of her hair and eyes, and the pallor of her skin. As she strolled through the reading room, behaving as if she owned it, she seemed fascinated by all the documents and books, but particularly *The Tale of Genji*. Roth watched her intently studying the book through its locked glass cover, its beautiful, snow-covered landscapes, its parasol-hefting noblewomen, its splendid kimonos. She took notes in a little red book. Roth wondered who she was, whether she could read the language or whether she was just fascinated by the images. He imagined her to be a graduate student or perhaps a young editor working on a new translation of the book. He resolved that he would introduce himself to her and ask. But she didn't stay long. He saw her ask the Hooligan Librarian if she could take out the "Shining Lord," but the man said no, that wasn't allowed; the book was "too delicate-like." She asked to see some other manuscripts in the collection; no, the man told her, those weren't available.

"Check back Monday," he told her. "How's that soun' like a good idea?"

Roth was there on Monday, but the girl wasn't.

And neither was the library.

THE CONFIDENT MAN'S STORY, PART III

The sirens should have alerted him, but Roth didn't even notice their wail until he arrived at the place where the entrance was supposed to be. Where the library had been were mounds of rubble, charred manuscripts, the shell of a building with its windows blacked out, smashed in; firefighters were moving deliberately but slowly through the wreckage as if there was no longer any urgency to their mission. The air was thick and dark, suffused with the stench of burned paper, which flurried in the breeze like black snow. The site was bordered by yellow caution tape, and when Roth tried to get a closer look, he couldn't get past news reporters, gawking spectators, and police officers, who were trying to push everybody back so they could gather what appeared to be already beyond salvaging.

I had heard of the fire at the Blom—when he was still working, my dad often directed me to interesting news stories about libraries. He told me about the legendary Belgian library of Jean Népomucène Auguste Pichauld, a fictional library full of imaginary books. He taught me about tragedies that had befallen famous libraries throughout history—the great fire in Alexandria in 48 B.C., the destruction of the Louvain Library in 1914, the fires set at the Los Angeles Public Library in the mid-1980s. He told me about the destruction of obscure libraries as well—those in Norwich, in Lynbrook, Long Island, and on the East Side of Manhattan at the Blom. Roth told me that the story of the Blom fire made all the New York papers and television stations.

An investigation was conducted, arson suspected but never confirmed; the fire could just as well have been caused by the library's antiquated electrical system and generally shabby condition. What remained of the building was demolished, the ground was cleared; within a year, another building rose, condominiums, and soon there was no sign that the Blom Library had ever been there. There was no Girl in the Library anymore, no Hooligan Librarian, no *Tale of Genji*. Roth had witnessed an interesting beginning to a story, perhaps, but nothing more. That was the problem with trying to write about reality, Roth thought—the modern human condition, whatever that may have been, didn't follow the arc of a good plot: characters appeared then drifted away; conflicts remained unresolved; imaginary love affairs stayed imaginary; even as dramatic an incident as a fire blazing through a strange old library was rendered banal or inconclusive in explanation. If anyone wanted to know who the Girl in the Library might have been, what might have happened to the Hooligan Librarian, if anyone wanted a more compelling story than an unexplained fire and a pile of rubble, ash, and blackened books cleared away to make room for condos, he'd have to invent a story.

"And that's what I did," Roth told me. "I made up a story."

By now, I had finished my beer, and the 106 Bar was filling up. Couples were drinking pitchers, guys from the neighborhood were watching football on TV, hollering at the screen as they ate handfuls of wasabi peas from small wooden bowls, a jukebox played "People of the South Wind." Roth had taken off his charcoal gray gatsby and hung it on the back of his chair. He was an especially good-looking man, I began to think, one who inspired confidence as much as he demonstrated it, who held within him the promise of success, the kind of man I wouldn't have minded seeing myself become in fifteen years if I could figure out a way to clean myself up, keep myself fit, and make a pile of dough.

"Why're you telling me all this?" I asked.

"Patience, Ian," said Roth.

I was feeling buzzed from the Guinness, and I was no longer in any rush to leave the bar. I had nowhere else to go but home, and no one was waiting for me there. Roth asked if I wanted to hear about the story he wrote, and when I told him I did, that I was a sucker for stories, he handed me another twenty and told me to buy us a second round.

THE CONFIDENT MAN'S STORY, PART IV

Jed Roth started the novel *A Thief in Manhattan* as an original modern tale, but one that encompassed elements of classic adventures he loved—fights and chases, shoot-outs, a mysterious damsel in distress with a surprising secret. It began with a library much like the Blom, a hooligan librarian, a lovely, pale woman admiring *The Tale of Genji,* and a man at the next table wondering what it all might add up to.

It didn't seem like much to build a story on, Roth thought, but *Genji* was the book that had invented novels, so it didn't seem like a bad place to start. Roth tried to imagine himself back at the Blom Library, then asked himself, "What if?"

And maybe that was a good way to write a story, he

thought—start with reality, take a vicious left turn, slam on the gas, never look back. Maybe all stories started with "What if?" *What if* the Girl in the Library's interest in the *Genji* wasn't some passing fancy but a long-held personal obsession; *what if* Roth's interest in the Girl wasn't an idle reverie but a deep passion, the sort of love at first sight he'd read about in novels but never truly experienced? *What if* the Hooligan wasn't just a librarian but also a thief who was planning to steal *The Tale of Genji?* *What if* every time the Hooligan said a manuscript was out or "unavailable," he had actually brought it to a crooked appraiser's office and fenced it? *What if* Roth had seen the Hooligan Librarian pilfering valuable documents from the Blom, heard the man discussing the *Genji,* then decided he would steal that book for the Girl himself? *What if* he actually involved himself in the story?

Roth imagined himself as the hero of a classic thriller, one in which a naïve young man stumbles upon a crime and soon finds himself in a situation beyond his control. He imagined hiding in the Blom Library until late in the evening, crouched in darkness among the stacks, inhaling the aroma of all those ancient volumes, breathing some of the same air and dust that had once been inhaled by Shakespeare, Chatterton, and Marlowe. He imagined watching the Hooligan Librarian insert some precious document into a metal case, lock it, then head out.

And then, in his imagination and in the story he was beginning to scribble as fast as he could because now he was getting excited, he was following the Librarian, yes, tailing that hooligan, and here they went—now out of the musty library, now onto the rain-puddled sidewalk, now into the subway station, now onto the uptown 6 train, *Excuse me, miss, excuse me, sir, hold that door.* He imagined himself keeping an eye on the metal case as he squeezed his way through the crowds at Grand Central, then onto the Times Square shuttle, *Pardon me, sorry, pardon me.* He imagined emerging from another subway all the way down at Delancey Street, out into a windy, rain-soaked night, neon light now quivering in puddles, pedestrians clutching tightly to black poppinses, some of those poppinses blown inside out. He imagined keeping to the shadows; trying to stay warm and dry in his gogol; hiding in the doorway of a bodega. He imagined himself watching the Hooligan Librarian pounding the buzzer on a panel in a doorway across the street; the door clicking open; the Librarian disappearing inside the dilapidated six-story building.

The faster Roth wrote, the more ideas kept coming. "What if?" he kept asking himself.

What if?

Up five flights of rickety stairs where the Librarian was headed, there was a seedy fencing operation masquerading as a manuscript appraisal service. Stacks of dusty manuscripts were piled on lopsided shelves, and jewelers' loupes and magnifying glasses were scattered on a long desk. Behind the desk, Roth imagined, there was a woman about seventy. She wore thick Joan Didion glasses and her silver hair was parted down the middle and gathered in a tight bun. She was straitlaced in appearance, but she swore like a sailor; every other word out of her mouth seemed to start with an F. Roth decided that the fence would be Iola Jaffe, sole proprietor of Iola Jaffe, Rare Manuscripts and Appraisal Services.

Roth felt himself immersed in the story now, could imagine his characters' physical appearances, their names. Once

Norbert Piels—yes, Piels would be the name of the Hooligan Librarian—once Norbert Piels had finished cutting some deal with Iola Jaffe, he would exit the apartment, step out into the rainstorm with his case, hail a cab. And Roth, or whoever the hero was—he hadn't come up with that name yet but Roth was as good a name as any—would catch a taxi too. And then, *zhooooom,* a game of Follow That Cab, detective stuff, noir thriller, 1940s, a lady cabdriver: *"You keep a good tail on that taxi, there'll be a twenty in it for you, sugar."* Across Delancey they ride, up the West Side Highway, exit at Ninety-sixth Street, windows foggy, wipers going, north to Tiemann Place, where two taxis stop: *"Keep it." "Thanks for the change, mister—say, you know, I get off work at twelve." "Some other time, precious."* The two men emerge from their taxis; one heads for a droopy prewar mid-rise, the other follows at a distance. Roth stands under a streetlamp, watches Norbert Piels enter his building, waits for a light to go on, *look, there's one,* fourth floor.

In Roth's story, he stands there all night, watching. Waiting for morning. Then, early the next day, the skies clear, and Norbert Piels lumbers out of the apartment building, heading for the 125th Street elevated train platform. Our hero follows him down the street, up the escalator, onto the platform. The southbound number 1 train arrives, doors open, people jostle to get on. Piels, too big and bulky for the gatsby he's wearing, tries to shove his way past, but our hero shoves him back: *'Scuse me, pardon me, bugger off, how's that soun' like a good idea?* In the confusion, Roth reaches into the Librarian's pocket, grabs his keys, pockets them, and the train doors close. Roth doesn't board the train but Piels does, and it starts rumbling south. Roth or whatever his name is runs for the train station stairs, down to the street, and catches a cab: *Blom Library, Thirty-third and Lex, and make it fast.* When he gets to the library, he tries Norbert's keys, then opens the door. He enters the reading room, waits for his eyes to get accustomed to the dark. And then he sees it under glass: *The Tale of Genji.* The "Shining Lord." The illustration on display is so lovely, the shimmering cover magnificent. But there is only a moment to admire, because the Librarian is approaching the door, the door is opening, and *bam!* Roth brings his fist down on the glass. It shatters, the alarm sounds, and our hero grabs *The Tale of Genji* and runs for the back door, down the stairs, out to the street.

Taxi!

Back to Delancey Street, back to Iola Jaffe and her rare and most probably stolen manuscripts, up the stairs to the sixth floor—*What is this?* Roth wants to know. *What is it worth?* Iola Jaffe, a grim-visaged figure all in black, lips pursed as if she just tasted something foul, hisses: *How much is this* Genji *worth?*

Iola Jaffe sighs, contemplating. "No one ever has any questions about literary merit," she says. "No one asks about provenance or cultural relevance. Just 'how much?' World full of Philistines! How much? Twenty years ago, the price at auction for one like this was six point six million. That's how motherfucking much."

"And *today,*" Roth asks, pressing her, "how much would *this* one be worth *today?*"

"Today?" she asks.

Iola Jaffe steps into another room. There are sounds of clattering, the mewing of cats—she's the sort of woman who would keep cats. When she returns, she's holding a loaded .38-caliber canino.

"Today, I'll take it for free," she says, and directs Roth to put the manuscript down. He backs away, raises his hands. But then he reaches forward and lunges for the gun. They wrestle and the gun flies to the floor. Iola goes for the canino, while Roth goes for the book. He grabs it, throws open the door, and runs out. Iola fires her weapon; hammetts whiz past Roth's head as he races down the stairs, fourth floor, third floor, second, first. He pushes the door hard, shoving Norbert, who has just arrived, and knocking him to the ground. "Wot you done?" Norbert Piels asks, his eyes wide. Manuscript under an arm, our hero jumps into a taxi: *Step on it, driver!*

THE CONFIDENT MAN'S STORY, PART V

The crowd at the 106 Bar was thinning out. The game on the bar's TV was over; the sports fans were heading home. The bartender shouted, "Last call." Roth and I were nearly done with our fourth beers, and he was winding up his story. He had, in fact, managed to put elements into it from just about every genre he loved. In the cat-and-mouse game between the narrator, the Hooligan Librarian, and Iola Jaffe, there were elements of espionage fiction; in the chase for the manuscript, he had found a sort of treasure hunt. In the hero's seemingly futile search for the Girl in the Library, Roth modernized tales of knights. And in the climactic confrontation, which he borrowed from one of his own short stories, the one entitled "A Desolate Field, Beneath a Golden Cross," hero and villains fought it out for the *Genji,* which was buried outside Manhattan in the titular location. The scene was an updated and fairly brutal Western shoot-out in which the hero offs his foes before hopping a train to find his girl.

A Thief in Manhattan didn't sound like the kind of story I'd write or read, and certainly not the sort I'd mention when trying to impress anybody. Back then, I tended to define my tastes in opposition to whatever was deemed either brilliant or popular; the quality or success of a work was probably directly proportional to how much I envied it. But Roth was a talented storyteller, one confident his listener would follow him wherever he went. So I was surprised when he told me he had been unable to find anyone to publish his novel.

Times were different in publishing fifteen years earlier, when he wrote his book, Roth said, and the smarmy, pretentious agents and publishers he approached felt *A Thief in Manhattan* wasn't sufficiently literary. It was just a fun page-turner that didn't aspire to be anything more. Roth told me that he supposed he could have tried to find some pulpy, less-esteemed publishing house, but after one literary agent's particularly savage assessment, he just gave up.

"Which agent?" I asked.

"Geoffrey Olden," said Roth.

"What did he tell you?" I wondered if Olden had been as nasty with Roth as he had been with me.

"Something characteristically imperious, unctuous, and snide," said Roth.

When Jed Roth began sending his manuscript around, the Olden Literary Agency was brand-new, Geoff Olden having just left the venerable Sterling Lord Literistic to form his own agency. Olden was not yet thirty and had only half a dozen clients but already had the attitude of someone who had been in the business for decades. Olden invited Roth to his Soho office, an invitation that Roth foolishly mistook to mean that Olden was interested in his work. Sitting behind his desk, Olden crossed his hands over Roth's manuscript, studied Roth through his eckleburgs, and said that "no serious house in New York would ever consider publishing this in its current form," and that there was only one way any publisher at all would consider doing so.

Which way was that? Roth asked.

"If every word of it was true," said Olden. He smirked, then slid the manuscript across his desk back to Roth.

"Jackass," I said.

Roth put the manuscript in a drawer, deciding that he had no future as a writer, that his ideas were too hackneyed and unliterary. He still loved books, but he would no longer fantasize about writing them. From time to time, he might think back to the Blom Library and those strange characters he had seen there, but when he did, he would no longer wonder *What if?* He'd leave that question to people with more talent and imagination.

Instead, he became an editor, worked his way up the ladder at Merrill Books, a fixture of New York publishing since the early 1950s when James Merrill, Sr., founded it. James Jr., who was in charge when Jed Roth started working there had been an undergraduate at Yale during Merrill Books's early days, when it was primarily an old boys' operation, redolent of bourbon, cigars, and exclusive East Side clubs where men swam naked and discussed Great Ideas in steam rooms. Younger, energetic editors toiled for aristocratic elder statesmen and the occasional elder stateswoman. In the late 1970s, after Merrill Sr. stepped down and his son took over, the publisher maintained its prestige and also most of its previous editors. James Sr. kept an office where he penned his exceedingly honest and exceedingly uninteresting memoirs. The differences between Merrill Books, Sr., and Merrill Books, Jr., were predominantly ones of style. A somber, studious, and grubby downtown office became a slick midtown one located on a high floor of a steel-and-glass office building on Seventh Avenue.

Roth started at Merrill Books by opening mail, making coffee, answering phones, and getting called "Young Man" or "Boy" by Merrill Jr., who seemed to think that being called by name was a privilege his employees had to earn. Roth was passed over for promotions in favor of younger assistants, those with family connections or those who happened to be sleeping with one of Merrill's editors. Still, Roth persisted with a furious intensity and certainty of purpose, dutifully carrying out tasks that the other assistants considered themselves above. After senior editor Ellen Curl performed her annual ritual of firing her assistant, Roth applied for the position, and when he got it, did absolutely everything asked of him without complaint, working nights and weekends; went without sleep so he could read manuscript submissions; wrote detailed coverages; offered recommendations for or against publication that were remarkably canny. He lasted longer at this position than any assistant Ellen Curl ever had. Of all his talents, most useful was knowing the sorts of manuscripts Merrill Books wanted, not always the most entertaining books, not usually the ones Roth enjoyed reading, but ones that maintained the publisher's reputation. Soon, he began to acquire his own books, and although few were great financial or literary successes, most made a modest amount of money, and Roth enjoyed the cachet that came with being a respected editor at a respectable publishing house.

But after James Merrill, Sr., died, and other veteran editors including Ellen Curl began retiring, James Merrill, Jr., became more concerned with maintaining a financial legacy for his own children, fuckups the lot of them, than the literary prestige of the company his father had built. He severely reduced the number of books Merrill was publishing and formed a more commercial imprint, JMJ Publishers. Jed Roth had thought that the further he rose in the company and the longer he stayed, the more freedom he would have. The opposite turned out to be true. He found himself questioned at every turn, burdened with thankless assignments—diet books, ghostwritten celebrity autobiographies—as Merrill Jr. paid greater attention to the highly profitable JMJ Publishers.

When a six-hundred-page memoir, written by a two-bit thug and music business hanger-on named Blade Markham, arrived at Merrill Books, Jed Roth had been working there for over ten years. He had a spacious office with a dramatic view, a list of about three dozen authors, and also a new assistant named Rowell Templen, who had been foisted upon him by James Merrill, Jr., who was either sleeping with Templen or owed Templen's father a favor. Templen, an oily, sideburned twenty-four-year-old Princetonian, fond of velour blazers worn over V-neck sweaters and ties, had an obsequious air that, to Roth, rendered him immediately untrustworthy. Templen's accommodating manner and his way of meekly knocking before entering Roth's office could not disguise his ruthless ambition any more than the bottles of Listerine he kept in his desk and in his sport-jacket pockets could disguise his penetrating halitosis.

Jed was sitting at his desk, working through a gossipy Hollywood memoir as fast as he could, when Templen knocked twice, then entered with an intimidating tolstoy of pages.

"Time to read today, Mr. Roth?" he asked.

Roth said that he didn't, but asked what Templen had in mind. Templen showed him the title page of *Blade by Blade*. He said he knew that Roth didn't like to be bothered with submissions before they had been summarized, but he hoped Roth would make an exception. This book was brilliant, Templen said, so raw and so true; when he had read one of Blade Markham's prison scenes, he practically palahniuked all over his desk. Roth told Templen to put Markham's manuscript in his box and he'd look at it someday when he had the chance, but Templen said, No, Mr. Roth, there wasn't any time to wait—three other publishing houses were already considering the book, and he was sure it would sell by the end of the week.

Roth didn't know whether to feel angered or amused by Templen's presumption—in all his years as an assistant, he never told Ellen Curl to put aside her work—but his curiosity was piqued. So, after Templen closed the door to his office, Roth picked up Blade Markham's manuscript and turned to the dedication page. And then he burst into hysterical laughter.

THE CONFIDENT MAN'S STORY, PART VI

Jed Roth and I were walking up Amsterdam Avenue now, pass-ing shuttered storefronts, restaurants with chairs up on tables, all-night groceries populated mostly by hard-luck men and women standing on line for lottery tickets. Drunk Columbia University students were laughing too loudly, trying to walk straight lines as they searched vainly for bars that were still open. Roth said he had something he wanted to show me at his apartment, and I was too drunk to be suspicious anymore.

"So, what happened next?" I asked.

As we headed west on 111th Street toward Riverside Drive, I was trying not to slur my words; Roth, who I thought had drunk as much beer as I had, was still as precise as ever in his speech, as if he had already memorized his lines. His slacks and gatsby were as smooth as when the night had begun.

Roth said that he supposed he could have stopped reading Blade Markham's manuscript after a page or two, when it be-came clear to him that just about every word was "utter horse-shit," but he read the entire thing. He supposed, too, that he could have just told Rowell Templen that he had read *Blade by Blade* and that he wasn't interested. Instead, he channeled all the frustration he felt at the ignominy of editing diet, exercise, and celebrity books, all his anger at the direction Merrill Books and JMJ Publishers were taking, into marking up just about every page Blade Markham had typed. He noted every grammatical flaw, every preposterous boast. He worked past midnight, in-sisting that Rowell Templen stay until he was done. And when that time came, he called Templen into his office and proceeded to berate him for the better part of an hour, ostensibly to teach the punk a little bit about publishing and literature.

Everything about *Blade by Blade* was a lie, Roth told Templen, and if the young assistant couldn't or didn't care to sniff out the BS in Markham's manuscript, well, then, why didn't he either join the circus or go to business school? He didn't know whether Templen was gullible or just cynical, but either way, he didn't belong here.

The kid didn't flinch, just stood there the whole time, hands folded in front of his portnoy, the same arrogant, pinched lips, the same bored slouch, the same empty stare, the same tosses of his oily, shoulder-length hair, while Roth became more and more agitated. When Roth finally ran out of insults, Templen merely took the manuscript from him, said "Thank you, Mr. Roth," then walked out.

"The skill I had was one I hadn't realized was a skill," Roth told me as we turned north onto Riverside Drive. A faint halo rainbowed the half-moon overhead, and the neighborhood was silent save for the occasional whirring of a passing taxi or the footsteps of a doorman heading home at the end of a shift. Soon, Roth and I were the only ones on a long stretch of sidewalk.

"What skill?" I was walking with a jittery, drunken feeling; the streetlights were making crazy zigzags, as if I were looking through the viewfinder of a camera I couldn't hold still.

"The ability to tell not only if something actually happened, but, also, whether the telling is true," said Roth. "Because sometimes fiction lies too."

As we walked into the lobby of his five-story building, with its marble floor and staircase, and its cathedral ceilings, Roth flashed me a knowing look. In that look, I could see that he was trying to tell me that he and I shared this ability, this sense of knowing what was and wasn't true. I didn't know exactly how he sensed that about me other than remarks he'd perhaps overheard me making to Faye about *Blade by Blade* at Morningside Coffee. But if he could discern the truth of a manuscript by page two, maybe he could do the same thing with people.

"I was so sure everyone else would see what a fraud it was. It seemed so obvious to me," Roth said as we entered his elevator and he pushed the number four button. "I soon learned I was wrong."

THE CONFIDENT MAN'S STORY, PART VII

Roth was working at his desk on a Friday afternoon, ready to head home, when his door swung open.

"Busy, Jed?" James Merrill, Jr., asked, and before Roth could respond, Merrill told him, "There's someone I'd like you to meet."

In all my years of reading at open mikes, working at the coffee shop, and at private publishing parties, I had never met James Merrill, Jr. I knew him only from pictures in the Sunday Styles section—a man with a sophisticated, John Steinbeck mustache and tailored Savile Row suits—and from the other night at the Blade Markham party, when I had seen him pop a grape into his mouth. I associated him with a golden era of publishing, a time when men spoke with the vaguely British inflection of 1940s Hollywood film stars. But to Roth, Merrill was a dolt who had never edited a single manuscript on his own, perhaps had never even read a book of any length all the way through; he based his impressions of the books he published on their first and last pages and on the coverages his editors and their assistants provided for him.

Roth followed Merrill down the hall to the conference room, where Rowell Templen and Geoff Olden were already seated, drinking scotch with Blade Markham, who was boasting of having glugged slivovitz with snipers in Sarajevo and faced down fellow gangbangers in South Central LA.

"Tell it to ya' straight, son," Blade told Templen, who had asked him if he kept in touch with any of the people in his stories. "If I gave y'all the righteous answer to that, I'd have to waste all y'all, yo."

Roth surveyed the convivial conference room. It didn't take long for him to figure out that Jim Merrill and Rowell Templen had made a deal with Blade Markham behind his back. His mind reeling with thoughts of betrayal, he gritted his teeth. He shook hands with Blade, then seethed as Merrill told Roth that he had just signed a half-million-dollar contract to publish *Blade by Blade*. Apparently, Merrill said, "young Rowell" had discovered the manuscript on his own and had taken the initiative of bringing it directly to Merrill's attention.

"Young Rowell will be working directly on the book, but I'd like you to look over his shoulder a bit during the process," Merrill said to Roth, then added, as he always did, that the opening of *Blade by Blade,* probably the only part that he had troubled himself to read, was "a real knockout."

This news would have been humiliating enough, but when Templen looked up at Jed with an oily, smug, and victorious cheshire, and observed that he was sure he would "find Jed's feedback invaluable," Roth could not stand it anymore. "If you'll excuse me, gentlemen," he said, then walked fast out the door, letting it slam behind him.

Jim Merrill caught up with Roth when he was halfway down the hall and demanded to know the meaning of his behavior; exactly who did he think he was? Roth thought of trying to convince Merrill that Blade's book was a fraud, but after Merrill informed Roth that he had outbid three other publishers for the book and was planning to make *Blade by Blade* his lead title for the following autumn, Roth just walked away.

"You can't leave when I'm talking to you, Jed," Merrill said.

"Of course I can," Roth responded. "Because I don't work for you anymore."

THE CONFIDENT MAN'S STORY, PART VIII

"Well," Jed Roth said, handing me a glass of faulkner with two ice cubes in it as I sat on his living room couch, "now you have some idea why Rowell Templen has my job and I have none, why Blade Markham has a book contract and you have none, why we're two jobless men with enough free time to drink whiskey after midnight."

I clinked Roth's glass and swigged to the freedoms afforded to the unemployed.

Roth said his initial inclination after leaving Merrill was to start looking for another editing job, but he figured that he would probably find himself in a similar predicament, continuing to work in a frightened industry more concerned with its own survival than its legacy, one that had never quite lived up to his fantasy version of it anyway. He would spend more time improving the writing of celebrities who had been signed for their names, not their prose; more time ignoring obvious inventions in fake or exaggerated memoirs if those inventions would mean better sales. He would continue to live in a world of books, but would read fewer and fewer of them. When he had started out in New York, he'd read so much, but ever since he had begun working at Merrill, he read only the books that were relevant to his job, which wasn't really reading at all. He was unable to recall the last time he'd read solely for pleasure.

"So," I asked Roth as I sipped the whiskey that I certainly didn't need, "you would have published my stories if you could have?"

Roth laughed as if my question was so presumptuous and the answer so obvious that he didn't need to offer it.

"Of course not," he finally said, and when I looked at him, somewhat dumbfounded and more than a little defensive, he said, "No, Ian. You're a decent writer. You know how to take a story from your life and tell it in a way that makes it sound smart and sad and witty and real. You know how to do that, but in the end, so what?"

"So, you'd think that would be enough," I said.

Roth made a *peh* sound with his lips. "Why would you think that, Ian?" he asked, and in the suddenly fierce gaze with which he now regarded me, I could see the way he had tried to face down Rowell Templen, could now see the hint of his deep, well-concealed rage.

"Why would you think that would be worth something?"

Roth asked. "Writing a book can be a profoundly optimistic act; expecting someone to read, buy, and publish it is always a phenomenally presumptuous one. Why would a marketing department put money behind anything you wrote? Why would someone who didn't know you spend twenty-five dollars to read your stories of small people leading small lives? Your stories aren't unusual, Ian, nothing happens in them. Your characters don't do much; they rarely have anything of value at stake. You're not famous, you're not rich, you're not outrageously talented, you have no platform. Tell me exactly what there is about you that anybody would want to sell or buy?"

"So, that's what it's about now?" I asked.

"That's what it was always about," said Roth. "Selling books. You thought it was about charity?"

I glared at him, initially unable to speak. So this was where his story had led: some cynical advice given by an embittered man who thought he could apply his lousy experiences to the life of a total stranger. Who was he to judge me, him with his thousand-dollar Jay Gatsby suits and his cashmere gogol and his designer franzens. I went back and forth in my mind, cursing Roth and cursing myself, cursing Roth for his cynicism and myself for my naïveté, cursing him for what he said and myself for the fact that he might be right.

Roth saw how angry and frustrated I was getting and started to laugh, as if he had known exactly how I would react. "What are you sniggering about?" I asked.

He held up one finger, turned with a little flourish, then left the room. I finished my drink in one gulp and stood up, but before I could make a move for the door, Roth returned with a bound manuscript and tossed it on the coffee table in front of me. I glanced at the title page—"*A Thief in Manhattan,* a novel by Jed Roth."

"Read it," he said.

"Yeah, maybe if you find someone who wants to publish it, someday I might," I said.

"Now," said Roth, and then he said it again, slowly but forcefully: "*Now.* I want you to read it now, Ian."

"What time is it?" I asked.

"Read it now."

"Why should I?" I asked.

"Read it and I'll tell you," said Roth.

"What for?"

"Read it and you'll know." He saw my eyes settling back on the title page, then looking back up at him. "It doesn't cost anything to read," he said.

"It costs my time."

"What's that worth to you?" He reached into a pants pocket, pulled out his wallet, took out a hundred-dollar bill, and tossed it onto the coffee table. And when I didn't say anything, he tossed another bill in my direction, then another. When there were five C-notes on the table beside *A Thief in Manhattan,* I asked what the five hundred bucks were really for.

"A reading fee," he said. All he wanted was for me to sit on his couch, read his manuscript, then tell him what I thought. For that, he would pay five hundred dollars, and afterward, if I chose, I could walk out and we would never speak about this again. I looked at the manuscript. I looked at the money. Back then, five hundred seemed like a lot.

"All right," I said, and flipped to the first sentence: "She was standing in a library."

A THIEF IN MANHATTAN

Jed Roth was making another pot of coffee, I was about half-done reading his manuscript, and out the window, dawn was beginning to purple the sky that was becoming visible through the nearly bare trees in Riverside Park. Roth asked if I needed to take a break or if I wanted to take a nap and finish reading when I woke up. No, I said, I'd keep reading until I was done.

Looking back, knowing how long it had been since I'd gotten any sleep, I'm surprised I was able to stay awake. But once in a while, a story can work as well as coffee or speed. During my father's last months, he said the meds never did much; the stories I read to him were all that seemed to ease his pain. Now my headache was gone, my drunkenness, too, and even if I was not as awake and chipper as Roth seemed to be—he kept walking in and out of the room, whistling, refilling my coffee mug, offering sandwiches and other snacks, apparently amused by the idea of playing Jeeves—I wasn't ready to pack it in, and not just because of the five hundred bucks.

Loath as I might have been to admit it at first, *A Thief in Manhattan* was a great read. While I was blazing through it, I no longer felt angry with Roth for having insulted me; in fact, I forgot how angry I had been. No, it wasn't particularly literary. In a writing workshop, I probably would have ripped it apart—peopled by broad, outlandish characters, filled with unbelievable events. But it was fun and fast, and I just wanted to keep flipping pages to learn how Roth would make it all turn out. The man who had written this wasn't some cynical former editor; he was an ambitious and creative young man, one who loved books and adventures, and hadn't yet learned to stop asking *What if?*

Apart from the story itself, what I liked most about *A Thief in Manhattan* were Roth's knowing literary references, the sorts of details that might have seemed precious to some readers, but not to a librarian's son. Throughout, Roth employed a literary sort of slang; he called an overcoat a "gogol," a smile a "cheshire," and an umbrella a "poppins." He called trains "high-smiths," because they appeared so often in Patricia Highsmith's thrillers, and referred to money as "daisies," since in *The Great Gatsby,* F. Scott Fitzgerald describes Daisy Buchanan's voice as being "full of money." At the end of Roth's manuscript, he included a glossary of literary terms, but I didn't need to consult it much; the only one I didn't get was "canino," Roth's word for a gun, which he took from the name of a heavy in *The Big Sleep,* a book I had never read.

References to books appeared on nearly every page of Roth's novel. When the reader first encountered the foul-mouthed manuscript appraiser Iola Jaffe, she was looking up from the Riverside Shakespeare, specifically Act III, Scene ii, of *Othello,* where Iago tells the Moor, "Men should be as they seem." In the novel's climactic moment, when it appeared the hero was about to be shot dead by Norbert Piels, he was able to wrest the gun away, shoot his adversaries, Piels and Jaffe, then hop an 8:13 train, 813 being the Dewey decimal number assigned to fiction. The longitude and latitude of *The Tale of Genji's* location corresponded to the Dewey numbers for illustrated books and foreign reference works. I knew that Roth's book was probably filled with more clues and in-jokes I wasn't getting, but I was reading too quickly to try to figure out all of them.

I kept turning pages, reliving all the parts of the adventure Roth had told me, feeling surprised by all the plot twists that he hadn't. I felt "Roth"'s passion for the Girl in the Library, his sorrow at the sight of the Blom reduced to rubble after Norbert set it ablaze in a fit of rage upon realizing that Roth had stolen *The Tale of Genji;* I felt my heart thump when Roth was being chased by Iola and Norbert, felt both horror and catharsis when Roth shot them dead, then buried them in the desolate field beneath a golden cross, and I felt elated when Roth was about to be reunited with the Girl in the Library. And when I read the last page and its final, charmingly hokey line, a question spoken in darkness by the Girl—"True love never has to end, so why shouldn't our story continue after the last page has been written?"—I couldn't help but think that Roth was talking about not only one love affair and one story, but about all stories, for a good story never has to end when it lives on in our minds. And I couldn't help but think that the reason why lately I had such trouble finishing stories was not because I wanted them to go on and on, but because I never really knew how to begin one. I wished I could learn how to start a story and see it through to the end so clearly that it could live on after the last page.

A MODEST PROPOSAL

"So?" Roth asked. I put the manuscript down on the coffee table and took a long look out at his view of Riverside Park.

"So what?" I asked.

"So, what do you think?"

I considered, then told Roth the truth, that I thought *A Thief in Manhattan* was a good story. To earn the five hundred dollars that was still on the coffee table, I told him that the book was a little violent and amoral for my tastes. Then I made some obvious points about his story's plausibility: I said that maybe I wouldn't have made all the Dewey decimal references—one was fun; three was overkill. I told him that I had a basic sense of most of the characters, but maybe Roth could have described the Girl in the Library better and told more about what happened after his hero reunited with her. Iola Jaffe and Norbert Piels were amusing foils, but without knowing their backstories or motivations, I ultimately grew weary of Iola's profane rants and Norbert's cruelty; I saw only glimmers of their humanity, never saw them as fully realized characters. The hero, too, Roth, wasn't sufficiently defined. I said that I couldn't tell whether the character was supposed to be a naïve, inexperienced guy in over his head, or whether he'd been conning the reader from the beginning and knew a whole lot more than he was letting on. I also told him that I didn't necessarily see why, even in an escapist caper, burying a valuable manuscript in some desolate field outside Manhattan made much sense, and when Roth muttered something about statutes of limitations and the fact that he liked to add "little turns of the screw" to his stories, I told him that, even so, a safe deposit box would have been better. But mostly, I said, my opinions didn't matter much, because *A Thief in Manhattan* was an entertaining story, and one that he could probably publish if he still wanted to—so what was he planning to do with the book?

Roth took a seat next to me on his couch, put his feet up on his coffee table, and then said that, actually, he himself wasn't planning on doing anything with the manuscript. He asked if I remembered what Geoff Olden had told him about it.

I did: "No serious house in New York would ever consider publishing this in its current form, and there was only one way anybody ever would—*if every word of it was true.*" I could hear Olden saying that, cackling in his imperious, unctuous, snide, know-it-all way.

"Man, what a jackass," I said.

"No, Olden was right," said Roth, adding that *A Thief in Manhattan* was, in fact, too implausible, too slight, and too shallow. Fiction had to be plausible, more so than the truth. And Roth's novel wasn't plausible.

"That's why the book will be published, yes, but not as fiction, Ian. It will be published as a memoir."

I laughed a little when Roth said that, thinking he was making a joke about *Blade by Blade*. But when he stared straight at me, I saw he wasn't joking.

Wait, I said, beginning to put it together, did Roth really mean to say that he would try to pass off his novel as truth, that he would present everything—the chase scenes, the gunfights, the search for the Girl in the Library—as a memoir?

"You'll say it all really happened to you?" I asked.

"No," Roth said, and then he smiled. "No, Ian. We'll say it all happened to *you*."

I tried to play it off like I still thought he was joking, but now he was regarding me even more intensely, as if I'd become his coconspirator. And somehow, I felt as if I already had.

"Yes, you'll say *you* wrote it," Roth continued. He kept repeating that word *you* as if he were slapping me in the face with it. "*You*'ll say it all happened to *you* just like it did in the book.

And if *you* agree, Ian, here's what will happen next. Agents will want to represent *your* book. Publishers will want to buy *your* book. There will be reviews of *your* book, there will be interviews with *you,* and then . . ."

"Then what?" I asked.

"Then what? Then, when a hundred thousand copies of *your* book have already been shipped to every bookstore in America, *you*'ll say that every word in it is a lie, that it was all made up. And here's the part *you*'ll like, Ian. When people ask why you did it, why you took a book full of lies and pretended it was true, you'll tell them that you did it because it was the only way to get anyone to pay attention to *your* stories. And soon those stories you wrote, the ones no one would publish because they were too small and no one knew who you were—everyone will want to publish them. Because you'll be somebody then, Ian. You'll have a name."

I couldn't tell whether he thought I was the stupidest guy in the world, or the cleverest and most cynical. He seemed to be suggesting that the two of us had a lot in common, had been implying that ever since we'd sat down at the 106 Bar and he'd told me his life story, and I had no idea whether he thought he was paying me a compliment or the nastiest insult he could devise.

"Why me?" I asked.

"Because you're the first person I've met who might hate *Blade by Blade* even more than I do," Roth said. He told me that he'd been coming to the café before I'd noticed him. He had heard me mouthing off about Blade Markham, and that's when he'd come up with the idea of taking *A Thief in Manhattan* out of its drawer. After he saw the name on my Morningside Coffee badge and remembered it from the few stories of mine he had read, he made a habit of coming into the café during my shifts, ostentatiously reading *Blade by Blade* and leaving large tips, waited to see what, if anything, I'd do. He said he hadn't been sure of his plan or that I was the right one to execute it. In my stories, the protagonists were too ineffectual; they always preferred to wait for events to take advantage of them than to seize them and create their own destinies. But when he saw me charging toward him at the café, when I grabbed his book out of his hands and whipped it down Broadway, he knew I could do it.

"You must think I'm pretty desperate," I said. It was a stupid thing to say. We both knew I was desperate. Roth didn't contradict me.

"Anyway, what's in it for you?" I asked.

"Revenge, of course," said Roth.

"On Merrill?" I asked.

Roth nodded. "Merrill, Rowell Templen, Geoff Olden, the whole pack of 'em. Take your pick."

And when Roth could see that I wasn't completely satisfied with his answer, he added, "I could make up something more romantic, Ian, something that might appeal more to your Midwestern sensibilities. But that's it, really. If this works the way I know it will, Blade Markham might well survive it. He will probably thrive. And so will you, Ian. But Jim Merrill? No. That little bastard Rowell Templen? Not him either. Because once people look more closely at the other 'true stories' Merrill has been publishing, no one will trust their word again. And then people will start looking at what other publishers have been putting out."

Roth's idea was funny in a sick sort of way, but I still felt there was something he wasn't telling me, still felt that all this seemed like a whole lot of trouble to go through just for a bit of revenge, no matter how detestable or gullible the Merrill Books crowd was—sure, they believed Blade Markham's book, but Roth's was even more far-fetched. Roth must have been reading my mind again because he said, "Oh, one other thing I should mention, Ian. If we do this together, I'll also be taking twenty-five percent."

"Of the book?" I asked.

"Of both books," Roth said. "My book and your stories. Call it a gamble. If I'm right, both of us come out with quite a bit of money."

"And if you're wrong?"

"That's the beauty of it," said Roth. "It's not high crime. It's not politics. No one's going to be breaking any laws. Only ethical ones, perhaps, but those don't come with prison terms. It'll just be a little publishing scandal, and outside of that tiny universe of authors, editors, agents, and readers, no one will give a damn."

But *A Thief in Manhattan* had been rejected years ago, I said; no one had wanted to publish it when Roth had first written it.

"Ancient history," said Roth. Besides, he added, it was a different book now.

How much had he changed, I asked.

"Just the word *novel*," he said. "That's all I needed to change."

I looked at the manuscript again. I looked at Roth. He seemed so confident that I would say yes. I wasn't sure if I felt more frightened by the thought that his scheme would work or the thought that it wouldn't, that I would ruin whatever reputation and self-respect I might have had for nothing, or that lying would make me as successful as Blade Markham.

"No," I finally said—there was no way it would work and no way I'd try it. I stood up, grabbed Roth's manuscript, and thrust it back at him. I thought I was flinging it hard, but he caught it and smiled, then set the manuscript back on the table as if I'd lobbed him a Frisbee.

"Why don't *you* do it if it's such a killer idea?" I asked.

"I'm too old for the part," said Roth. "No one would look at me and think I'd be chasing girls and hopping freight trains. Besides, the publishers all know me. And I'm not a writer anymore anyway. I'm not the one writing stories that everyone on the planet is rejecting while my Bulgarian girlfriend gets her stories published."

"She's not my girlfriend anymore," I said, getting angrier now, "and she's Romanian. And you probably know that. And you probably just said that to get at me." No, I told him. I could feel my headache returning, the fatigue curtaining down again. Roth would have to find someone just a bit more desperate than me, just a bit dumber, or just a bit more cynical.

I was at the door, hand on the knob, when I heard Roth's voice, as calm and measured as it had been all night and all morning.

"Oh, Ian?" He was staring at me again. "You remember what I said before? That talent of mine? Knowing when people are lying?"

I stared back at him.

"You're doing it now, Ian," he said.

"You go straight to hell," I said and walked out the door.

EFFECTIVE MEDICINE

My resolve was firm as I approached 112th Street, but when I reached 113th, it was already beginning to weaken. My thoughts had been clear on Riverside Drive, but when I turned east toward Broadway, I could already sense both mind and sight blurring, the sidewalk below me starting to tilt. The sun, up full now, was far too bright, but my army jacket was too thin for the cool, damp air. My chest felt cold, and yet my forehead was damp with sweat. How much coffee had I been putting in my body? How much scotch and beer? How much cynicism had Roth slipped into my mind like so much Rohypnol? How much self-doubt?

I needed someone to talk to, someone to run the whole story by, someone to tell me I had done the right thing by walking out, and that all I had to do was trust myself and that everything would turn out fine. Anya would have said something like that—*you heff sotch grett tellent, Ee-yen; you shoult trost in dett.* I would have liked to talk to Anya, to have one more of those bed-time conversations we used to have when both of us seemed to be heading in the same direction. But my life with Anya was now just one more thing on a long list of things I'd screwed up or thrown away.

I knew what my father would have told me; he believed in honesty at all costs—"Call up the hospital and tell them they didn't bill for that last procedure, Ian." But I didn't know what was more relevant: the fact that he would have told me I had done right by refusing Roth or the fact that my dad was dead and that, in the end, all his honesty and sage advice hadn't given him much except maybe some peace of mind.

I wound up at Morningside Coffee. Joseph was on a stool by the register, munching a bagel as he halfheartedly tried to memorize lines for another show in which he probably wouldn't get cast. Faye was finishing up a phone call and handing a customer a postcard for her gallery show. Joseph scowled as I entered and nudged Faye, who looked at me, raised one eyebrow at Joseph, then cheshired in my direction. For one more moment, I felt the floor firm beneath my feet; then it gave a sudden tilt and flung me down hard. I crashed into the Confident Man's old table, where the whole story had begun.

I woke up in darkness on a cold bed of concrete, my face pressed against burlap coffee sacks someone had meant to serve as pillows. I heard laughter and muffled conversations overhead. It took me half a minute to realize I wasn't in Roth's apartment anymore. A dim, distant light illuminated a steep metal ladder. I rubbed the sleep from my eyes, stumbled to my feet, stepped on the bottom rung of the ladder, and started to climb toward the light.

It was nighttime in Morningside Coffee; another day had already passed, the last customers were leaving, and Joseph was turning the sign on the door from OPEN to CLOSED. Faye was slinging a beat-up red vinyl bag over a shoulder and stuffing it with her postcards. She looked as though she was heading out for the night, but when she heard me mounting the stairs, she turned and said, "Thought you were gonna sleep till morning, Sailor."

"Sailor" was Faye's nickname for me, something she'd heard in some song, read in some book; apparently, it was a cultural reference I didn't get. She asked if I wanted coffee, flashed me a knowing "You're hungover and I'm not" smile. Joseph wasn't smiling, though—as always, my presence seemed to bug him, as if I were an uninvited guest at his party, one who'd palahniuked on his couch then passed out, while he'd had to clean up the mess. I started to thank Faye for giving me the burlap coffee sack pillows and letting me sleep in the basement, but Joseph interrupted.

"Didn't you used to work here?" he asked me.

Look, I said, trying to placate him; all I wanted was a cup of water and then I'd be on my way.

"Cup costs fifteen cents," said Joseph.

I began to reach into my pocket for money, but Faye took fifteen cents out of her change purse, whipped the coins in Joseph's direction, then told him to go home; she'd deal with the rest of the cleanup.

"I don't like the way you clean, woman," Joseph said. He sighed and told Faye he'd see her in the morning, but her "friend" had better be gone by then. He lingered in the doorway for a moment, watching the two of us, then glumly walked out toward his big black Citroën, which was parked outside. Faye poured me a glass of water and told me that Joseph really wasn't as nasty as he appeared to be and he really did have people's best interests at heart; when you really needed him, he always came through. She said she was sure I could have my job back if I wanted it. I thanked her but said no, I had to figure something else out; I wasn't going anywhere as long as I worked here.

Faye left me alone to brood in the Confident Man's old seat while she grabbed a pail of dirty water and a mop. She whistled a seventies tune as she washed the floor. Joseph was right about one thing: she sure did a lousy job—she left puddles every-where, and her paint-spattered boots made tracks wherever she clomped. Was she pretty? A lot of our regulars seemed to think so, but I hadn't taken the time to look at her that closely before. Her features were harsher than any thirty-four-year-old's should have been, and her skin looked as though she were aller-gic to sunlight—she spent all her days in studios and her nights in cafés. Plus, I still wasn't sure if she was straight or not. But either way, I couldn't stop watching her, so amused by the world, so comfortable in her own body, so confident even in her own clumsiness.

When I was done drinking the water, I got up, grabbed a rag, and started wiping down the tables and counters. Faye asked if I was reconsidering her suggestion about returning to work. No, I said, I just needed to focus my energy on something simple and productive, had to think about something other than the hours I'd spent with the Confident Man.

"With who?" Faye asked with a laugh, and after I ex-plained, she asked with a grin if he'd "had his way" with me.

"Just about," I muttered.

I wound up revealing much more than I'd intended. Faye was still the perfect audience—paid close attention but never seemed to judge; asked questions, not because she was nosy but because she was interested; remembered little details I'd told her months ago. In this city, people paid two hundred daisies an hour for that kind of listener. I had no idea how Faye felt about me, but she seemed to genuinely like listening to my story, which is something every writer hopes for—a reader who gets so caught up in the story that she almost forgets who's telling it. She understood that even a tragedy can be funny if you tell it right. Finally, when we were done cleaning up—a far better job than I'd ever done when I'd been paid to work—I asked Faye the question that had been obsessing me before I blacked out and woke up in the cellar.

"You'd understand this, Faye; you're an artist," I said. "Let's say you had an opportunity to get your work in front of more people than you ever thought you'd reach, a chance to get more money than you thought you could ever get, but you had to compromise everything you thought you believed in. Would you do it?"

Faye appeared to contemplate my question for a moment or two. "Would I have to kill anyone?" she asked.

"No," I said.

"Would anyone get hurt?"

"No."

"What would I have to lose?"

"Just your integrity," I said. "Would you do it?"

"Wouldn't anyone?" asked Faye.

I said I wasn't sure.

We walked out together and I waited for Faye to lock up. I figured that we'd keep talking—I certainly didn't want more liquor, but I would have bought Faye as many drinks as she wanted with one of the bills Roth had given me. But when we reached the 116th Street subway station, Faye said that since I was going uptown and she was headed downtown, she guessed she'd see me around, "Sailor." Didn't she want to join me for a drink? I asked.

"Nah, I'm not gonna be your Betty," she said. When I said I didn't understand, Faye asked if I'd ever read the *Archie* comic books; Betty was the nice girl who Archie called whenever foxy

Veronica was unavailable. I said it was over between me and "Veronica," then felt myself flush. Faye raised an eyebrow and said she had work to do tonight, but maybe she'd see me again at her opening at the Van Meegeren. She handed me a postcard for her show. At the top of the subway steps, she advised me to stay away from hunky strangers in coffee shops, then raced downstairs before I could kiss her goodbye.

"Carry on, my wayward son," she said with a laugh.

As I watched her clomp out of sight I felt more alone than I ever had in this city.

IN SEARCH OF MYSELF

I had no job, no money, no girlfriend. I was considering tracking down Jed Roth when something unanticipated happened: I started to write. One morning, after waking up well past noon, I showered, dressed, and, feeling newly refreshed, I sat down at my computer and began typing as if I'd been doing it every day of my life.

I didn't write about myself particularly, didn't write about growing up in my little Midwestern town, the son of an Indiana State librarian and an Indiana University law student who died before her son had even learned to write his name. I didn't write about escaping inside a father's world of books and stories. I didn't write about a boy who had been looking forward practically his entire life to moving out of Indiana, then getting the call from his father asking him to come back home. I didn't write about a father dying too young or a young man saddled with too much responsibility, about selling a house and everything inside it, then moving to New York to fulfill a dream. In the stories I wrote, there were no sweet, ambitious Romanian writers with tragic life stories; there were no frustrated, overweight actors working as café managers; no wiseass baristas with paint-spattered jeans, concert jerseys, and work boots; no suave authors of unpublished adventure novels with nefarious schemes to scam the publishing world.

But, though none of the stories I wrote was autobiographical, they all contained elements with which I was familiar: a kid and a dying parent; dreams of leaving a small town behind; a man and woman fighting to remain in love while their careers seemed headed in opposite directions. And there was a story about a man struggling with whether to give up what little artistic integrity he had left because he had met someone with a plan that sounded too good and evil to be true.

In the past, writing had always seemed difficult, required pots of black coffee and extensive channel-surfing breaks, long walks to clear my head. Now I wrote for hours at a time, played music as loud as it would go—Bobby Womack, Beth Orton, Astor Piazzolla. My favorite was Charles Mingus, and I decided to name my collection of stories after one of his songs—"Myself When I Am Real." My laptop began to feel like a musical instrument; Mingus tapped keys and so did I. I felt confident, not only in my ability to write stories and see them through to the end, but in my ability to do the same thing with my life. I could find another job, that wouldn't be hard; I could make my rent, millions of other people did; I would fall in love with someone else, and someday I'd look back at this period as the one that had prepared me for the rest of my life.

Whenever I finished a story, I would slide it into an envelope, send it to agents, publishers, and magazines, even to Miri Lippman's *The Stimulator*. When I walked in or out of my apartment, I felt no trepidation when I saw my mailbox. If someone didn't want my story, eventually someone else would. And when the phone rang and I heard Miri Lippman's voice on the other end, I knew I was right. At first, I wasn't sure that it was really Miri and not someone playing a joke, but when she introduced herself and said she didn't believe she'd met me before, I knew, yep, that was Miri Lippman all right. She told me that she had an open slot for her Lit-Stim series—was I interested?

If I'd gotten Miri's call during my first years in New York, I would have celebrated all night. But I was newly disciplined, and took it all in stride. I scribbled the date on my calendar, the only item on that calendar save for Faye's gallery show and jury duty, and then I got back to work. I finally felt like I was on my way.

HOW IAN MINOT GOT KISSED, GOT WILD, AND GOT A LIFE

When I got to the Van Meegeren Gallery for the opening night of Faye's show, I immediately understood why she sent me home the night I'd tried to get her to linger with me at the top of the 116th Street subway steps. The reason wasn't because she thought that I was some scummy humbert or that she was playing hard to get; it was just that the show explained what I needed to know about her a lot better than any conversation over soda pops could have. Faye must have known that after I'd seen her work, I wouldn't see her the same way anymore.

Back at the coffee shop, Faye was always up for hearing my stories, but she never seemed to like talking to me about herself or her art—"Let's talk about you, champ, my life's boring as a mofo." I had no idea she was downplaying her talent. Back then, whenever I said my writing sucked or was going poorly, I meant it.

I arrived at the gallery late. I'd been working on one of the stories I was thinking about reading at Lit-Stim and hadn't wanted to stop in the middle, and after I got off the C train at Twenty-third, the walk to the gallery took longer than I'd expected. Heading west, I smiled, thinking of the last time I'd been in this neighborhood—for Blade Markham's party. When I read at Lit-Stim, maybe Geoff Olden would come. "Good luck with all your future clients," I'd say, then toss both his business cards right in the trash.

It was opening night for about a dozen gallery shows in a gutted industrial building, and the Van Meegeren was located on the third floor. The crowds milling about in hallways or sneaking unfiltered vonneguts in stairwells were dressed a little more funkily than those I used to see at book parties when I'd worked in catering. Still, the behaviors and demeanors were familiar, every conversation characterized by its participants' desire to find better conversations elsewhere. Heads bobbed and weaved; eyes scanned rooms and halls; whenever someone new entered, people whipped around to see who it was. Like the writers at any book party, the artists were easiest to find, self-consciously dressing down—ripped kowalskis and torn

Levi's—or dressing up, in gatsbys and ascots, all ironic. The whiff of high school was inescapable.

The gallery where Faye was showing her work was a small, white, windowless box of a room with an office attached—in most of the galleries I passed, some officious panza was manning phones or handing price lists to prospective buyers, but in the Van Meegeren, nobody. The crowd was smaller than the ones in the other galleries I'd passed too; a few people would break their stride to glance at Faye's work, but no one stopped to hang up their jacket. Faye's snacks were grim—just a scattering of tired pastries from Morningside Coffee, and Joseph was the only one eating them; he had a turnover in his mouth as he slipped on his immense black gogol, congratulated Faye on his way out to a casting call, then glowered as he lumbered past me.

Even in the most poorly attended galleries, artists adopted façades of preoccupation, turned their backs to the entrances, focused intense concentration on even their most trivial conversations, lest anyone think they were disappointed by the meager turnout. Not Faye. She didn't do pretense. The moment Joseph was gone, she stepped into the gallery doorway, took a big swig from a bottle of wine, then cast her eyes skyward and demanded where the hell everyone was. When she glimpsed me approaching the gallery, she smiled. I was wearing a blazer and had shaved for the event, but Faye was wearing her usual boots, blue jeans, and concert jersey. No baseball cap tonight—that was the sole indication that opening night was a special occasion. Weren't people supposed to dress up for gallery openings, I asked as I kissed her hello. Nah, she said, if people were looking at her instead of her art, that was a problem. Then she thrust the wine bottle into my hand and told me she had to leave to take a piss. She warned me not to drink all her wine, since she had only one bottle left.

"Sell what you can, Sailor," she said with a wink. "You couldn't do any worse than me."

I stood alone in the gallery doorway, holding Faye's wine bottle, and watched her red hair bounce as she stomped down the hallway. Up ahead, I could see a line for the bathroom, so I wandered into the gallery. I've never known much about visual art, can never figure out how long I'm supposed to look at a painting, and frequently count to sixty in my head when I'm in front of one, so it will look as if I'm actually getting something out of it. I planned to do the same with Faye's work.

The dozen framed pieces each measured about two feet square. They seemed to be copies of famous works with which I probably should have been familiar: a smoky portrait of some sullen, Dutch tradesman—maybe a Rembrandt?; overlapping disks of bright colors—Kandinsky?; a woman with a cloudy sky where there should have been a face—probably Magritte. The prettiest one looked like a Wyeth—a pastoral landscape, a little family graveyard behind an old country house, a long white car on a distant road. But each painting had been violated, its frame broken or smashed and held together with wire, pipe cleaners, and Scotch tape; sections of paintings had been chipped or torn away. Visible underneath were crude sketches or cartoons, the sorts of drawings Faye tossed off while supposedly working at Morningside Coffee. In a corner of the landscape, there was a cartoon of Dorothy from *The Wizard of Oz* with a thought bubble over her head ("There's no place like home").

Forged in Ink was the title I'd given Faye's exhibit, but now that I was seeing her work up close, I understood that it was

a bad and pompous one; it totally missed her sense of playful-
ness. The works here encompassed her personality perfectly—
irreverent, self-deprecating, honest in their own way.

"*Konbanwa,*" said Faye by way of a greeting when she
returned, then glanced at the bottle I was still holding.

"You drink all of it?" she asked, and when I shook my head
no, she raised an eyebrow, then grabbed the bottle and gulped
down a third of it before handing it back. I took a swig, then
gazed at her paintings, searching for something insightful to say.

"So," I began. My eyes had settled on a pointillist landscape,
ducks and paddleboats operated by top-hatted men on a rip-
pling pond, and a big hole in the center revealing polka-dot
ducks drawn in crayon. "So, you take the copy of the old painting, tear it, and slap it over one of your drawings?"

Faye shook her head. "Nah," she said, "I do both. The old
and the new."

It took some time for it to dawn on me that everything I was
looking at was her original work—each exquisite brushstroke
in each old master painting and each squiggle in each napkin
doodle. Now I felt like a moron for having underestimated her
work every bit as much as I had underestimated her—the more
I looked, the more I wanted to keep looking. Her works were
fakes, but at the same time, they were real. She seemed to be trying to fuse the two to create art that was more than either one or
the other.

"Yeah," she said, "some of it sucks, some of it doesn't; what
else can you say? There's nothing more boring than listening to
people try to talk about art. It just is what it is; good or bad, it almost always fails."

"Fails at what?" I asked.

"At becoming something real," she said. "That's what artists try to do—you copy and copy and copy, and someday maybe you finish faking it and you learn how to make something real."

The crowds in the hallway were thinning out; no one was in line for the bathroom anymore. "This party's pretty much cashed," Faye said as she finished the wine. "Wanna grab some grub?"

We split a slice of cherry pie at the Empire Diner. Conversation was effortless, as it always had been between us. But by now, it seemed as though we both had become different people to each other than we had been at the coffee shop—me, now a genuine writer with newfound confidence in his work; Faye, now a legitimate artist whose sarcastic veneer no longer concealed her talent. She told me more about her art than she ever had—drawing and painting had always come easily to her, she said, so she had never valued her skills, and neither had her parents, both of whom were gone now. As our conversation continued, we still talked in the same self-deprecating manner, but more out of habit than conviction. We weren't coffee-shop slackers anymore; we were now New York artists, laughing and arguing, hands grazing each other's, eyes locking on each other's. When we left the diner and stepped out onto Tenth Avenue, neither of us asked where the other was headed; we both knew.

We kissed in the back of a taxicab for the whole fast ride up the West Side Highway to my apartment building, kept kissing when we got in the front door and when we reached the top of the stairs. In front of my apartment as I fumbled with keys, Faye suddenly pulled away from me.

"Just so you know, Sailor," she said, "I don't do sex on first dates."

But when I told her that I'd just come to see her show, so the evening didn't really count as a date, she stopped, then pretended to ponder. "Oh, right," she said. "Then it's no problem; let's go."

A TRAGYCAL INTERLUDE

Faye and I met in front of the KGB Bar sign on an unseasonably warm December Monday. On the Lit-Stim blackboard outside, my name was listed below that of the memoirist Hazel Chu. No, I hadn't dreamed my conversation with Miri Lippman; I was a stimulating writer after all.

I must have been studying the blackboard for a full thirty seconds before Faye delivered a "Hey, did you notice I'm here too?" tap on the shoulder. She was wearing a denim jacket over a short black-and-white zebra-print dress, the fanciest outfit I'd ever seen her in, as if to tell me that she knew I thought this would be an important evening. But when I put my arms around her and kissed her, she backed away. I tried to hold her hand as we walked up the steps to the front door, but she wasn't into that either.

"Enough of this phony boyfriend-girlfriend crap," she said. "I'm about to yack."

In the weeks that followed the first night Faye and I spent together, we saw a lot of each other. I don't know if it represented some sad commentary on my poor perception of human behavior or some greater truth about the depths of human complexity that demure, brunette, Romanian beauty Anya Petrescu had been the incorrigible sex fiend who enjoyed raunchy chinaski, the more public the place the better, while redheaded, boot-clad, smart-ass Faye, who sported a tattoo of a twilight flower on a shoulder, eschewed displays of affection whenever anyone else was around and enjoyed quieter, more chaste moments in darkness underscored by "Dust in the Wind." Still, Faye's and my relationship deepened, and I kept writing at a furious pace. Her work was somehow inspiring me. When Faye slept over, I would get up the moment after she'd fallen asleep and start typing. We rarely made plans—sometimes, she'd come over after her coffee-shop shift or stop by on her way to the Van Meegeren, but she never slept over at my place two nights in a row. "I don't like sequels, Sailor," she told me.

I always felt when we were together that our relationship could go on like this forever. Spending time with her seemed almost too easy, as if we'd skipped all those first steps that couples are supposed to have, as if we had loved each other as kids, gone our separate ways, then returned to each other as adults who were through with games and already knew each other's secrets.

Tonight, I would be reading a brand-new story, one I hadn't sent to Miri Lippman. Like all the stories I had been writing, it had its basis in reality. The lovers in my story were a woman with more beauty and talent than she liked to admit and a man on the rebound, just beginning to trust his own voice. It was about how the two of them could work together to make something real. I had titled the story "After Van Meegeren," and dedicated it to Faye. Our plan was to celebrate after tonight's reading; Faye said that for the first time, she would take me back to her place and she would show me more of her art, which I had been asking to see. She was almost done with a new project, and she said she thought I might appreciate it.

Outside the KGB, as I walked beside Faye, I tried to lower my expectations for the night, to keep my mind from leaping ahead to agents and publishing contracts and six-figure fraziers. I tried not to think about who might be in the audience, the compliments they might offer about my work. I tried to stop thinking about how I would handle my fame—whether I would snub everyone who'd rejected me in the past or act with grace and humility. I tried not to speculate about what might happen between Faye and me if women at the KGB were interested in me—bibliophiles, author groupies, who knew? I tried to tell myself that being invited to read here was enough, a first step that I shouldn't take for granted. I almost believed it as we entered the bar.

The place was as packed as it always was on Lit-Stim Monday, but I sensed something different about the crowd, something I couldn't quite identify. I practically tripped a half-dozen times as I searched the bar for familiar faces, then looked down to the ground so that nobody could see I had been searching. I tried to focus on the lit candles in the menorah in a south-facing window, looked away only when the imprint of the flames began to dance before my eyes. I glanced over to Faye, then down at the manuscript pages in my hand, almost tripped again, thinking maybe I was just nervous about reading in public, something I hadn't done since my first year in New York.

"It'll go fine, right?" I asked Faye, who was taking a seat at the bar. But Faye wasn't someone to approach for reassurance. I wished I could act as cool and unconcerned as she had at her gallery opening when no one had bought any of her work.

Oblivious or unsympathetic to my mounting trepidation, Faye was already trying to place an order with the bartender. She asked how much a draft cost, and when the bartender said nine bucks, Faye laughed, then asked for two waters. When she got them, she demonstratively poured them onto the floor, unzipped her bag, produced a bottle of cheap faulkner, and refilled our glasses.

"*Kanpai,*" she said, and clinked her glass against mine.

"*Kanpai,*" I said, but my hand was shaking.

It was just nerves, I told myself as I kept looking for Geoff Olden, for Rowell Templen, for any Knopf editor, any Inkwell or ICM agent, any Harper publicity director I might recognize. But the only familiar sight was Miri Lippman's head, her atwood bobbing as she spoke to a crowd of college students, all dressed better than the usual Lit-Stim crowd—clean-shaven guys wearing neckties and gatsbys; young women in stockings and golightlys. And as Miri Lippman turned to the bar and I waved at her, it dawned on me that, with the exception of Miri, Faye and I were just about the oldest geezers in the joint.

"Ian Minot?" Miri asked as she approached us, and when I nodded, she "introduced" herself.

"I'm just jazzed we got an audience; weather's been so good lately. Plus, with the holidays and all," she said.

The word *holidays* didn't register at first; then the menorah in the KGB window took on new significance, made me look again at the crowd of college kids. And before I could fully process the fact that it was the first night of Chanukah, which meant that half the publishing world was on vacation while the other half was lying low, knowing no serious business in publishing was ever conducted before the first of the year, Miri was telling me that she, too, would be on her way home soon to light candles with her nephews. She said she hoped she would be able to hear my story, but that depended on how long Hazel Chu wanted to read. Hazel taught at Columbia and she was giving her students extra credit for attending. Plus, her parents were in town, and they'd never heard her read in public before.

My shakiness gave way to a sick empty feeling, as if I no longer had to anticipate the worst; it was already happening. I had been invited to read at what I thought was one of the most influential literary venues in New York, but on a night when it wouldn't matter; I felt like Crash Davis in *Bull Durham*, breaking the record for home runs, but in the minor leagues, where nobody gave a damn.

Still, I told myself, at least Miri had chosen my work, might even select one of my stories for inclusion in *The Stimulator*, might put my photograph on her "Stimulating Events" page. Searching for more hopeful signs amid my gathering sense of doom, I asked if Miri would mind if I read a new story tonight.

No, Miri said, she trusted my judgment. And when I pointed out that I was glad she trusted me even though she had only just met me, Miri said, well, if she didn't trust my judgment, she certainly trusted Anya's.

I flinched. "Which Anya?"

"Petrescu," Miri said. "When I told her we had an open slot, she suggested I call you." Miri asked if I'd heard which publisher had won the auction for *We Never Talked About Ceauşescu*. And after I said I hadn't, Miri said she'd love to chat more, but she wanted to start on time, so she could get home.

I downed my drink in one gulp, and then Faye poured me another. "Thanks for the introduction," she snapped. I considered apologizing but was too involved in my own thoughts. From that moment forward, I walked through the evening in a daze, half-deaf to the applause that crackled through the bar after Miri introduced Hazel Chu, who stepped to the podium and began to read.

Several weeks and a dozen lifetimes ago, I would have come here with Anya and we would have mercilessly mocked Hazel Chu—her declamatory, pause-laden style peculiar to the literary reading form, all diction and no drama, her Roget's vocabulary, describing clouds as "cruciferous" against an "oleaginous blue sky." We would have giggled at her tortured metaphors, obviously flogged in some workshop; we would have kicked each other every time Hazel used the word *sinuous*.

Tonight, I found no humor in Hazel's reading. She may have read for an hour or just a few minutes; to me, it was all one endless stream of words and laughter, then applause. Hazel may have written something brilliant or dreadful—I had no idea. All I knew was that one moment, KGB was full and the crowd was alive and Faye and I were at the bar and Hazel was at the podium; the next moment, I was at the podium, and the bar was just about empty. Hazel had taken the audience with her, save for the few stragglers who didn't seem to realize they were allowed to leave before both authors had read. Even Miri exited noisily while I was thanking her for her "generous" introduction: "Although I don't know his work, I know people who do."

My recollection of standing at podiums in the glare of spotlights during open mikes was of being unable to see individual audience members, just blackness and glare. But tonight, I could see everything, as if I were appearing on a stage after a show was over and the houselights had been turned up. I could see Faye, and I could see the bartender; mostly, I saw empty chairs. One seat at the end of the bar was occupied by a man in a dark gogol and a broad-brimmed capote who didn't even look up when I stepped to the microphone.

I smiled in Faye's direction as I prepared to read the dedication of "After Van Meegeren." But before I got the words out, I heard a clattering. The bar's door swung open, and I heard a loud, whispered *saw-ree, saw-ree* as Anya Petrescu made her way past the empty chairs. Her beautiful, ruthless eyes sparkled as she took a seat in the previously empty front row. She put her bag on the floor, then looked up at me, smiling. I smiled back at her, then looked over to Faye, who was regarding me with an increasingly contemptuous glare. I could almost see the warmth and trust she had begun to show me evaporating. Veronica had arrived; Betty was throwing back hooch.

I skipped the dedication.

I read my story more quickly than I had rehearsed it, skipped over parts I now saw were repetitive, glanced at Anya, then at Faye, before returning to the manuscript, where I struggled to find my place. The story was less polished than I remembered, its insights less profound, and I took solace only in the fact that neither Miri Lippman nor anyone with apparent influence in the literary world was here. As I read, I found myself feeling both hatred and affection for Anya, wondering if her recommendation to Miri was a peace offering, an invitation to start over, a farewell gift, or just a reminder that I would never be her equal. I wondered too about Faye, whether she would be flattered, amused, or revolted by the fact that I had written a story that was, in a way, about us. I wondered also whether she could guess that Anya's entrance caused me to omit my dedication.

The final sentence of "After Van Meegeren" was meant to be a laugh line—outside a man's apartment, a woman says she doesn't have sex on first dates, but when the man reminds her that this hasn't even been a date, she smiles and says, "Oh, right, then it's no problem." But I rushed the line, so much so that no one in the audience realized the story was over, and not until I mumbled "Thank you" did Anya begin to applaud, and then the rest of the half-dozen or so spectators followed suit. Faye clapped too, though she didn't put down her whiskey to do it.

And then the bartender stepped out from behind his bar, unplugged the mike, and began shoving the podium into a corner, and someone turned up the music on the sound system. The candles in the menorah had already burned down to their wicks—the evening was over before I had even decided whether I would speak first to Anya or to Faye, hoping against hope some editor or agent would step between us.

I began walking toward Faye, but Anya intercepted me— oh, how *byootiful* my story had been, *Ee-yen,* she said, how *luffly,* how *gledd* she was to see I was writing again. And as she hugged me and I felt her body against mine, as I saw the sparkle in her eyes, I thought of how much I missed her effusive compliments, how much I missed our relationship's drama, how much I wanted to grab her hand, run for the john, and lock the door behind us, just like old times. Faye was always so honest and direct, never offered a compliment I didn't deserve, and something was still so narcotic about Anya's presence. Even if her enthusiasm was phony, I needed it now.

"Heard you sold your book," I said, but Anya said she didn't want to talk about that. She was nothing more than a *"fekk,"* a *"one-heet* wonder." The true joy was to be found in writing, she said; everything else was *deestrection.*

I asked if she'd sold her story collection to Merrill Books, and she responded quickly, as she always did when she was relating ostensibly unimportant information. No, those *chip besterds* hadn't offered enough *mah-nee;* she'd sold it to *Dotton.* And, though I didn't ask how much *Dotton* had paid, she allowed that the *mah-nee* was *complittly rideekyouluss* and, don't tell *ennybody,* but she would have taken *heff* of what they ultimately wound up *payink.* But all that sort of talk was so *borink,* what she really wanted to talk about was me, how *goot* I looked, how healthy, had I *poot* on some *wett*? Was I *seeink ennybody*?

I looked over to Faye, wondered whether she could hear us, assumed she couldn't. I looked at the few people still in the KGB, the man in the capote at the end of the bar, a few of Hazel Chu's students, still drinking beers, probably under twenty-one and amazed they hadn't gotten carded. Anya had come alone, seemed to be in no rush. I needed affection, reassurance, and she was flirting with me the way she used to on our first dates. Was I *seeink ennybody*?

"Not seriously," I mumbled to Anya, adding that I still thought about her a lot. What about her?

"But of course I'm *seeink* someone," Anya said with a sigh, she couldn't *stend* to be alone. She joked that she was *mono-phobeek,* but her new relationship wouldn't *lest* long *eezer;* her *new luffer* was too *eentense.*

At the bar, Faye hopped off her seat and slung her red vinyl bag over a shoulder as if she'd heard exactly what I had said to Anya about my relationship with her not being serious and she now knew I was a phony and a jackass. She took one long look toward the end of the bar, pulled a baseball cap out of her bag, put it on, then started walking fast to the exit without looking back. When I called her name, she didn't turn around.

Anya sauntered alongside me, unaware of my predicament. I was trying to walk with her and catch up to Faye at the same time, but when Faye shouldered open the back door and started heading downstairs, I quickly whispered goodbye to Anya, kissed her cheek, then scampered out the door and down the stairs, yelling, "Faye! Faye, wait a second! Faye, would you hold on?" I practically slammed into Blade Markham, who was entering the building.

"Easy there, *compadre,*" Blade said with a laugh, either not remembering who I was or not caring anymore.

As Faye walked outside onto Fourth Street, on which a light rain had begun to fall, I froze on the stairs. Blade walked past me, taking two steps at a time, boots clacking, truth cross beating against his chest. I turned to see him look up at Anya and greet her with a smile, a peace sign, and a gruff "What up, dawg?"

Anya laughed. I wasn't sure if she was laughing with or at Blade, until I saw the two of them making out on the stairs. Over Blade's shoulder, Anya smiled at me, rolled her eyes, just as she had after Geoff Olden had introduced himself to her at the KGB and given her a pair of business cards. But I took no comfort; Olden was now her *edgint,* Blade was her *luffer,* and I was *complittly* alone. I could hear Blade tell Anya that their "peeps was waitin, yo" as I ran out into the rain.

Faye was already waiting at a bus stop, and once I caught up to her there, the M15 was approaching. Faye's facial expression was sullen, more tired than angry, and it didn't change when her eyes met mine.

"What's the matter, Arch?" she asked. "Veronica split town?"

I smiled, but Faye didn't smile back.

I desperately tried to explain, to apologize, to say that the night hadn't gone as I had anticipated and what I really wanted to do was forget about it and start over. I said I knew I was a heel, but Faye wouldn't even give me the satisfaction of acting angry. She just seemed disappointed, as if she now knew that I was no different from all the liars and cheaters she must have known before me. She'd dated guys like me, she said, guys who said they cared more about her than about getting famous, more about their art than about making money, but I was lying, maybe even to myself.

No, I told her, she had me figured all wrong. I did care about her, was still looking forward to seeing more of her art. I was searching for the one thing I could say that would break through to her, make her believe me, but in her eyes I could see that she had already boarded the bus, its doors had closed, and it was pulling away fast.

"Faye," I said, looking at her pleadingly.

"*Jigoku ni icchimae!*" she said, then called me *usotsuki.* But when the M15's doors opened, she didn't deem it worth the trouble to speak to me in any language, not even English. She just slipped her MetroCard into the reader and walked to the back of the bus. When it began to move again, I could see her red hair and her baseball cap framed in a window. For a moment, it looked as though she might have been crying, but I figured it must have been the rain.

I could say that I felt as if I had just lost everything, but that wouldn't be quite right, for it would imply I had something to lose. Instead, I now understood that I had had nothing in the first place—the stories I had been writing weren't worth a damn. If someone on the street had come up to me and asked who I was and what I did, I wouldn't have known what to say. There was a person I wanted to be, and a person I had been, but in between those two, I felt as if I were nobody at all. JUST A FAG

The rain was beginning to fall harder. As I walked slowly back to Fourth Street, I took out my cellphone, removed a card from my wallet, and dialed the number that was printed on it. A recorded message informed me that my jury duty assignment for the following day had been canceled. No, not even the Appellate Court of New York County could distract me from my plight.

On the front steps of the KGB, the man I'd seen at the bar wearing a capote was skimming some pages and sipping a scotch. When he looked up and revealed himself to be Jed Roth, I can't say I was surprised. I sat down on the steps next to Roth as if this was where I belonged, the place I always knew I would end up. Roth was skimming the manuscript of "After Van Meegeren," which I hadn't bothered to take with me after I had finished reading.

"It's another good story, Ian," Roth said. "But it's just too quiet, too small. A quiet little story about people living quiet little lives. Tough to get anyone interested in it when the author doesn't already have a name."

I turned to Roth.

"So," I said. "Tell me again how all this is supposed to work."

Roth put down his glass.

"Right," he said, "shall we begin?"

II fiction

"Yes, it's very wicked to lie . . . But I forget it now and then."

PIPPI LONGSTOCKING

MY LIFE AS A FAKE

When we got back to his apartment, Roth acted differently than he had on our last night together—more focused, less patient; now that I seemed willing to follow him, he seemed to feel there was no need to turn on the charm. The apartment was brighter and less atmospheric than I remembered it. But the manuscript of *A Thief in Manhattan* was on his living room table, in the same spot where he had placed it after I'd flung it at him. A newly sharpened red pencil lay beside it.

When I sat down on the couch, Roth offered only water; when I asked for something stronger, he pointed to the coffee-maker.

"Just coffee or water? Those are my options?"

"Tonight, we're working, Ian," he said.

I took a glass of ice water.

I still had huge misgivings about Roth's plan, but I needed distraction and a paying gig fast. Just about anything would have beaten waiting tables, tending bar, or pouring coffee; plus, the money Roth was offering was better—a thousand daisies a week. I now figured that Roth was right about the stories I had been writing—they were too quiet, and if nothing else, working with an experienced editor like Roth might give me insight into bigger stories, where the stakes were higher. Probably Roth had also been right when he said that his plan really would draw attention to my work. Writers seemed to be getting rich plagiarizing stories or making them up; I'd spent the better part of a year saying the very same thing, boring Anya and Faye and whoever else would listen.

Still, as Roth sat across his coffee table from me, I kept asking questions, which he answered in clipped tones, as if I were wasting time.

"What if I change my mind about this?" I asked.

"Then you change your mind about it," he said.

"So, the thing is, you won't let me tell anybody," I said.

"You can tell anyone anything you please, Ian," said Roth.

"Anything?"

"Like what? Like Jed Roth gave you his old novel and asked you to put your name on it and pass it off as your memoir?"

"So that's it," I said. "You don't think anyone would believe me."

Roth shrugged. I could see he didn't care. I wondered if I could ever say anything that would faze him, if I would ever ask him a question and he wouldn't know the answer.

"But what about my stories?" I asked.

"We'll get to that," said Roth.

"So that's not really part of your plan." I informed him that finding a good publisher for my stories was the only reason I was even considering working with him.

But Roth said the plan remained the same, had always been and would always be the same. I would make Roth's story my own, it would be published, and then I would declare it all to be a lie. And after the ensuing scandal, everyone would want to read the stories that were really mine. But that was step five, and what was the point of discussing step five when we hadn't gotten through the first four?

"So, what's step one?" I asked.

"Read it," he said, tapping the manuscript of *A Thief in Manhattan* with the fingers of one hand.

"We already did that one," I said.

"You remember it?"

When I said I more or less did, he asked me to tell him the plot. I was bad with plots and it took only a minute for me to recount what I remembered—guy walks into a library filled with rare, valuable manuscripts; sees a girl admiring a famous old book, *The Tale of Genji;* observes some hooligan librarian stealing manuscripts; follows him to the office of a foul-mouthed manuscript appraiser who's fencing the documents; realizes he might be able to steal a document himself without being suspected; sneaks into the library and rips off the *Genji* for the girl; returns to the library one final time. The girl isn't there, and the place has burned down. Cat and mouse; cloak and dagger; chase, chase, chase, until the librarian and appraiser catch up to the guy outside Manhattan in the desolate field where the book has been buried beneath a golden cross. In the end, the guy shoots the librarian and appraiser, catches the 8:13 train, goes off to the site of the library, finds the girl. End of story.

I thought I got the plot pretty much right and was actually feeling rather smug about it, but Roth regarded me with contempt, then pelted me with questions—well, did I remember the name of the library?

No, I said.

Did I remember that the Hooligan Librarian was named Norbert Piels? That Iola Jaffe was the manuscript appraiser? That her office was located on Delancey Street? Did I remember the street address?

Did I at least remember the name of the narrator of the story? he asked. The name of the thief?

No, I said.

Well, then he'd give me a little hint, Roth said—the name was Minot. He spelled it out for me. I-A-N M-I-N-O-T. This was my story now, he said.

And then he picked up his red pencil, crossed out "A Novel by Jed Roth" on the title page, and replaced it with "A Memoir by Ian Minot."

MY COUNTERLIFE

I wanted to move on to step two as quickly as possible, but in the first weeks, Roth seemed to view his main responsibility as being to slow me down. Rushing smacked of desperation, he said, and the only thing that could jeopardize the plan was trying to reach the end of it too fast. The project couldn't be a simple matter of putting my name on a manuscript he'd written, and then, at the appointed time, revealing that it was false—I had to know the whole story inside and out as if I had written it myself.

To ensure that I would work at his pace, he paid me by the hour, not the job, which would be over only when he said it was. I was to edit just three pages a day, and retype them myself; as long as I maintained his basic story and characters, I could change as much or as little as I wanted.

I arrived at his apartment between nine and ten every morning, and worked at the computer in his office—a spare, clean nook with good light, a desk, a comfortable swivel chair, and a view of the park. Roth left me alone most of the time. I would stay until five, and he was usually back by then, sometimes sipping a takeaway cup of tea from my former place of employment. He'd look over the pages I had copied and printed out, then pay me in cash.

In the beginning, I worked as little as possible on the story, typed the pages fast right when I got to Roth's place, changing little other than the occasional comma or phrase, after which I worked on editing my own stories. Then I'd gaze out at the snow falling on Riverside, or snoop through Roth's belongings, curious whether I might learn something he hadn't told me. But I found nothing that contradicted his stories—on his shelves were copies of books he had edited alongside some of his favorite classics. In his drawers, none of which were locked, were marked-up manuscripts he had worked on; there were files of financial documents that went back nearly a decade, pay stubs from Merrill Books, holiday cards from Francine Prose and Miri Lippman, photos of Jed with Jim Merrill, Jr., during happier days, copies of some of Jed's early stories with long, evocative titles ("A Desolate Field, Beneath a Golden Cross"; "Blood Is Thicker Than Nothing") that he'd placed in magazines and literary journals.

At the end of my workday, when Roth would look over my manuscript pages, he wouldn't ask why it had taken eight hours for me to finish, just, "Are you sure that's all you want to do?" or "You're certain you like it just the way I wrote it?" I would shrug and say yes, but by the end of the week, I was getting bored, both with the job and with Roth's story, which was thinner than I remembered. Though the plot remained amusing, the characters were too broad and lacking in substance. Roth didn't seem to give a damn about the people in his book; I couldn't empathize with any of them. Iola Jaffe was a foulmouthed harpy; Norbert Piels, an illiterate dunce; the Girl in the Library was a schoolboy's fantasy; Roth's hero was too suave and unflappable to be believed. I had trouble deciding whether to make changes or to leave everything just as Roth had written it and get on with my own work. The more I looked at how long it would take to complete the book at this pace of three pages a day, the more I started to add details—a line of dialogue I'd overheard, a little descriptive flourish, backstories for each character.

As the days drew on, I spent more time on *A Thief in Manhattan,* less on my own work; if I was really going through with this plan, then I wanted the narrator's voice to be my own. Roth's manuscript didn't offer many details about his lead character, who had been named Roth but had little in common with the man I saw every day. His Roth seemed more sketch than fully realized human being, as if a screenwriter had created him, uncertain of who would wind up playing the role in the movie.

I began adding details from my own life—I gave the novel's hero not only my name but my history: a childhood in a tiny, rural Indiana hamlet between Terre Haute and Indianapolis, a law-student mother who died young, a deceased librarian father. I gave him a hot Eastern European ex-girlfriend, too, and when it came to describing the Girl in the Library, I made her a sexy smart-ass with a baseball cap, boots, paint-spattered jeans, red hair, a concert jersey, and the tattoo of a twilight flower on a shoulder. For one of the chase scenes, I even used my knowledge of the freight trains that used to pass through my hometown.

I began to work longer hours and Roth paid me for overtime. I took research field trips, went to the New York Public Library microfilm reading room, where I studied whatever I could track down about the history of the Blom Library. I couldn't find much—a 1951 piece about the library's history; items about various accidents that had struck the library over the years; obituaries from the *Times* for Chester and Cecille Blom; an "Also Worth Noting" listing in a 1974 travel piece about "Undiscovered New York," and then the Metro pieces about the Blom fire, which hewed to the story Roth had already told me, that arson had been suspected but never confirmed, and that the most valuable manuscripts—the first editions, the Shakespeare folios, *The Tale of Genji*—had been destroyed. One afternoon, I took a taxi from Roth's apartment to the site of the Blom Library on Lexington to see the condo building that had replaced it. The trips didn't help me to add much to the manuscript, but the story did begin to feel more real and true, the characters more sympathetic.

Soon, Roth began taking me on his own field trips— Lessons in Lying, he called them. He said he had little doubt in my ability to fess up to the whole story when the time was right but was less certain about whether I could bluff agents and publishers and, later, journalists, all of whom would be necessary for our plan. He took me to Atlantic City, where he won three hands at a blackjack table; to swank parties and clubs where he quietly but confidently talked his way past bouncers; I stood beside him in a supermarket checkout line where he handed a cashier a ten-dollar bill, took his change, then claimed he had given her a fifty.

"You didn't give me any fifty," the cashier told him.

"I did," said Roth. He stared at her until she reached into the cash register for more change.

Roth said he didn't care about the few bucks he made here and there from these little "lessons"; he was after "far bigger game." In fact, he wrote a check to the PEN American Foundation for the daisies he'd won at blackjack, didn't pocket the excess change he'd received from the supermarket cashier—he handed it to some homeless dude on our way out of the store. What he really wanted to do was to show me the right way to tell a lie—the secret to a good one was the perfect combination of self-confidence and understatement, that delicate balance between offering too much and too little information. The point was not to be able to anticipate or predict everything, but to behave as if you could. The same was true of writing, he said, and, as I delved further into the manuscript, he paid more attention, simplified what I wrote; he liked bold, improbable proclamations relayed in short, declarative hemingways, the fewer adjectives and metaphors the better. And though I bristled at each red line Roth drew through my sentences, when I retyped them and read them back to myself, they did sound better.

On my way out of Roth's apartment at night, he would loan me books, memoirs mostly, and I'd read them on the bus and at home. I read *In Cold Blood, Go Ask Alice,* and the memoirs of

Casanova. I read *Blade by Blade,* too, saw how artfully each memoir was constructed. I began to see my own definition of truth evaporating, saw the artistry and artifice in all I was reading, saw how a lie is not only what you say but what you omit, and by the time I was half done rewriting *A Thief in Manhattan,* I was almost convinced that just about every memoir I had ever read was bunk. Even the truth began to seem fake—telling the truth is one of the best ways to disguise a lie, Roth told me; what makes it a lie is why you're telling it.

A month into the project, my self-confidence was soaring— I had faith in Roth, in the books he had edited. I had faith in the clothes he wore, all the daisies he seemed to have, the confidence he had and that he also inspired in me. On Roth's advice, I started dressing better, not exactly like him but not like me anymore either. I got a haircut, shaved every other morning. I even got fitted for glasses and bought a pair of black-framed franzens.

I maintained Roth's three-pages-per-day pace, but instead of seeming like too little work, it seemed like almost too much. I felt like an apprentice artist, painstakingly copying the work of a master, and I had to work late to get the pages done. I also began to question the parts of the story that hadn't made sense the first time I'd read the book. Why would a man who didn't speak proper English find employment at a library, I'd ask myself, and rewrite the Hooligan Librarian's dialogue. How could our hero know that a train would arrive at just the perfect time to save him? I'd wonder, and leave the time vague. And why would anyone bury a valuable book beneath a golden cross in some desolate field outside Manhattan? As if there was really any undeveloped land left near Manhattan anyway.

Late one night, when I was halfway through the manuscript, Roth was working on a scene I'd rewritten. In it, the hero escapes with *The Tale of Genji,* but instead of burying it under a cross, he takes it to a bank and locks it in a safe-deposit box.

Roth quietly read and reread my pages, marking them with his red pencil. Finally, he put them down and looked at me. Why had I changed the scene? he asked.

Roth listened as I offered my confident explanation—his version was more entertaining, but mine was more plausible. That's why he and I were well suited to each other; he had good plot ideas, but I knew how to place them in the realm of believable human behavior. Didn't he think my version was more realistic?

Roth remained calm, but he regarded me with an increasing intensity that began to resemble anger. Yes, he said, I was right; mine was more *realistic.* Also, he added, it would be even more *realistic* for there to be no stolen manuscript. Also, it would be even more *realistic* for there to be no fire. Also, the chase scenes were *unrealistic,* didn't I think so, particularly the one with the train. Maybe I was right, he said, maybe the librarian at the Blom shouldn't be a hooligan, maybe he should be a fussy and fastidious bookworm who wears bow ties, high-waters, and wingtips, and maybe Iola Jaffe shouldn't swear so much when she appraises book manuscripts—maybe she should smack the hero with a purse instead of face him down with a gun, and maybe a better story would be of a young man who sits in a library fantasizing about meeting a girl admiring *The Tale of Genji* but never speaking to her. Or, maybe an even more *realistic* story would be one about a young man working at a coffee shop, dreaming of publishing a book but never actually writing one, watching his Ukrainian girlfriend do it while he serves java to punters; maybe that would be the most *realistic* story of all.

By the time I figured out that Roth was mocking me, he was just about done. What the hell had we been doing here all this time? he demanded. What the hell was the point of all this, Ian, what did I think we were doing? Writing something realistic? Hadn't I learned anything? Hadn't he said that the way to write was to ask *What If,* then lay on the gas? I was writing like a guy who had run a red light but kept looking back to see if the cops were catching up.

Well, shouldn't we just leave out the patently ridiculous parts? I asked. Wouldn't that make the book easier to sell?

Did I know anything about selling books? Roth wanted to know.

No, I said, but still, there was no way anybody would believe this book.

"No, there isn't," he said, "and that's because you're not writing like you trust the story. Because part of you is still a small-town Midwestern boy who doesn't know how to tell a lie. You'll never succeed in telling one if you don't act like you trust it yourself."

Yes, he said, I could make his story more "believable," but did I know what would happen then?

No one would publish it? I asked.

Maybe they would, maybe they wouldn't, Roth said, but the point was that no one would care if my story was true or not. And if no one gave a damn about whether something was true, then they certainly wouldn't give a damn when it turned out to be false. Had I missed the entire point of the plan? The point was not to tell fewer lies, but to tell bigger and better ones, to tell bestseller lies, not mid-list lies, to state those lies boldly, clearly, without apology. He wanted to see fewer safe-deposit boxes and more golden crosses in empty fields; he wanted to see more hooligans, hunchbacks, wizards, and dwarves.

"Don't worry about anyone thinking your story's false," he said. "Try writing a story they'll want to believe is true."

Then Roth apologized for raising his voice. In fact, he said, he felt bad for me.

"Why bad?" I asked.

"Because now you'll have to start over from the very beginning."

THE HAPPY COUPLE

And so I began again, typing all through the winter. Roth made corrections, encouraged me to expand my ideas and eliminate everything that felt too quiet. Our workdays lasted twelve hours at a minimum, and by the end of them I was exhausted. Everything became an argument—I agreed to keep his desolate field and his golden cross, and he grudgingly allowed me to get rid of the gratuitous reference to its longitude and latitude; he insisted on keeping the improbable names of Iola Jaffe and Norbert Piels but assented to lishing some of the former's monologues and eliminating some of the latter's tattoos; I argued that the end of the book, in which "Roth" and his Girl reunited, was too hokey and romantic, but Roth convinced me to leave it as it was—readers liked happy endings, he said, stories where heroes got what they wanted.

When it came to developing biographies for the characters of Iola and Norbert, we rejected almost all of each other's suggestions, so that when we finally arrived at stories both of us could live with, I had no idea who had come up with the ideas. We decided that Iola Jaffe had not always been a crooked manuscript appraiser; she had once been an academic, who turned to crime when she'd failed to find a publisher for her research into the origins of the novel and had been rejected for tenure by her university. And Norbert was no mere hooligan—he'd been one of Iola's most promising students and research assistants, an ex-con whom Iola had nurtured, but he'd suffered a severe head injury when a shelf at the Blom had collapsed on him. Even though he no longer spoke proper English, and recognized manuscripts only for the money they could fetch, he remained loyal to Iola, and still played the role of her research assistant, albeit in a very different context.

One of our biggest arguments came in regard to the fates of Iola Jaffe and Norbert Piels. "Roth" had shot them dead in his story, but though I was willing to put my name on a thief's autobiography, I wasn't about to say that I'd killed anyone, even a fictional character, even in self-defense. So Roth let me leave Iola's and Norbert's fates vague, but he advised me to hang on to his original draft; someday, I might find that his version worked better.

Midway through the third draft, the book became as much my obsession as it had once been Roth's. *A Thief in Manhattan* haunted not only my waking hours but also my dreams, until I could almost see the Girl in the Library, could see flames rising, books in ashes; I could see the Hooligan Librarian and the Foul-Mouthed Manuscript Appraiser, I could hear the voices of

"Norbert Piels" and "Iola Jaffe" and could now understand how they had gotten to be who they were. I could see the desolate field and the golden cross and *The Tale of Genji* buried beneath it. I could feel the thump of the approaching 8:13 train in my chest, feel my heart racing as I tried to catch it. I could feel myself becoming the author of *A Thief in Manhattan,* book in hand, leaping off a train, then running to find the Girl in the Library.

As winter drew on, I couldn't find any time to work on my own stories. It seemed as if just about all I did was type, read, sleep, and run every morning and night back and forth between my place and Roth's. On Sundays, my one day off, I went shopping. I bought slicker shoes, better gatsbys that Roth had shown me in catalogs. I moved out of my West Harlem studio and found a better apartment in Hamilton Heights, a two-bedroom on the top floor of a newly rehabbed condo building with good light on a secluded block that looked like the sort of place where a serious writer would live. I bought a desk with a good chair, bookshelves, which I filled with classics, and when I grew weary of staring at bare walls, I took a trip to the Van Meegeren Gallery. Even though Faye wasn't there, I paid cash for my favorite of her paintings—the fake Wyeth that depicted a country house, a meadow, a graveyard, a white car on a distant road, and a little doodle of Dorothy Gale from *The Wizard of Oz.* It reminded me a little of home, and I thought having it on my wall would inspire me.

Sometimes on the Riverside jogging path, women would smile at me or ask for directions. I was always polite but never broke stride long enough to begin a real conversation. I felt as if I was at the midway point between who I was and who I sensed myself becoming. How could I have described myself anyway?

As a former barista in a scam with a confident man? Or as the author of *A Thief in Manhattan,* a novel that would pose as a memoir before I would reveal that it had been a novel after all? The man I really wanted to be was the one I would become after all that was done, the author of the short-story collection that had been written by a fake memoirist now finally telling the truth.

By the time I ran into Anya Petrescu again, on a Sunday in early spring, I was nearly done with my final draft of *A Thief in Manhattan.* The fourth rewrite was my idea; Roth had said it was good enough to start sending to agents, but I felt the book wasn't ready. I wanted one more draft to make the writing tighter, the characters more vivid and sympathetic, the pace even faster.

I was in ABC Carpet & Home looking for a queen-size proust to replace my crappy pull-out couch, when I saw Anya with Blade; they were looking at prousts too. Blade had an arm draped over one of Anya's shoulders and she had a hand on his waist. I couldn't understand any of the words either was saying, but I immediately recognized her Eastern European inflections and his affected street patter. They were moving in perfect synchrony, the sure sign of a couple that has been having chinaski for some time.

In her black golightly and tights with her backpack over both shoulders, Anya was lovely as ever; in his baggy, hip-hop jeans and steel-toed boots, Blade was still a joke. But what struck me most about them was how small they appeared in comparison to how I had remembered them. He was no taller than I was, and she was a good deal shorter than that.

Ee-yen!

I had been intending to let the two of them go about their business, but Anya spotted me, gave a little yelp of delight, clapped her hands, then dragged Blade over to meet me. As she spoke, she seemed to be attempting to appear more confident than I remembered her, which had the effect of making her seem less so. She used to tell me how *goot* I looked, how *moskyoolar* and *mennly,* but this time, when I was dressed in an off-white linen gatsby, new jeans, boots, and franzens, she didn't comment about my appearance. Instead, she talked about herself as if she could see that I had become the person who needed to be impressed. If Blade remembered who I was or that he had almost thrown me out of Geoff Olden's window, he didn't show it. He was soft-spoken, deferential, called me *blood, bro-ham,* and *compadre;* apparently, I looked like someone worth knowing.

Anya took off her backpack, put it on a bed that she and Blade had been eyeing, and pulled out a galley copy of *We Never Talked About Ceaușescu;* it would be published in the fall. She was so *nerf-ous* about the book, *Ee-yen,* she said as Blade rubbed her back with husbandly concern; she was sure that *eff'ryone* would *hett eet,* that *refyooers* would *reep eet* to shreds and call her a *tellentliss leetle fekk.* She handed the galley to me, said I could *tekk* it as long as I *promeesed* to come to her book party and to buy a *feenished* one when *eet vas pobleeshed.*

I took the book, flipped through it, stifling a laugh when I got to the back cover and read each laudatory blurb; they had all been written by Geoff Olden's clients. The one in the biggest type was Blade Markham's ("Man, this is some righteous shit, yo!"). But I kept a straight face—a blurb from Blade would look good on *A Thief in Manhattan* too.

This time, unlike our last meeting at KGB, I was the one who cut it short. I pecked Anya on the cheek, shook hands firmly with Blade, then bought the proust that the two of them had been looking at, before I headed home to rest up for my next week with Roth. On the uptown highsmith, I cracked open my galley of *We Never Talked About Ceauşescu*. I spent the afternoon and half of the evening reading it over cups of tea. And when I was done, I was pleased to note that I hadn't been wrong about Anya—her stories were beautiful, timeless, profound; her writing, if this was possible, was even lovelier than she was; each character was deeply human, each hemingway was exquisite, each metaphor resonant. I closed the book thinking I had lived an entire life in Romania with a wonderfully talented, creative, and generous spirit.

At the same time, I thought that night as I turned out my bedside lamp, Anya's stories seemed quiet and small. And I couldn't imagine them selling all that well.

AN AGENT

"So what's the next step?" I asked Roth.

Little green shoots had appeared on the branches of the trees outside his living room windows; the early morning joggers on the paths below were still exhaling steam, but they were wearing only sweatshirts or light jackets. I could make out silhouettes of boats chugging down the Hudson River. Roth and I had stayed up all night; now dawn was fading, and we were sipping from flutes of champagne, two copies of the final draft of *A Thief in Manhattan* on the glass table in front of us.

It was done—300 pages of heart-stopping adventure and utter hokum in which I, Ian Minot, stole *The Tale of Genji,* escaped my adversaries, and got the girl. There they were—two thick stacks of paper with my name printed on the title page, and by now, I felt as if I had actually earned that authorship. I had never written anything this long, had never, even in a short story, paid so much attention to each sentence, had never experienced the frustration and exhilaration of working day after day on the same project. I felt as if I had crossed a finish line and was only beginning to come down from a runner's high.

Roth was wearing a silvery jacket and slacks, sleek and slippery like the skin of some serpent. He wore black, square-toed shoes, and a black silk shirt with one button undone. He had the aspect of James Bond emerging from some death-defying battle into a Monte Carlo casino, and now here he was, ready for the baccarat tables and a roll in the hay with Fatima Blush. I still longed to have that same unflappability—I was wearing the same gatsby and slacks I had worn for today's session, and they were good ones, but now they had creases in them, and when I looked down at my shoes, I could see they needed a good shine.

"What's next?" he repeated. "We get you an agent." His voice was low and a bit rough, the one hint that he hadn't slept.

"Who?" I asked.

Roth cleared his throat—he seemed to like this game, liked knowing the lines I didn't; he wore the same smile I had seen him wear on Broadway in front of Morningside Coffee right after I'd chucked his copy of *Blade by Blade* halfway down the block. I fancied that maybe I'd looked a little like he did now when I saw Anya with Blade in the bedding department of ABC.

"Who would you think?" asked Roth.

"You know more agents than I do," I said.

"Then tell me characteristics," he said.

I paused before answering, pondered, wanted to reveal myself to be the good student he'd trained. I took another sip of champagne.

"Someone young," I said. "Someone hungry and inexperienced, desperate for their first deal."

Roth looked me up and down with a knowing nod, suggesting that my description more closely matched myself than the agent he had in mind. "Very clever, Ian," he said. "Also very wrong."

Roth finished his champagne, put his flute down on the table, then walked to the window seat, where he sat and gazed out over the park. He was in his early morning mode, a time when words seemed to come more slowly and had a hint of confession about them, as if for the first time he was revealing secrets about himself.

"Let me tell you a story with a moral," he said as he turned back to me. Fifteen-odd years ago, Roth said, he didn't have much cash, but he hadn't wanted his family's money to bail him out either. So every week when he bought groceries, he switched tags on the most expensive items. Before he approached the register, he tried to find the person who looked like the dumbest, least experienced cashier, assuming they wouldn't notice what he'd done.

"Know what happened?" he asked.

I shook my head.

"I got busted every time."

He smiled as if his meaning was evident, but I wasn't getting it. "So, what's the moral?" I asked.

"That the least-experienced people are the ones you have to watch out for," he said. "The smarter a person seems and the more powerful they are, the easier it gets to trick them. Because they wouldn't dream you'd ever dare.

"No," continued Roth, "we'll get you a smart agent, a veteran, the cockiest one we can find. Taking him down will be as easy as swatting a fly."

He listed names of agents, all of whom I'd heard of, most of whom had sent me rejection letters—Ira Silverberg, whose agency had sent me a form letter, even though he'd seemed excited about my stories when I'd told him about them while tending bar at a party for one of his clients; Kassie Evashevski, whose encouragement that if I wrote a truly great story, she'd "love to see it" fell flatter each time I received the same letter; Nicole Aragi, who sent me a handwritten paragraph explaining how sorry she was that she hadn't liked the "rubbish" I had written. Roth said that all of them could do a great job for us, but when he mentioned Geoffrey Olden, I asked if he really thought Olden would fall for it.

"Why Olden?" he asked, but we both knew the answer; Roth wasn't the only one who wanted revenge.

GETTING GEOFF OLDEN

Though I relished the idea of duping Geoff Olden, I had reservations about trying. After all, he'd read *A Thief in Manhattan* when Roth had submitted it as a novel. But as always, Roth's confidence allayed my concerns. People in publishing had short memories, he said, Olden especially. He barely remembered books he had rejected months ago. Olden turned down dozens of novels every week; there was no way he'd remember one he'd read in an afternoon more than a decade earlier, let alone one that was now a memoir.

Roth told me that he knew how to get just about any agent in New York to represent our book, but if I wanted Geoff Olden, he would take a bit more work than most of the others. Some agents responded well to flattery, some responded best to their clients' recommendations, some were horny humberts who were interested only in good-looking authors and asked potential clients to submit photos, while other agents, most of them really, were just looking for books with that elusive combination of commercial potential and literary heft.

Geoff Olden was not particularly different from the rest of the agents—he understood the usefulness of everything Roth mentioned; all successful agents did. What distinguished him was his need to always be proving someone else in the industry wrong. He measured his worth by the successes he had had with authors his competitors had overlooked. The phenomenal sales of *Blade by Blade* were delicious, but not nearly as much as the fact that they had come after more than a dozen other agents had turned the book down.

Roth and I didn't approach Olden directly; instead, we crafted query letters to the agents Olden most despised, hoping these letters would earn immediate and insulting rejections. We sent sample chapters from Roth's earliest and most overwrought stories and *A Thief in Manhattan* drafts, pages from my least-consequential stories, comparing them favorably to works written by the agents' most celebrated clients ("Dear Mr. Wylie: In my coffee shop romance, you may well find themes reminiscent of those in Salman Rushdie's *Midnight's Children*"; "Dear Mr. Parks: In my depiction of contemporary New York, you may hear echoes of Jonathan Lethem's descriptions of Brooklyn"; "Dear Mr. Simonoff: Since I assume you've grown weary of representing Joompa Laheeri . . . [*sic*]").

I had expected that the agents would send back the same curt form letters that I generally tended to receive. But the letters Roth helped me write must have gotten under their skin. Within weeks, we had assembled a portfolio of damning rejections from a Who's Who of literary agents who lambasted the author of *A Thief in Manhattan* for his poor manners, his bad taste, his lousy grammar, and his ham-fisted writing style, which, three agents said, would "never find an audience in today's market." We bundled the letters in a packet and sent them to Geoff Olden, complimenting him on having the foresight to recognize what other agents had overlooked. Roth said that once Olden had read our letter, he would ask his assistant, Isabelle DuPom, to shoot me a quick email, requesting my complete manuscript.

On the morning I got the email from Olden's office just as Roth had predicted I would, I FedExed a copy of *A Thief in Manhattan* to him with a short, fawning note, then returned to Roth's apartment, where I asked Jed how long I should expect to wait for Olden's response.

Jed looked at his watch. "About seventy-six hours," he said, and when I laughed, he shrugged, a little irritated, it seemed to me. Wasn't I done doubting him? Wasn't the script playing out exactly as it had been written? Wasn't I done fussing about longitudes, latitudes, 8:13 trains, and seventy-six-hour estimates? He asked if I wanted to bet whether he would be right or not, and when I told him I didn't, he suggested that I take the next seventy-five hours off; when the seventy-sixth arrived, we would get back to work.

AN UNEXPECTED GUEST

I had told Roth that I wouldn't gamble about when Olden would respond, but I probably should have taken that bet—for Olden didn't call in seventy-six hours; he called the very next afternoon, when I was jogging south along the Hudson River.

I knew it was Olden before I answered; hardly anyone ever called me on my cellphone anymore, and Roth's number never appeared as "restricted." Geoff told me that he had just finished reading *"Thief"*—the man seemed fond of abbreviations—and found it to be *muy bueno*. The conversation, despite taking place more than a day early, went as Roth had predicted. It began with compliments: Olden said he liked the terseness of my writing, how no words were wasted; it would be easy to read on a Kindle or a Nook; he liked the depth and humanity of my characters; the book was nonfiction that read like fiction, which was the best and rarest of finds, akin, he said, to a tofu product that really tasted like meat. But he said that he did have some changes to discuss before he would agree to represent me. Could his assistant, Isabelle, arrange a time for lunch?

"At Miguel's," he said, just as Roth told me he would refer to Michael's Restaurant.

When I was done talking to Isabelle—I wondered if she was one of those beautiful, golightly-clad women who'd ignored me at the Blade Markham party—I started running, didn't even stop to catch my breath when I got to Roth's apartment building. I slapped the UP button for the elevator, and when the doors didn't immediately open, I took the stairs two at a time until I reached the fourth floor, where I slid down the hallway before arriving at Roth's door, which I slapped hard with my palm. I heard a rustling, then footsteps approaching.

Roth was wearing a black murasaki, belted at the waist, and black socks. He wasn't wearing his franzens, and he looked older and more tired than usual. Apparently, I had interrupted him, or woken him up. I had never seen Roth without his glasses. Or his pants. He stood in his doorway, regarding me expectantly.

"Olden called," I said.

Roth nodded brusquely as if to ask why I was telling him what he had already told me would happen.

"He asked to set up a lunch," I said, and when Roth appeared to be expecting new information, I told him that he had been right; we'd be eating at Michael's.

"Wanna go out?" I asked. "Get a brew? Celebrate? My treat?"

Roth's weariness took on a more impatient tone.

"There's nothing to celebrate yet, Ian," he said. "We'll discuss it after the weekend."

Roth began to close the door, then stopped.

"Oh, and Ian?" he said. "Next time we're not scheduled to

work together and you have something you want to discuss: call first."

I nodded and told him I'd come by next week at our usual time. But when I walked out of the building, I couldn't help feeling embarrassed for having bothered him. I had begun to think that he and I were friends, but apparently, this was only a business relationship and we were just using each other for what each of us wanted. I would become a published author and he would get his money and revenge. I had been hoping that there might be more to it, but that's all there was.

MEETING AT MICHAEL'S

When I met Roth the morning before my lunch with Olden, Roth was back in his usual form. He told me that the key to winning Olden's trust was to refrain from acting either too eager or blasé. I was to let Olden decide who he thought I was; he treated people as if they were manuscripts. He liked to talk about how awful books had been before he got his hands on them, how unpolished and untutored his writers were before they had met him.

As for me, now that Roth had convinced me that Olden wouldn't recall having read *A Thief In Manhattan* before, I had only two questions.

"What if he recognizes me?" I asked, remembering the night at the KGB and the Blade Markham party.

"He won't," Roth said. "When he met you before, you were

nobody. Now you're a potential client. To Olden, those are two completely different people."

"What about my short stories?" I asked. "Can I mention them to him?"

"Not yet," said Roth.

"When?" I asked.

"You'll know."

I arrived at Fifty-fifth Street intentionally about ten minutes late, and was seated with Olden at his usual table. He was wearing a pale yellow sport coat over a black shirt and was eyeing one of his two watches—he wore a Rolex on one wrist, a red, blue, and green Swatch on the other. The two watches, one expensive, one not, was a fashion quirk that Roth told me Olden had picked up in Milan. Olden looked peeved at my tardiness, but when I caught his eye, he was all smiles and cackles.

"You don't look like a thief," he said as he shook my hand.

"Neither do you," I said.

He liked that joke; cackled louder. *"Bueno conocerte, ladrón,"* he said.

Michael's tablecloths were white, its chairs black leather with wooden frames and armrests, and the air was thick with talk of books and deals. Nearby, Olden informed me, the director of Knopf publicity was showing a new catalog to the nonfiction reviews editor of *Publishers Weekly,* who was taking notes on a pad. David Hirshey, executive editor at HarperCollins, was forking a chunk of salmon as he sat across from an author who wore a black T-shirt under a blue blazer and was muttering something about soccer. The ICM superagent Esther Newberg was dining with Patricia Cornwell.

As for me, I was wearing an old Ian Minot outfit—a wrinkled white shirt that was now a little small in the shoulders and too loose around the stomach, battered jeans, a flimsy belt, and scuffed boots. The only stylish touch was the franzens. Roth had said that either dressing up or down for Olden would be a waste of time—Geoff said that anyone who didn't dress like him was a "fashion victim" no matter what they wore. But I liked dressing down; later, when I would wear my new gatsbys to meet Geoff, he could take credit for my transformation.

Olden didn't talk about *Thief* during the first part of our lunch, and I didn't talk much at all. Editors and industry reporters kept coming over to shake Olden's hand and schmooze. He didn't introduce me to anybody, though, just waited until they were out of earshot, then talked smack about them—which agent was sleeping with which editor, whose novel was tanking on *Bookscan,* whose wouldn't "earn out," whose magazine wouldn't last, who was about to get fired. He pointed out to me the agent with the eating disorder, the one with a coke habit, the one who had been justly hit with sexual harassment charges, the one who was having an affair with the editor of *The Stimulator.* He gestured to each of the writers he spotted and explained why he'd been right to reject their work.

I nodded and smiled through Geoff's bitter monologues, kept smiling through my beet-and-goat-cheese salad and my poached halibut and Geoff's *"El bistec, por favor,"* but I could barely contain myself when he seemed to start talking smack about me. He said he'd just gotten back from a "SpeedFuck" in Key West. He took lots of free trips—he twirled a sea scallop on the end of a fork—free trips were viewed as perks in the industry, but he hated them. The moment you started getting something for free, you didn't want it anymore. He loathed booksellers' conventions and book fairs, all those slutty publicists getting drunk on expense accounts and getting fat on hors d'oeuvres, behaving as if publishing were a sorority rush; he hated all those lascivious foreign publishers acting as if every American thoroughfare were the Reeperbahn, cutting short meetings so they could return to their hotel rooms and watch pay-per-view porn. When the economy went down and took half the industry with it, he wouldn't miss any of it. The worst part, he said, were the SpeedFucks—three-day weekends in resorts where writers paid hundreds of dollars for the privilege of having their work evaluated by "industry professionals," meaning him. One had to try to find constructive things to say about manuscripts so that their authors would feel they had gotten their money's worth. But Olden said he didn't even need to read the pages an author had written in order to critique them; he needed only to look at the writer. He could instantly recognize the permed, overweight women with their romance novels; the doughy, middle-management men who thought they could write thrillers; most of all, he despised the scruffy young men who thought they were better than the others, fancying themselves literary authors as they droned on about tending bar or pouring coffee, as if such experiences were meaningful or unique.

"See, with you I knew right away you were a good writer," Olden said.

"How?" I asked.

"Your glasses," he said, then went on to tell me why he thought my book was special. But now I was listening with only half an ear. The other ear and a half was already replaying Olden's diatribes as I thought of all the daisies but mostly the time I'd wasted on hoping to win over the likes of Geoff Olden, who disdained not just my stories but me. I thought of the literary seminars I'd attended when I first came to New York, the tickets I'd bought to book fairs. I fought the desire to walk out of Michael's, to say that any triumph that might come at the end of my ordeal was not worth this humiliation. I kept telling myself that I was only playing a role and reciting lines, that Ian Minot wasn't sitting here, ordering a trio of sorbets, that Geoff Olden was lunching instead with the author of *A Thief in Manhattan.*

Over coffee, Olden offered his criticisms of *Thief*—too long, he said, book groups rarely chose books longer than 250 pages anymore; the opening was slow, it really needed to grab people; the conclusion was too abrupt, *let us savor it more;* there were too many swearwords—most readers were women and they didn't like characters who swore; the title needed work too. As he criticized both Ian Minot and the author of *A Thief in Manhattan,* I wasn't sure which of us felt more resentful.

When the check came, Olden eyed it, raised his eyebrows, and whistled. He put down his platinum card, then handed me three pages of typewritten notes. As I scanned them, I kept thinking about how each of us should and would react—Ian versus the author of *Thief.* The author, the one whose glasses I was wearing, was a hustler, a rogue, a bit of a romantic, too— a man who believed in love and art and didn't care how much something was worth or what some agent thought about his story as long as it could get him back to the woman he loved. Then there was Ian, the schlep in the wrinkled shirt and scuffed boots; he wouldn't have been granted entrance to this lunch in the first place. The only person remaining was me, the man who was not yet done being Ian Minot but who was not quite ready to be the author of *A Thief in Manhattan*. So I just thanked Geoff for his notes and didn't say anything else; I figured I'd let him decide who I was supposed to be, and get back to work.

REVISING THE DRAFT

Geoff asked if I could return *Thief* to him in two weeks. But the day after our lunch, when I went back to Roth's place, I couldn't summon the motivation. Isabelle DuPom called me at Olden's behest to ask how I was doing, and I told the truth—that I was working to return the manuscript to her boss at the appointed time and that making the changes was harder than I'd anticipated. Isabelle asked if I needed more time, and though I said no, I'd meet the deadline, I continued to fritter away days. After a week passed, I began to panic when I realized that half my time had elapsed, and I had not come close to cutting *A Thief in Manhattan* down to the size Olden had requested.

I spent the following week cutting and rewriting, chopping this paragraph and that, lishing entire chapters. But when the next Monday arrived and I reread my work, I realized that I had made the book worse. The shorter manuscript took longer to read; it lurched from incident to incident; Iola Jaffe and Norbert Piels were as shallow and cartoonish as Roth had initially written them—their actions were not only improbable but also dull. The book was becoming one that Roth had warned me about— no reader would care whether it was true or not, and so wouldn't feel betrayed when I revealed it to be false. I considered calling Olden to ask for more time, but because I knew that I had to become the sure-of-himself author of *A Thief in Manhattan,* because I knew that I had to be an actor and not a reactor, had to act like something big was at stake, I vowed that I would send in the revised manuscript to Olden the following morning as promised, no matter how much work was left.

I must have spent hours pacing in front of Roth's window, watching the wind blow the bright green leaves of the London plane trees, watching the ripples in the Hudson River, watching traffic zooming south but getting backed up in the northbound lanes on the Henry Hudson Parkway, watching the sky brighten as the sun rose behind Roth's building. Cut about fifty pages, Olden had told me; lose the swearwords; change the beginning, the ending, the title. I watched the sun dip into the river, watched the sky grow dark and the trees disappear into its blackness. I saw southbound traffic stall, then ease up, watched the separation between river and sky evaporate.

Finally, in a blaze of inspiration and swagger, I returned to the original manuscript, glanced at it for just a moment. On the computer screen, I selected the entire document, then changed the font from twelve-point to nine, switched from Times to Palatino. The page count was now just about 250. Olden hadn't liked the first paragraph, so I lished it and started with the second. Olden didn't like the swearwords, so I figured what the hell, and just cut all of them out except for Iola Jaffe's. He had found the conclusion too abrupt, so I added some paragraph breaks. I looked at the title, wondered what was wrong with *A Thief in Manhattan* anyway, and just changed it to *The Thieves of Manhattan*. I wrote a note to Olden thanking him for his input—cutting it down really improved the pace, I said. I saved my document, addressed my email to Olden, then clicked SEND.

Before I headed out of Roth's apartment, I paused in the living room, where Roth was gazing out over Riverside Park. "Did you make those changes Olden wanted, Ian?" he asked.

When I told him yes, Roth nodded, then said he had faith that whatever I had done would meet with Olden's approval.

"But Ian," Roth added, turning to me. He hoped that I hadn't worked too hard on the manuscript; just about all I really had to do was change the font and the type size, cut the swearwords, and rearrange some paragraphs, and Olden would be happy as long as I gave him credit for improving the book. For a moment, I felt angry that Roth hadn't told me about this, but then I smiled, knowing that I had passed another test. The plan was going forward as smoothly as Roth said it would, and I felt certain that it would work.

THE ART OF PUFFING

"Tanto mejor," Geoff Olden said as he sat across from me in his Soho office clutching *The Thieves of Manhattan* to his chest, *"Tanto tanto mejor."*

The offices of the Olden Literary Agency were sleek, elegant, and understated, as though Geoff Olden had art-directed them for a film in which he played the starring role. Aside from Geoff's clothing and accessories, everything was black, white, or silver—white walls, black floors, chrome details on his furniture; his receptionist and junior agents wore black, white, and gray—so that Geoff's mustard yellow blazer and matching eckleburgs stood out as the splashes of color in his otherwise black-and-white world.

"You're a courageous man," Olden told me. "*Muy valiente.* Only a man of great courage could write something so true."

He put down the manuscript, reached across his desk to shake my hand, then, apparently thinking better of it, stood up, walked around the desk, and pulled me up into a hug. I could feel his chest heave as he cackled.

Olden didn't listen to me any more than he had at our last meeting. Now that I had signed a contract with him, he talked about his other clients, tried to impress me with the company I would be keeping. The names of his authors went right past me until he told me of a "young Russian writer" whom he had signed up as a "low-value/high prestige client." Some of his clients' books, he said with a wink, meaning that he was referring to *The Thieves of Manhattan,* were projects that publishers liked because they could become commercial blockbusters. Others, he said, helped to establish or confirm agents' and publishers' reputations as arbiters of literary taste. Publishers didn't always expect to make a lot of money on these sorts of books, and far fewer of them were being published than in years past, but every house had to put out some. The greatest thing, he said, was to find a book that did it all—won every award, made every year-end Top Ten list, and still sold like the dickens.

Geoff didn't need to tell me he was referring to *We Never Talked About Ceauşescu,* but he did anyway, holding up the galley with the ghostly image of the Romanian flag superimposed over a photograph of New York Harbor and the Statue of Liberty. On the flyleaf was a sultry black-and-white portrait of

Anya taken by Annie Leibovitz. I wondered how much she'd had to pay Leibovitz for that photo, then thought probably nothing—Anya knew how to get people to do things for free.

Geoff said *"Ceauşescu"* had already been chosen as an alternate selection for the Book-of-the-Month Club; it was an IndieBound pick; Big Box Books had chosen it for its "3B's Breath of Fresh Writers" program; rights had been sold in more than a dozen countries, though not yet in Anya's native Romania; the audiobook was being recorded by Stockard Channing; Gwyneth Paltrow's film company, which needed a "prestige project," had already put a bid on an option; *Redbook* would be running an excerpt. Plus, advance praise for Anya's book was stellar—starred reviews in *Library Journal, PW,* and *Kirkus.* Every blurb Geoff had gotten for the book was incredible too, he said, especially the one from Blade Markham.

Geoff's enthusiasm for Anya's work wouldn't have bothered me so much if he had said something, anything positive about *Thieves,* but it was clear that he didn't regard its author and *Ceauşescu*'s in the same light—Anya was the genius and I was the hack who would make some money for a publisher so it could sign up more "good writers" like her. Even when he was flattering me, Geoff couldn't help but remind me that I would never match Anya. I hated him for this. And when the time came for me to reveal the truth, I knew I wouldn't feel the least bit bad about having betrayed him.

BURNING DOWN MY MASTER'S HOUSE

Geoff Olden sent out *Thieves* to half a dozen publishers on a Friday, then called me during my morning jog to tell me not to expect anything exciting to happen soon. One of his most important jobs, he said, was to "manage authors' expectations." Then he told me he had to take another call—the art director of *Lucky* was on the line. "Masako" wanted to do a photo shoot with his "Russian author," but he wouldn't say yes until he'd approved the photographer, something upon which he'd been insisting ever since *Details* had published pictures of Blade Markham shirtless, just as the author had requested, but had airbrushed out his gang and prison tattoos.

When I called Roth to ask how long I should expect to wait for Geoff's call, he said that if Geoff didn't call within a week to tell me about a deal, it would be time for us to find a new agent.

"Things happen quickly or they don't happen at all," Roth said. "When people think there's money to be made, they don't wait around."

Three days later, my phone rang and, when I picked up, I heard Isabelle DuPom—"I have Geoff Olden on the line," she said.

"You'll want to sit down for this," Geoff told me.

When I met Olden at his office, he was oozing more self-satisfaction than he usually did. He was wearing his eckleburgs up on his head. He rubbed his hands, then tapped the fingertips of one hand against the palm of the other. Every move he made seemed rehearsed to create maximum suspense.

"I've only had the manuscript out for seventy-two hours, and I already have three offers, Ian," said Geoff. "But there's one on the table from Merrill, and I think we'd be *loco* not to take it."

I regarded Geoff blankly. "Which editor?" I asked.

Olden cackled, put his eckleburgs back on, then looked at me as if ready to play an ace.

"Rowell Templen," he said. He waited for me to look either interested or surprised, but something felt wrong to me.

"This is a win-win-win-win, Ian," Geoff continued. "Rowell's young, he's smart, he's still hungry, he's an up-and-comer. What do you think of him?"

"What do I think of him? I think you're sitting on him," I said, and when Geoff seemed not to understand, I said, "That guy's an ass."

Geoff smiled oddly. "I'm sorry?" he asked, and so I launched into every reason why I didn't want Rowell Templen working on my book: *Thieves* wasn't the right project for some oily opportunist only four years out of Princeton and only two years out of the Columbia Publishing Course. I was remembering something Roth had told me—one day, everything Templen had edited would be more closely scrutinized. I figured I needed a more experienced editor, one with an unassailable reputation.

"I'm not sure you heard me. I don't want to work with him," I said. "Who else have you got?"

"Do you know who Rowell Templen edits, Ian?" asked Geoff.

I said I knew he edited Blade Markham.

"And what do you have to say to that?"

"I'd say it serves them both right."

"Do you even care how much money we're talking about here?" asked Geoff. And now it was my turn to smile as I thought about the story Roth and I had written, of a man who risks his life just to bring a rare book to a girl he saw once in some strange library.

"If you read the last chapter of my book, I think you'd know the answer to that one, Geoffrey," I said.

I kept speaking at the same volume and pitch, but Geoff's voice was becoming louder, his gestures more frantic. Outside the office, I could see Geoff's junior agents beginning to take an interest in our discussion. They passed his door with greater frequency, loitered by the water cooler. Isabelle DuPom seemed to be focusing with unprecedented intensity on whatever rejection letter she was ghostwriting for Geoff; anyone paying such close attention to her work must have been eavesdropping. Geoff closed his office door.

"Are we going to have a problem here, Ian?" he asked.

Ian Minot might have been intimidated; the author of *The Thieves of Manhattan,* not so much.

"That's up to you," I said.

Olden's face flushed. "You are nobody, Ian," he said. "You have no track record, no platform. Do you understand your position?"

I told him that I did, and that I didn't work for him, and that I didn't want Rowell Templen editing my book. And before I had even completed that thought, I knew exactly what I would say next. It was like taking a dive and realizing there's a parachute on your back and all you have to do is pull the rip cord.

"If Merrill Books wants the book so bad," I said, "let Jim Merrill edit it."

There it was—Jim Merrill, the celebrated editor who, according to Jed, read only the first and last pages of anything his company published. He'd be perfect.

"Jim Merrill has not edited a book in twenty years," said Geoff.

"He'll edit this one," I said. "You call Jim Merrill. Tell him I want as much money as he gave Blade Markham for his book. Plus one dollar more. And you know what else? You tell him that I don't want a one-book deal. You tell him I want two. I want one for my memoir; the other for my short stories."

Geoff's face lost its ever-present cheshire. "You're gonna blow the one chance you've got, Ian," he said.

"Only losers get one chance," I said. "I'm gonna keep getting 'em. Either Jim Merrill buys the books, edits them, or they're out and you're out. You call me when it's done.

"You'll excuse me," I added, remembering Roth had said exactly that when he walked out on Merrill Books rather than help Rowell Templen edit *Blade by Blade*.

THE FABULIST

In the past, after I had done just about anything that I considered to be uncharacteristically bold, I immediately started to regret it. Moments after I had thrown Jed Roth's book down Broadway, then lost my job, I was already wondering if I had done something stupid. This afternoon, I had no second thoughts, in fact I kept gaining confidence with every step as I jogged to the Broadway-Lafayette subway station. I could take on anybody, I thought; I was in a zone. Throw me a basketball, I'll nail every free throw; pass me a pool cue, I'll sink every shot; introduce me to any woman, I'll tell her my story and she'll fall in love with me. I didn't play basketball, though, I didn't know of any pool halls nearby, and as for women, I was out of practice; when I flipped open my cellphone, I saw only two names of people with whom I wanted to share my tale.

I arrived at Morningside Coffee shortly after five, always the slowest part of the day save for closing time. When I peered through the window, I felt as if I were gazing into a past I had gladly left behind, a world of small people leading small lives—smart, well-turned tales, perhaps, but nothing anybody would really want to read about. *LIKE THIS*

Joseph was behind the counter, looking slower and heavier than ever. Faye wasn't even pretending to work; she was sitting on a stool behind the register, sketching in a notebook; she didn't look up when I came in.

I strutted toward the counter, one hand in a front pocket of my butter-colored suit jacket. Joseph spotted me first. He looked me up and down, seemed to understand in one glance that I had moved on while he was standing in place.

"Nice duds," he said with a smirk.

Faye still wasn't looking at me, so I kept talking to Joseph even though he was behaving, like always, as if he had something against me, maybe because my presence reminded him that he would always be stuck here, now 325 pounds and still counting.

"Hey, man," I said, "get cast in any shows?"

"Hell, no," he said, adding that he had all but given up acting. The only times he ever got cast was as a funny fat guy. He'd

liked acting because he thought doing it would allow him to escape his life, but what was the point if you only ever got to play
the same role, and never got a chance to play a hero? Joseph
sighed, then asked the question I was waiting for—"What
about you? Sell any books, man?"

"Maybe I did." I brushed a speck of lint off my jacket.

"Lucky you," said Joseph. He shuffled to the sink, while I
leaned on the counter where Faye was sketching, effortlessly as
always. She was drawing a landscape—water, a bridge, a clock
tower. Maybe when she was done with it, I could buy it from her
gallery and put it on my wall, I thought.

"Sell any paintings, Betty?" I asked.

"Hell, no," Faye said, still sketching.

"You're lying," I said. "I know for a fact you sold at least
one."

Faye stopped drawing, then looked up at me. I never understood how much she must have liked me before until I saw
how she was looking at me now. For a moment, I wondered if
I'd lost even more than I realized that last night with her at the
KGB.

"What do you want, Ian?" she asked.

I tried small talk, told her I was just passing by and wanted
to see how she was doing.

"I'm doing shitty, Ian," she said, "but why would you care?"

"Well, we never really had a chance to talk." I thought I had
gotten pretty good at BSing by now, but Faye could see through
me: I had come here to brag and make her feel like she had
missed out on something, but now I just felt petty and small.

"So, how's your Ukrainian?" she asked.

"Romanian," I muttered.

"Whatever works," said Faye. "Look, Ian," she told me, "I'm seeing someone else anyway. I was even when we were going out."

Joseph smiled, and in that smile I could see that Faye was telling the truth.

"Why didn't you tell me?" I asked.

"Because I thought I might've liked you better," she said. "Turns out you fooled me; I just liked your stories.

"For a while, I thought you were an honest, decent guy," she continued. "Then you showed me who you really were, no different from the rest of them. I was upset for a while, but it was really my fault. I'm over it now anyway. Whatever. It's done."

"I just thought you'd like hearing about something that happened to me today," I said. "It's another good story."

She paused for a moment. I could see her deciding whether she wanted to hear the story. But no, she was done with fakes like me.

"Why don't you tell them to someone who still cares about you," she said. "You should go back to your Ukrainian; you guys deserve each other." She didn't look up when I walked out the door.

Now the only person I wanted to talk to was Anya, but I needed two fitzgeralds at the 106 Bar before I could call her. And when I heard Blade's recorded voice on her number, I needed another.

"Yo," he said. I could imagine him throwing his hands out, flashing his phony gang signs. "This here's the number for Blade Markham and Anya Peh-tresh-KOO. Y'all wanna rap with *Anya,* press *one.* Y'all wanna talk with the *main man,* press *two.* Y'all wanna suck *mah dick,* you press the motherfuckin' *three,* yo."

I didn't leave a message. To tell the truth, I was laughing too hard. The woman I had loved had left me for a fraud, and now I was a fraud too; it was pretty funny. I sat at the bar for hours, ordering fitzgeralds until the bartender told me I'd had enough, and did I need a taxi to take me home? A taxi might have been a good idea. That way I wouldn't have fallen asleep on the train and woken up at 207th Street to see Blade's grinning mug staring down at me from the subway ads.

By the time I got home, morning had arrived, and my cellphone was ringing. "I don't know how I did it, but I did it, you *ladron culo,*" Geoff Olden said with a cackle. He asked when I would be available to meet Jim Merrill, Jr., at the Century Club. "Oh, and *por favor?*" he said after we had set the time and date. "Those short stories of yours better be good, Ian. I already told Merrill they were."

THE HONORED SOCIETY

I met Geoff Olden and Jim Merrill, Jr., at the Century Club on Forty-third Street and Fifth Avenue, a relic of Manhattan's artistic and literary past. New York city law decreed that cigars could no longer be smoked in the club, but the cloakroom still smelled of them and so did the doorman's jacket; women were now admitted to the club, but the place still exuded an old boys' clubhouse, a place where men gathered in dim, smoky light to drink, chortle, and discuss the serious business of literature and art out of the sight of their wives and mistresses. The ghosts of onetime members Winslow Homer, the architect Stanford White, and the late railroad magnate and manuscript collector Chester Blom seemed to swoop in and out of the dining room and bar.

Michael's Restaurant may have been located less than a mile from here, but entering the Century Club was like stepping fifty years into the past. The difference between the two was that of new publishing versus old. It was that of JMJ Publishers versus Merrill Books, between the works of literary titles that Jim Merrill published under his old company's name and the diet and exercise books JMJ published to keep Merrill Books solvent. Here at the Century Club, there was no overt discussion of deals or bottom lines, no crass displays of publishers' catalogs. It was a place where cash was rarely seen and money exchanged only via scribbles on club members' accounts. Conversations were confidential, muffled by carpets. Men wore corduroy blazers and sipped brandy from snifters; waiters in slightly frayed uniforms called members by name and spoke to them in low, respectful tones—"Right this way, Mr. Minot," "Good afternoon, Mr. Merrill," "Pleasure to see you again, Mr. Olden,"

A concierge directed me up the stairs to the bar, where Geoff Olden was sitting beside Jim Merrill, Jr., who wore a powder blue suit with a pink, four-petaled boutonniere. Olden was dressed more conservatively than usual: black suit, gray shirt buttoned to the neck; the only color was the yellow frames of his eckleburgs. The bartender was serving a fitzgerald to

Merrill Jr. and asking whether Mr. Olden would be having "the usual." When Olden said, *"Si, señor,"* the bartender took down a cordial glass and poured a Lillet.

To me, Jim Merrill, Jr., had the respectable air of an old-school gentleman—narrow, salt-and-pepper steinbeck; tan, weathered skin that suggested summers spent on yachts; and a deep, soothing voice that told you at once how welcome you were at his club and how unusual it was for him to invite anyone new to it. To Jed Roth, Merrill Jr. was an unworthy inheritor of a great name, knew only what drinks to order, what sort of outfit to wear to lunch, and what tie to wear to dinner. But I couldn't help but feel flattered by the way Merrill looked at me, as if he were granting me the privilege of marrying his daughter.

"Mr. Minot," Merrill said, standing to greet me.

"Compañero," said Geoff Olden. He tried to step between me and Merrill, but it was clear that the latter viewed my agent as merely a means to an end, something unpleasant yet necessary to the process. Like the presence of women or the absence of cigars, Geoff Olden was to be tolerated at the Century Club, never truly accepted.

"Ian, I'd like you to meet Jimmy Merrill," said Geoff.

"It's Jim," Merrill told him curtly, then assessed me with a satisfied, proprietary smile, as if a brand-new car had been delivered to his building, and he found the vehicle to his liking.

"Well," Merrill said as he shook my hand, "well, well, well." He turned to Geoff, then gestured to me. "Now, *that* looks like a writer," he said. "Welcome aboard, my friend."

Merrill asked what I would be drinking. I ordered a fitzgerald, and he smiled approvingly. Yes, he seemed to be thinking, that's a writer's drink.

"What a book, what a life," he said, adding that the first page of *Thieves* "certainly set the scene," and that my last page "really packed a wallop."

"But you know something?" Merrill asked as we clinked glasses. "I'm even more excited about your short stories."

MY FRIEND JED

I was still feeling buzzed when I arrived at Roth's place in the evening to tell him about my meeting with Merrill. The apartment looked emptier than before, and when Jed spoke, the walls seemed to reverberate with the hint of an echo.

He stood by his kitchen counter, uncorking a bottle of champagne, then poured the contents into two chilled flutes. He regarded me with an unfamiliarly distant look—the intensity of our months working together had been replaced by something approximating nostalgia or perhaps regret, as if he had already moved on to the next chapter. When I told him of the argument I had had with Geoff Olden, the way I had swung a deal for my short story collection, when I told him about the fitzgeralds I had quaffed with Merrill at the Century Club, Roth reminded me of my father during his last months, when I had read him my stories and told him my plans. Though my dad wouldn't say what he was thinking, I thought I could tell—my stories made him happy, granted him momentary escape from his world, but he knew he would not play any part in them; I would be moving on without him.

But not until Roth sipped his champagne and told me how much he'd miss me after all this was over did I realize that he seemed to view the evening as the beginning of a farewell. He said that we'd be meeting even less frequently now, and rarely in public. He didn't want to run the risk anymore of people recognizing us and thinking we were working together. The best con-artist teams were usually made up of mismatched pairs, Roth said, an old black man and a young white girl, a bag lady and a fresh-faced kid; as for us, we could now almost pass for brothers.

I hadn't really thought past this point, had figured that I would keep meeting with Roth, working at his desk, that at least our business relationship would continue, that after this project, he would have another scheme. But no, we would be going our separate ways—25 percent for him, 15 for Olden, the rest for me.

Roth and I stood side by side at his window, looking out over Riverside Park, two men in light-colored gatsbys, black shoes, no ties. I asked Roth what he might do. He said he had no immediate plans; he'd stay in New York for a while, but then, when some "things" had "sorted themselves out for better or worse," he would move away. This New York was so different from the city in which he'd grown up. Manhattan was all about money now, all about trying to make enough of it just to survive. He'd still have money, but there would be fewer and fewer things he would want to buy with it.

I asked Roth if he'd ever work in publishing again. No, he said, that business was dying. Books would never disappear entirely, there would always be places to buy them, libraries where you could read them. But for him, they had lost their romance. He wondered if that day when he had stumbled upon the wreckage of the Blom Library had been a sign of what was to come, a world he had sought erupting in flame, then being reduced to ashes. He said he might start some new business in Europe, maybe in London, or perhaps in some other foreign country whose language he didn't speak, one where it would take him a lifetime to understand what old traditions were passing, so he wouldn't regret their disappearance. Now, the only relevant regret he had was that he wouldn't be able to see Geoff Olden's and Jim Merrill, Jr.'s faces when they learned the truth about *The Thieves of Manhattan*.

The two of us stood before the darkening sky, the leaves and the branches of the London plane trees slowly but inevitably fading into night. I couldn't help but feel some regrets too, not about Geoff Olden, but about Merrill, a man whose name I had once respected. He was putting his money and faith in me, and I would repay him with the truth—that he had trusted a liar.

"Second thoughts?" Roth asked. I nodded.

"Remember this," he said, and as he spoke, I could see another flicker of the anger he usually hid so well. "When you were already a writer and a pretty honest, stand-up, wholesome Midwestern guy, you were invisible to Jim Merrill, Jr. At best, you were some hick serving coffee somewhere he would never have gone. Only when you became a liar and a thief did he ask you to his club, buy you a drink, and tell you that you were a writer.

"No matter what happens, never forget that, Ian," said

Roth. "You'll follow the plan exactly as we discussed. When the time is right, you'll tell everyone it was all a lie."

"When will the time be right?"

"Don't you think you'll know that?" Roth asked.

Yes, I said, I would. "But until that time comes," I said, "if Merrill or Olden or anybody else asks whether or not the story is true..."

"Here's the funny thing," Roth said, interrupting. "They'll never ask you."

Roth finished his champagne and rolled the stem of his flute nimbly between thumb and middle finger. "When all is said and done, book people don't know much about the lives real people live. They think the only Manhattan is the one they live in. They've read too much, lived too little. They think everyone acts like they're part of some big story. Just keep acting like you're part of the story you've written, Ian, and they'll believe it's true."

Act like you're part of some big story, I thought as I finished my champagne. Yes, I knew how to do that now.

MY OWN SWEET TIME

The rest of the summer lurched by in haphazard fashion—spurts of frantic action separated from each other by long stretches of aimless slothfulness, euphoric moments closely followed by days of desolation. There were interviews with publishing industry magazines, furious email exchanges with copy editors, strategy sessions with publicists, meetings with Merrill and Olden to discuss potential covers for *The Thieves of Manhattan,* and follow-up meetings when those covers didn't meet with the approval of buyers for the chain stores. I had my picture taken by top-notch author photographers: Marion Ettlinger for the U.S. market; Jerry Bauer for overseas. And yet none of this happened in an orderly way. My days were absolutely full or utterly empty; weeks were chaotic or just plain blah; on my calendar, July was a mess of scribbles and cross-outs, but August had nothing on it save for the launch party for *We Never Talked About Ceaușescu.* Jim Merrill spent his August in Nantucket; Geoff Olden in Rhinebeck. I had more free time and ready cash than ever, and less of an idea of what I might do with it.

Roth had prepped me for the ups and downs of publishing, the stops and starts. This was an old plodder of an industry vainly struggling to move at twenty-first-century speed, he said. Sure, you could now pdf your manuscript to your editor instead of delivering it to his or her office, and yes, you could edit your book on a laptop at Starbucks instead of scribbling upon parchment with a plumed ink pen, but some aspects of publishing couldn't move any faster than they had a thousand years ago in the days of *The Tale of Genji.* Novelists couldn't write any quicker, and authors of memoirs couldn't live their lives any faster. Though one could speed up individual steps, the whole process required too many of them to kick the business into a higher gear. Magazines were reviewing books for issues that would be coming out six months from now, publishers were signing up manuscripts that wouldn't be in bookstores for years. What seemed like a good idea for a book in outline form now might well be irrelevant when the *Times* reviewed the finished version three years later, if the *Times* would even review it, if the

Times would even have a book review section, no sure thing given the declining circulation numbers of newspapers nationwide; if the editor of the book would even still have a job at the publisher that had employed him or her when the contract for the book had been signed—if the publisher itself hadn't been folded into some conglomerate or been driven out of business entirely. In the past half decade, half a dozen magazines about books had launched and folded, replaced, for the most part, by book blogs, which no one knew how to make money off of. And, though the Merrill Books autumn catalog was already labeling me a "bold new voice in the world of memoirs," no one, other than Roth, myself, the copy editor, and maybe Jim Merrill had read any of *The Thieves of Manhattan*.

This pace might have been inconvenient for the industry as a whole, but it was phenomenally useful to the con artist who knew how to exploit the flaws in a world that spun at two different speeds. By the time the truth behind *The Thieves of Manhattan* would be revealed, all the checks would be cashed, and *Myself When I Am Real* would be in the hands of a copy editor.

Nearly a year had passed since I had gone with Anya to hear her read at KGB's "Literal Stimulation," and now I was walking into the Big Box Books on Broadway for the launch event of *We Never Talked About Ceauşescu*. When I worked up the street at Morningside Coffee, I was greeted every morning by the sight of a scowling, even-bigger-than-life cardboard Blade Markham in 3B's window; tonight, his picture was gone, replaced by a giant cutout of Anya's book cover. Blade Markham was here in person, though, standing with his hands in the pockets of his baggy jeans at the front of the store near the podium. Geoff

Olden was shaking hands, smiling, passing out pairs of business cards.

A familiar crowd was here—Anya's editor, her publicists, creative writing students from Columbia, and a few unsuspecting bookstore customers trying to make their way past the crowd to get whatever book they had come here to find, probably *Blade by Blade*. Isabelle DuPom was standing beside Geoff Olden near stacks of *We Never Talked About Ceauşescu*. Isabelle and I had dated for a few weeks in late July and early August, but we were a bad match. She was my agent's employee and she had a book manuscript she was hoping to sell—exquisitely crafted but hopelessly small stories about her childhood in Montreal; I was an up-and-coming author with a big book on the way. We went to movies, attended readings, made exuberant yet passionless chinaski, and talked about books and writing, but when I was with her, I couldn't escape the feeling that something was phony about our relationship, realizing too late that the phony thing about it was me.

Out the window of the bookshop, I could see traffic on Broadway, could see the café, too. For a moment, I thought I saw Faye in her baseball cap and paint-spattered jeans peering through the bookshop window—wishful thinking on my part. I longed to tell her stories again, but I knew she was no longer interested in hearing them.

I took my place behind the back row of folding chairs, most of which were filled when Blade Markham took the stage and bent down to speak into the microphone that had been positioned at Anya's height. Blade spread his arms out, then flapped them at his side, like a quarterback trying to silence the home crowd. He asked everyone to "give it up for Anya Peh-tresh-KOO, whose first book, *We Never Talked About Chow-Chess-Koo,* just *dropped,* yo."

Blade applauded, hands above his head, and then the audience joined in. Anya embraced Blade before stepping to the podium. Something was shining on the ring finger of her left hand—apparently, she and Blade were engaged.

Anya had just started to read when Blade spotted me and walked fast in my direction, truth cross thumping against his chest. I didn't know whether Geoff or Anya had told him I was here, whether he recognized me from the furniture store or from Geoff's apartment, but when he asked me to "step outside for a minute, son," I sensed he might want to roll me once and for all. I whispered that I was here to listen to Anya read, but he slapped me hard on a shoulder—"You've heard Anya read before, my man," he said.

Once we were outside the bookstore, though, Blade smiled, then put out his hand. "I been *readin'* you, bro; I been reading your *words,*" he said. He added that he wasn't through with *The Thieves of Manhattan,* which Geoff had sent to him, but it was "righteous as hell," and filled with *wheeze-dom.* If called upon to do so, he would be more than willing to deliver "props" to me in the form of a blurb.

I thanked him, then looked through the window at Anya. I couldn't hear what she was saying at the podium, and yet I could see the hold she had over the people in her audience—they seemed as if they would follow her anywhere. I confided to Blade that I had seen the ring on Anya's finger, and I congratulated him.

Hell yeah, he said, Anya was steppin' tonight, and now she

was "sportin'" his "*bling,* yo," and god*damn* did he love that woman. He said that the three of us had to get together some time and "throw back a couple coldies," and I said I'd be happy to. He told me to wait two weeks to call, because next week was gonna be crazy.

Why would next week be crazy? I asked.

"Just watch your television box, son," Blade said as he shook my hand again. "Just keep an eye on that TV box, yo."

HONOR LOST

When I learned that Pam Layne had made *We Never Talked About Ceauşescu* her next book club choice, Blade's words about the "TV box" made more sense. Anya and Blade's phone was bound to be ringing off the hook, and I could just imagine the photo spread being planned for *People* magazine—"America's Hottest Literary Couple."

Strangely, when I read of Anya's good fortune on page two of the *Times*'s Arts section, I didn't feel jealous. Layne's selection of *Ceauşescu* for her talk show seemed both inevitable and just, like Nelson Mandela winning the Nobel Peace Prize or Kate Winslet nabbing an Oscar. The world of bestselling authors and their books no longer seemed unattainable—today, it would be Anya's turn in the spotlight; next, it would be mine. I foolishly fantasized that Pam Layne might even ask Anya whom she had dated before Blade—a year from now, when *Thieves* would be published, people might remember my name.

I tuned in early to the show, and shut my windows and

blinds so I would be able to hear and see everything on my new flat-screen. I sat on my black leather couch with a beer and take-out Chinese food, considered the time Anya and I had spent in my West Harlem studio, Anya scribbling while I stared at my computer screen. I imagined what it must have felt like to be the Beatles in Hamburg.

Then the jaunty Pam Layne theme music began to play, Layne's logo popped onto the screen, and there was Pam in the spotlight, delivering her opening monologue. I didn't pay much attention to what she was saying—something about the power of a good story to transform us and to make us believe; I just kept waiting for Anya, whom Pam said would be "visiting us after a short break."

Pam Layne had been a child actor, had appeared in movies or on TV for nearly forty years, but when the first commercial break was over and Anya appeared in a black golightly, tights, and pumps, she appeared to be the one who truly belonged on television. As Pam introduced Anya, who smiled demurely as she walked to her chair, I noted that the show's set appeared starker and less welcoming than it usually did. When I had seen Blade and a half dozen other authors on the show, they sat opposite their host in comfortable chairs in front of a roaring fire, like old pals meeting in a living room, nibbling cookies, and talking over old times. Pam would describe how she had come to learn about whatever book she was featuring—it was always one that had been recommended by "this gal I met in the check-out line"; "my darling assistant, Mabel." Layne liked to tell her viewers and her studio audience to imagine themselves at a Girl Scout camp outing, holding hands in front of a fire, and listening to stories. Come on, she'd say, kick off your shoes, crawl in your sleeping bag, *let's listen*.

Today, the set was configured as if for a Sunday morning political talk show. Pam Layne's short, frosted blond hair looked sharper and more severe than it usually did. Pam and Anya were seated behind desks. Still, the camera adored Anya, and so did the audience, gasping when she told Pam about how she had come to write *Ceaușescu;* she described the desolation she had felt at her ailing father's side, reading her stories to him, knowing she would soon become an orphan. Yes, I felt proud that Anya's stories had made me fall in love with her long before America was doubtlessly doing the same.

Anya finished telling her story, blushed, wiped her eyes, and looked to Pam. And then Pam Layne looked directly back at her. "Why are you lying to us?" Layne asked. Anya emitted a nervous chuckle. "Why are you lying to my audience, Anya?" asked Layne. I had thought that Layne must have been joking, but then I saw the shell-shocked expression emerging on Anya's face. I felt my own heart beginning to beat just a bit more strongly as I saw Anya's hands start to shake. The camera cut to a close-up of Pam Layne.

"We'll be right back," she said.

My mind began to reel, my stomach started churning, I dropped my chopsticks and didn't pick them up—I didn't feel like eating anymore. I stood and paced my floor, then, after the break, sat back down as Pam Layne spoke directly to the camera. This woman sitting beside her was a fraud, she said; everything Anya Petrescu had said before the break was a lie.

Anya's skin was pale. Upon her face was an expression I

didn't recognize—shame, perhaps embarrassment. She looked as if she wanted to be anywhere but on the set of the show.

"Now, tell us the truth, Anya," Pam Layne said.

Anya seemed to be fighting back tears. Another unfamiliar expression—when she felt like crying, the Anya I knew always let those tears flow down her cheeks, let them stay right where they were until I wiped them away.

"Are you from Bucharest, Anya?" asked Layne.

I shoved my plate of food out of my line of vision; even the sight of it was making me ill.

Anya bit her lip. And then she shook her head, mouthing a word yet not giving voice to it.

"Anya, are you from Bucharest?" Layne asked again, and this time I could hear Anya's voice, which sounded more foreign to me than it ever had.

"I'm not," said Anya.

Members of the studio audience shook their heads in disbelief. My entire body felt dizzy. In the audience, Blade Markham was holding one hand over his truth cross, the other over his mouth.

"Where are you from, Anya?" Pam asked.

I couldn't hear Anya at first, and Pam couldn't either, but the second time Pam asked, I heard Anya's voice loud and clear.

"Maplewood, New Jersey," she said.

Another gasp from the audience, another gasp from me, another from Blade Markham.

"And is your name really Anya?" asked Pam.

Another no from Anya; her accent was gone, along with it the voice that had called me *Ee-yen* and told me how much she *luffed* me. She looked fragile and small, and I had the sensation that I often had when I was with her, that I wanted to fix whatever was wrong, to give her the happiness to compensate for all the misery she had felt growing up in Bucharest.

"No, it's Anna," she said.

Pam Layne looked piercingly at Anna Petrescu. "And why pretend your name was Anya and you were from Hungary?"

"Romania," said Anya.

"Why, Anna?"

Anna took a breath. "Because I thought no one would read my stories if I was just some rich kid from Maplewood, New Jersey," she said.

Pam Layne held Anya's book up to the camera, then slammed it down on the table. The camera closed in on Pam, who said she had half a mind to take Anya's book and throw it into her fireplace. She spoke to the camera about truth and trust and inviolable covenants between authors and readers. But I couldn't watch anymore. I felt mixed up and afraid, as if I only now understood the gravity of what I myself had done, what I was still doing, and all that I had left to do. I shut off the TV and called Jed Roth. And when he didn't answer, I jogged as fast as I could to his place.

OUTSIDE ROTH'S

"So explain to me exactly what some counterfeit Eastern European has to do with you?" Roth asked. I had caught up to him in front of his building right when he was about to enter with a cup of takeaway tea.

What did it have to do with me? I asked. I was still out of breath; I was speaking faster than I was thinking, and my thoughts had been racing along at a pretty good clip. It had everything to do with me, I said, everything to do with both of us.

"Then explain to me exactly what you think will happen," Roth said. "Tell me the cause and effect."

I thought it was obvious, but I told him anyway, nervously running my words together: Anya was represented by Geoff Olden. She had appeared on Pam Layne's show, and everything she'd said about herself to me and, more important, to everyone else had been revealed to be a lie because she hadn't thought people would buy her books if she admitted who she really was. And here's what would probably happen, I said: people would stop buying her book, and no publisher would give her a chance to write another. No Olden client would be safe; every one of his authors' biographies would be scrutinized.

Roth smiled, then led me by the shoulder across Riverside Drive and into the park, where he sat on a bench that faced toward the Hudson. The park was filled with sounds of children laughing as they swung on swings or ran through sprinklers; dogs barked as they scampered across fenced-in lawns; and yet the end of summer was approaching. In the air, I could inhale the imminent arrival of the first day of school—it smelled like freshly cut grass, newly poured asphalt, and leaves just getting ready to fall.

"Now," Roth said, sipping his tea as I sat beside him, "tell me exactly who will discover this truth."

"People," I said. "Anybody."

"Which people? Which anybody?"

"Some fact-checker," I proposed.

"Publishers can't afford to employ fact-checkers," said Roth. "Try again. Who else?"

"Journalists," I said. "The same people who found out about Anya."

"Which ones?"

I said I didn't know, but as more people read our book, more people would start examining it. Maybe it would be a reporter, or someone at Merrill Books or Olden's office.

"And what exactly will these 'people' find out?" Roth asked. "That your name isn't really Ian Minot?"

"No, that's true," I said.

"That you didn't come to New York from Indiana?"

"No."

"That a library didn't burn down? That no hooligan worked there? That there's no such thing as *The Tale of Genji*?"

"No, you know that's all true too." Usually, Roth's confidence was reassuring; today it just irritated me. "I mean everything else," I said. "The chases, the golden cross, the desolate field, the eight-thirteen train."

"And who other than you or me can prove that any of that's not true?" he asked.

I didn't say anything.

"Who?" he asked again.

I thought for a moment.

"Tell me, Ian," said Roth.

I kept thinking.

And then I thought some more.

Well, I thought, who really did know much about how I had spent my first years in New York? Faye didn't. Neither did

Anya, no more than I knew where she was from when she had talked to me in that accent, making believe she thought Blade Markham was the one from *Mepplewood,* New *Jairsey.* Maybe the truth was that they both were from *Jairsey.* Maybe they had planned everything out way in advance. As for me, I wasn't very good at maintaining contacts—my parents' deaths had taught me that nothing was permanent and so I tended to drift in and out of people's lives, mostly out, and my adult life had seemed to be a series of freestanding episodes linked only by their main character, something agents often complained about in letters to me when they were rejecting my work. Maybe Roth was on to something; maybe he had known all along that he had chosen the right man.

"But someone," I said.

"Yes, someone," Roth said. "You."

And then Roth told me that on the night I had gone to hear Anya read at the KGB Bar, he had been there too. He had known right away that everything she was saying was false, he said. It was that skill of his again, the one he had mentioned to me on the night we met—being able to see truth or falsehood even in fiction. For Anya, it had only been a matter of time before she was discovered; she was lucky that the wheels of publishing turned so slowly. By now, at least she had already cashed her checks.

"You see," Roth continued as he took another sip of tea, "your little Bulgarian friend? She told the worst sort of lies— the ones that are so easy to disprove, the ones that can be destroyed with one simple phone call. You're telling enormous lies, but they're so entangled with true stories that it would take years of work to pull out each individual strand to discover which is fact and which is fiction."

I didn't want to tell Roth he was right, so I shut my mouth. But as I added up the lies, I couldn't find the one that would give us away. The stories about who I was and where I came from were true; the characters in *The Thieves of Manhattan* were fictional, and what fictional character would stand up and say that Roth and I had created him or her? Would whoever had been working at the Blom Library when Roth had seen the girl there file suit, saying, "I'm no hooligan"? Sure, there were details that could have tripped us up, cute little flourishes about latitudes and longitudes that had been included in Roth's original, now stored safely away in my files, but I had insisted we eliminate them in the final draft.

"No, Ian," Roth said, "there's only one way this lie could unravel before its time, and there are only two people who could make that happen—you and me. As long as we remain calm and patient, as long as you stick to the story, everything will fall out just as it has been planned. It will all happen as it was written, Ian."

I watched the leaves flutter in the breeze, I watched boats sailing along the Hudson. I listened to children and dogs, to joggers passing. Roth stood up and took his empty tea container to the trash can. I could still hear his voice even though he wasn't speaking to me now.

"Just as it was written," I heard him say. I reminded myself to be patient and calm. I continued looking out at the river and the trees, trying to reassure myself that I was still in control.

III
memoir

Now we find, too late
That these distractions were clues.

ERN MALLEY, *Palinode*

BRIGHT, SHINY MORNING

I spent the better part of a week debating whether I should call Anya. She still exerted a pull on me, still made me want to try to right every wrong in her life. True, that was Blade's job now, but I owed him a phone call too; we had planned to get together after that "crazy week" with the TV box, yo. But when I finally convinced myself that a simple phone call wouldn't hurt, I couldn't get either Blade or Anya on the line. Every time I called their number, I got a busy signal or a voice mail message that said the mailbox was full. The next week when I called, a recorded voice said the number was no longer in service. So I just gave up.

The autumn passed with a passel of stories about a seemingly never-ending series of literary hoaxes—a drug addict and ruffian had exaggerated his criminal past; a purported gang-banger from South Central LA turned out to be a prep school girl from the San Fernando Valley; a memoir of an abusive household was apparently a libelous childhood fantasy; a teenage boy hustler and lot lizard was really an actress in a wig and sunglasses; a Holocaust survivor wasn't raised by wolves; another survivor hadn't met his wife on the other side of a concentration camp fence; the supposed witness to a Jordanian honor killing was a con artist from the south side of Chicago; a Romanian writer hailed from the mean streets of Maplewood, New Jersey.

In the press, these hoaxes were viewed mostly as symptoms of a declining industry struggling for relevance and attention and a society of declining morals. The writers in question and their publishers were savaged as betrayers of the public trust. At one time, I might have found them despicable too, but now that I was one of them, and had dated another, I saw them as All-American rogues. Who hadn't fudged their taxes, embellished a résumé, or invented a tale to impress a date?

As Roth taught me, the idea of a true memoir was absurd anyway. How reliable was anybody's memory? Even if you could remember absolutely everything that ever happened to you, wouldn't you have to cut out 99 percent to create a story that someone would want to read? Wouldn't you have to lish all that eating and sleeping and Web surfing and staring into space? And wouldn't all that editing be a little like lying?

And besides, no one had been injured by the lies that these authors had told; theirs weren't tales of a president lying to a grand jury under oath, of falsifying information about weapons of mass destruction before the United Nations. This was just publishing; no actual laws were being broken.

As for Anya, her editor and publisher appeared on radio and TV to apologize for misleading their readers. They promised to issue refunds to any readers who had bought the book and felt they had been cheated. But when *Ceauşescu* stayed on the bestseller list and went into its third printing, no further talk was heard about that. By the time winter rolled around, Geoff Olden had sold *Jersey Girl,* a memoir that Anya would write about her ordeal, and the screenplay of *Ceauşescu,* which had been in turnaround, was put on the fast track at Paramount. Apparently, Americans could more easily relate to the story of a liar from Maplewood than a beleaguered orphan from Bucharest. As far as Blade was concerned, his story remained unquestioned, his reputation unsullied. Maybe he was just waiting for the right time to reveal the truth to drum up more interest in his next book.

I hadn't seen Jed Roth in months when the first galleys of *The Thieves of Manhattan* arrived at my door, six of them in a manila envelope messengered with a congratulatory note from Jim Merrill, Jr., on Merrill Books stationery. I had been updating Roth by phone about the book's progress—the Big Box Book Club selection, the "Breath of Fresh Writers" nomination, the stellar prepublication reviews, the foreign rights sales, Merrill's positive feedback on the stories I had revised for *Myself When I Am Real* ("Great opener!" "Nice wrap-up!"). Though Roth never seemed impressed or surprised by any of it, the arrival of the galleys seemed like cause for celebration. When I called to invite him out for a drink, I told him that I would treat, and that I wanted to meet at the 106 Bar, where our adventure began.

Lately, no matter what the weather, I jogged or walked almost everywhere I went, but the evening Roth and I were to meet, I took the subway, so I could study my galley for the whole ride. I still couldn't quite believe that everything was falling into place. The book's cover was based on my idea, a riff on Faye's artworks. At first glance, it appeared to be rather plain—"The Thieves of Manhattan" in an elegant white font on a black background—but the corners had been charred and pulled away to reveal fires blazing underneath. On the back was a sampling of quotes from the prepub reviews, a picture of me in my linen gatsby, and a glowing blurb from Blade Markham, who had come through as promised.

I arrived at the 106 Bar, and Roth was sitting in the same window seat where we had drunk our pints of Guinness just over a year earlier. He was talking on his cellphone, but when he saw me, he smiled, then put the phone away. He was still a handsome-enough bloke, but he looked a little more disheveled than I remembered him being on our first night together. His gatsby appeared just a bit shabbier too. I couldn't tell if he really looked worse, or if I was seeing him differently now that I felt myself to be the suavest, most confident guy in the whole bar, someone who recognized that though the suit Roth wore was no doubt expensive, it was really more appropriate for warmer weather.

Roth embraced me when I entered the bar, and when I handed him his copy of *Thieves,* he smiled and nodded with the satisfaction I expected. But I couldn't help noticing some undercurrent of regret or resentment, as if perhaps what he had always wanted was coming true but far too late and not in the way he had intended. I couldn't shake the sensation that part of him was miffed about something, perhaps that my name was on the cover. Once, he had been a young man who would have given anything to see "A Novel by Jed Roth" on that book instead of "A Memoir by Ian Minot." Certainly, some of that ambitious young man remained; not all of him had succumbed to cynicism and age. Even as I sat there in a sharper gatsby than Roth's, and gleaming black shoes, part of me was still the old Ian Minot who had just arrived in Manhattan vowing that he wouldn't leave until he had succeeded.

Roth and I had little left to discuss—whatever I could say about *Thieves* sounded like either a boast or something he already knew. He gave me advice I had heard before, catchphrases I had memorized. I imagined how writers must feel when they return to their hometowns to see the teachers who inspired them. I imagined my own little Indiana town, my father's library, our house, his bedroom. Homey, comfortable, and yet so small.

Midway through our second round, Jed and I ran out of conversation and I was thankful when my cellphone rang. On the other end was Simian Gold, books editor of *U.S. News & World Report,* who said he wanted to set up a time to interview me about *Thieves*. I asked Roth to excuse me, told Gold to hold on, then stepped outside the bar to have the conversation on Amsterdam Avenue, where I stood under the canopy of the Chinese takeout joint next door and watched the light rain that was beginning to fall.

Gold sounded British, and, in staccato tones that at first made me wonder then dismiss the notion of whether he might have been wise to Roth's and my act, he asked when I might have time to meet and discuss the book. The connection was lousy, and I had trouble making out everything he was saying, but I did hear him tell me that his schedule was *woide* open and his deadline was *wikes* away. Still, since I was looking for a way to gracefully conclude my evening with Roth, I told the man that my schedule was clear too, and if he wanted to meet tonight, I could. He paused before agreeing, then suggested that we meet at the Hungarian Pastry Shop and Café up by Columbia University in about *fo'y-foive* minutes, and how did that sound like a good idea? I said yes, that sounded like a good idea indeed.

Roth was smiling when I returned to tell him the news, and it bugged me that, even now, I couldn't hide anything from him.

"*Time, Newsweek,* or *U.S. News*?" he asked.

I laughed, then added that Simian Gold was on deadline and we would have to meet tonight. I couldn't tell whether Roth knew I was lying so that I could bring our evening to an early end or whether I had gotten a whole lot better at making things up. Either way, Roth seemed relieved.

Our final hug lasted longer than our hugs usually tended to, as if both of us figured this might be the last time we would see each other for a long while. I shook his hand and wished him luck before I walked out the door, turned up my collar, and stepped into the cold, hard rain.

A MILLION LITTLE PIECES

I was looking forward to getting to the café early and warming up with a spot of tea and a slice of strudel while I prepared my remarks for the interview when I noticed a man about my height but a good deal bulkier step out of the shadows at 108th Street. Just as I registered the fact that something in his hand was glinting in the amber streetlight above, he was swinging the hand fast toward my head. *Bam!* I felt a sharp pain in my temple, and warm blood beginning to mix with the freezing rain sliding down my right cheek.

"Where is it?" the man demanded as my knees hit concrete.

He was bald under a dark tam-o'-shanter, wore a beat-up black leather Rusty James jacket and steel-toed boots. He pulled me up from the ground and back into the shadows of 108th Street from which he had emerged, then threw me hard against a brick wall. His eyes were small, black, and empty, and he had a swirling, dull red tattoo on one side of his face, and tattoos on his hands—strange tattoos, no obvious pattern to them, like maps of intersecting roads leading nowhere. In one hand, he held a gun.

"Where the *fook* is it?" he asked. The man raised the gun over his head as if to clock me with it once more. I raised my hands high and waved them.

"What the hell?" I asked, still waving. The bitter air had turned colder. The rain was now sleet. I was shivering, wet.

He cocked the gun, held the nose of it just millimeters away from my face. I tried to back up farther, but there was no place for me to go but into the wall. "Easy, easy, easy," I said. The sharp pain in my temple had already resolved into a dull but pulsating ache, and the blood and melting ice kept flowing down my face; all the while he kept asking, "Where is it, Ian?"

"What are you talking about? Where is what?" I tried to push the gun away, ease it down, but he kept it pointed at me; with his other hand, he grabbed me by my lapel. I put my hands back above my head and told him to just put down the gun; I wasn't going anywhere. Where could I go? But he kept it aimed right at me.

"Bring it to me *now,* and no one gets pulped," he said. "How's that soun' like a good idea?"

I reached for my wallet, proffered it to him. *Here, take it, take the whole thing.* He just smacked it away with the gun.

"No wallet," he said.

"You can have everything in it," I said, but he still wasn't budging, so I tried to yell something that would confuse or distract him—"Would you just put down the goddamn canino?"

For a moment, he looked surprised, like his cheeks would flush if they had more pigment in them. A thought seemed to ripple across his face as if he were remembering something.

"*Wot* you said?" he asked, and for just a second, no more than that, he dropped his gun hand a touch, maybe an inch. I shoved him hard against the building. I heard him yell something. Maybe a curse, I couldn't say for sure—I couldn't make out the sound over that of my beating heart. All I knew was that I was running fast against the light, across 109th Street, across 110th, running toward the café, wondering should I stop there, should I look around, see if Simian Gold was there and could help me? But no, the man was gaining on me as the sleet came down harder, pelting my face so that I no longer knew what was blood and what was water. I had no idea whether the pain I was feeling was from the pellets bolting down from the dark skies or from the place where the man had hit me with his gun.

I kept running, looking back, running, looking back. For a big guy, he sure was fast, and my shoes were too slippery and new for this kind of chase. I could hear the splashes his boots made behind me, but soon I couldn't tell whether those steps were mine or his or both.

I ran through the sleet toward home—112th, 113th, 114th. When I was back in Indiana, I used to hear that this sort of thing went down in Manhattan all the time, but it had never happened to me, not in all my years of living in the city. What were the odds of that, living way uptown as long as I had—surely my number was finally up?

"Ian!" He kept calling as if my name had only one syllable, *"Een!"*

For the first time it registered that he knew my name. Maybe I was getting a reputation, maybe everyone in the city was starting to recognize me, dressing too fancy, acting too slick. Before everything happened, before I met Roth, what would have been the point of robbing me?—I never looked like I had any daisies in my wallet, while now I must have oozed money. Look at me, I was just asking to get rolled.

Up ahead, I could see the 116th Street subway station, so down I went, hurdling the turnstiles just like I'd seen schoolkids do when I was working at Morningside Coffee, onto the platform, *come on, train, come on, train, come on, number 1 train,* and there it was, pulling in. I could hear the man's wet boots on the steps heading down to the platform just as the uptown highsmith stopped. I got on the first car, practically empty, too empty, no one to protect me now, *come on, doors, close, doors, come on, doors, close!* He ran toward the doors, but now the train was pulling out and I could see him running along the platform, trying to catch up. As we headed north, my heart felt as if it might erupt. The lights flickered in the train car, and I could see my reflection in a window, cheeks streaked with blood, rain, and sweat. Above me on a subway billboard advertisement was the image of a book cover, white type on a black background, and behind it, flames. *"THE THIEVES OF MANHATTAN:* COMING SOON FROM MERRILL BOOKS!"

THE DARKENING ECLIPTIC

I emerged from the subway at 168th, a mile north of my usual stop. I didn't want to get off too near my apartment, in case the man had gotten on the train after all. During my uptown ride, the sleet had turned into snow. I walked in darkness along Audubon Avenue, keeping out of the streetlights' spill, hands in my gogol pockets. I fished my phone out of my pocket and dialed the *U.S. News & World Report* number for Simian Gold.

Gold picked up, and when he did, I laughed. Gold would never believe what had happened, I said into the phone; it was like something out of my book. I told him I was running late, and I could either come by the café in a half hour, or we could arrange to meet another time.

"Where are ya, Ian?" asked the voice on the other end of the phone.

I was beginning to tell him where I was when he asked again.

"Where are ya, *ay*?"

I turned around. The man in the black boots, Rusty James jacket, and tam-o'-shanter was stepping out of the subway station; he looked right, then looked left as he held a cellphone to one ear.

"*Wot you said?*"

I quietly closed my phone as the man's voice came from up the street: *Wot you said?*

I ran into the middle of the street, hoping I could flag down a cab. I would have been better off with the scuffed boots or tennis shoes that Ian Minot used to wear instead of my slick dandy shoes. I kept nearly slipping then having to regain my balance as I ran over the whitening asphalt.

I thrust my right hand in the air, flailed it, *Taxi! Taxi!* Cars passed, honked their horns, swerved out of my way. *Taxi!* I held my phone in my right hand, tried to stop cars with my left. I wanted to call someone but couldn't slow down to make the call, and what would I say anyway? Should I call Roth? What could he tell me? The only adventures he knew took place in books. *Taxi!*

A gypsy cab skidded to a stop. I opened the rear door and got in. It was dry and warm and the driver was listening to a Haitian radio show.

"Where to, boss?"

"One Forty-first and Hamilton." Through the back window, I could see that the tattooed man had spotted me and was chasing us through the snow.

"How much you pay?" asked the driver.

"Whatever," I said, "just go."

"How much?"

"Forty bucks, forty-five, just go."

"For real?" The driver was grinning.

"For real," I said. "Just go fast, but not too quick, and don't go any usual way." Did people talk like this? They talked that way in *The Thieves of Manhattan,* but not in any life I'd led before now. The driver stepped on the gas; looking back, I could see the man getting smaller. Cars swerved to avoid him as he angrily gestured for a cab and the snow fell down harder.

"Someone following you, Boris?" asked the driver.

"They are, now that you mention it."

"For real?"

"For real."

People did talk like this; now I knew.

"Yeah," I said. "It's for real."

FRAGMENTS

The truth wasn't that I had no idea why the man was following me. Now I had too many ideas—some surprisingly close to the truth, some just utter madness—but they were all jumbled together, and my mind was woolfing too fast to stop and settle on just one. I thought what was happening to me was random insanity and I thought it had all been planned; I thought the man had confused me with someone else and I thought he knew exactly who I was; I thought someone was playing a joke on me and I thought I was in mortal danger; I thought I was imagining everything and I thought I had never seen the world so vividly; I thought it was fiction and I thought all of it was real.

The gypsy cabdriver screeched around corners, peeled out, made U-turns, weaved through traffic on the Henry Hudson, slid across four lanes of traffic to exit. He seemed to be having the time of his life.

"How you like that one, Boris? How you like that one?" he kept asking, calling me by a name he must have heard in some movie, laughing the whole while, until he turned onto my block, where he gunned the accelerator to seventy then slammed on the brakes. I felt as if I should give him a round of applause; instead, I gave him fifty bucks and told him to keep it.

"Anytime, Boris."

It felt good to be home—I couldn't wait to lock my door, sit down, monitor the video security system on my TV, see who was coming and going, remind myself of who I was. I would throw my clothes, a toothbrush, and a comb into an overnight bag, then take a cab to LaGuardia or JFK, get the next plane out, and salinger myself for a good long while. I wondered if this was what celebrity would be like, whether this was how I would have to live after *The Thieves of Manhattan* was published, with no place to hide anymore. What did I know about how authors really lived? In my lobby, I glanced at myself in the wall mirror. The wound at the side of my head was blacker than I had imagined, bigger too. My cheeks were streaked dark red, but my skin looked pale underneath.

I took the stairs slowly. My legs felt heavy now; they quivered with each step. I walked out of the stairwell, but as I approached my door, I froze. It was ajar, and light was streaming out. I peered through the crack and saw that my belongings were strewn over the floor: books, clothes, sheets, pillowcases, mattress. Someone was rustling through everything, and a voice, deep but unmistakably a woman's, muttered as my stuff kept falling to the floor.

What was she looking for? *Where was it,* the tattooed man had asked. But what did Ian Minot have except for clothes and money? The man hadn't wanted money. "No wallet," he had said. My mind was halfway to putting together the story when my cellphone rang. I reached into my pocket to mute it, but the woman rifling through my apartment must have heard the sound. She darted to the door, and I could see her now: silver-gray, every-which-way hair parted down the middle; sparkling, piercing, knowing eyes—and when those eyes met mine, I started running again, down the stairs. I looked at the number on my cellphone display to see who was calling—Simian Gold again. Simian Gold, was that even a real name? Did *U.S. News* employ a books editor named Simian Gold? Did *U.S. News* even employ a books editor? Every magazine seemed to be cutting its pages; some didn't even run book reviews anymore. *Simian Gold?* I waited to hear if the woman was following me; I didn't hear footsteps, and she had looked old, like someone I could outrun, but I didn't want to run anymore. I ran into the lobby anyway. The tattooed man was at the front door of my building, pressing buzzer buttons. He held his cellphone in one hand, and the phone in my pocket was still ringing.

I slipped out the emergency exit, and crept to the green dumpsters beside my building. Already there was a thin layer of ice and wet snow upon them. I crouched down and waited, wondering, should I run, *no, wait,* maybe now, *no, wait.* How long would it take the man to get buzzed in, climb the stairs, and find I wasn't there? *Count to ten.* I counted to ten, then sprang up from behind the dumpsters and ran toward 147th Street.

AWFUL DISCLOSURES

"Jed," I muttered breathlessly into my phone from the back of a taxi heading south on Broadway. "Come on, man," I was saying. *"Come on, pick up."* My taxi driver, an unkempt Eastern European with a week's growth of ginsberg, was moving slowly, hitting every light, and I turned around to check if anybody was following. Every car looked suspicious.

I heard a recorded voice on the other end of the phone line—"The cellular customer you are trying to reach is out of range." I tried again. "The cellular customer you are trying to reach . . . " Call 911, I thought. But then my mind started racing: What if the police asked too many questions? What if they wanted to know what I did for a living, what kind of books I wrote, what happened in them, whether they were true or not, whether I had committed the crimes I had written about?

I got out of the cab in front of Jed's building; the front door was open, and as I dashed into the lobby, I could hear Jed's voice ringing in my ears—"Oh, and Ian? Next time we're not scheduled to work together and you have something you want to discuss: call first." I dialed his number once more, but when I heard the recorded message again, I raced for the elevator, and when I saw it was in use, I ran for the stairs. Up to the fourth floor I went, my wet shoes slip-sliding along the marble floor.

"Jed!"

I knocked on his door.

"Jed!"

I stopped knocking, started slapping.

One more slap and the door swung open fast; it had been unlocked the whole time.

"Jed?"

But Jed was gone, and so were his books, his furniture, the paintings on his walls. I flicked a switch and the wooden floors gleamed in the glare of the lightbulbs overhead. All that remained was the view—Riverside Park, the black Hudson River, buses cruising north and south, and the snow falling upon cars, sidewalks, and trees. I flicked every light switch in the bedroom, the office, the kitchen, the bathroom—everything was gone. No flutes in the cabinets, no champagne in the fridge, no manuscripts or books, not even a sheet of paper.

By now I was pretty sure what was happening, what Roth had done. I took my phone out, called information, and asked for a number on Delancey Street—"Iola Jaffe Rare Manuscripts and Appraisal Services, please."

"Connecting your call, sir." I heard two rings, then a recorded voice.

"This is Iola Jaffe; I'm not here to take your damn call . . ."

I hung up the phone.

It was all becoming real.

A scrap of yellow paper was taped to Jed's bedroom door. On it were these words: "Ian, trust the story. Perhaps we'll meet again after the last page. Jed." The words echoed those in the last line of *The Thieves of Manhattan,* the words the Girl in the Library had spoken—"Why shouldn't our story continue after the last page has been written?"

I balled up the note, threw it right into the middle of Roth's empty living room, then hurried out and ran for the stairs.

I TELL YOU THESE THINGS ARE TRUE

I trudged east on 112th Street through the gathering snow, trying to make sense of everything that had happened. I felt like a fool. I had thought that *The Thieves of Manhattan* was a novel—that the real deception would lie in the word *memoir* on the book jacket. But Jed Roth had switched names and was somehow setting me up to make it seem as if I had written a memoir after all. "Everything will fall out just as it has been planned. It will all happen as it was written, Ian," I remembered Roth telling me. I hadn't understood what he had been saying. Now I feared that I had a pretty good idea; everything that had happened in the book was starting to happen to me.

But how true could the book really be? The tattooed thug in the Rusty James jacket didn't look like any librarian I'd ever met, but he sure looked like a hooligan. And he spoke exactly the way Roth had written him: *Ay? Ay? Wot you said? How's that soun' like a good idea?* Which had come first, I wondered, the actual hooligan or the one on the page? Was the woman in my apartment Iola Jaffe, the foul-mouthed septuagenarian manuscript appraiser? On the voice mail I had called, that sure sounded like the way I had imagined her speaking. Was there really a *Tale of Genji* buried somewhere in a desolate field beneath a golden cross? Iola Jaffe and that hooligan were certainly looking for something, and it wasn't money.

Maybe the book really did still exist, I thought. Maybe Roth had stolen it and hidden it somewhere, not beneath a golden cross, of course, but somewhere out of sight, like in the safe-deposit box I'd suggested. Maybe he'd kept it there until he'd found some poor sap to put his name to the book, add his story and make it his own, while he'd sell the "Shining Lord" for all it was worth.

Roth and I had spent so much time refining *The Thieves of Manhattan*—developing characters, establishing their motivations—but the basic story had always remained the same: A man walks into the Blom Library and sees a girl admiring a rare and valuable *Tale of Genji*. When he realizes that the Blom's librarian has been stealing manuscripts, he sees an opportunity to steal the *Genji* for the girl. He steals it, but when he returns to look for the girl at the library, he finds it has been destroyed by the Hooligan Librarian, who flew into a rage when he learned the *Genji* was gone. He buries the manuscript, then spends the novel evading his pursuers while searching for, and ultimately finding, the girl, bringing her the *Genji,* and winning her heart. Only in my version, the thief wasn't a suave customer named Roth, but a down-on-his-luck writer and barista named Ian Minot, son of a university librarian, with a Romanian girlfriend and a job at Morningside Coffee working alongside a sexy, baseball-capped artist and an obese thespian with dreadlocks and a goatee. I had thought that each of the details I had added made the story more believable. Probably they had. But they had also taken suspicion off Roth and placed it squarely on me, and I was starting to understand that just about all of my relationship with Jed, every "editorial session" we had ever had, was just part of one great big setup.

Still, all this seemed like a whole lot of trouble for Roth to go through no matter how much the *Genji* might have been worth, and I was getting dizzy trying to pull out the strands to determine which might be true. The Girl in the Library looked and talked like Faye in my version of the story, but who was she really? Roth had said he wanted to exact revenge on the publishing industry that had supposedly betrayed him, and he did seem to know that industry well enough, but did he really hate it so much? Why all the fuss about agents and publishers when my name would appear on the manuscript without them, when I had already signed my confession, agreed to take the fall? I needed someone to discuss this with, but who? Olden? Merrill? Admit to my lies and sabotage my career before it began? The police? With my name on the autobiography of a thief? I felt glad that I had insisted we at least cut out the scene in which the hero shot Iola and Norbert dead; now if the police ever caught up to me, they wouldn't think I was a murderer. I needed time to figure everything out, but I didn't have that either. Not with Iola Jaffe at my apartment; not with the Hooligan Librarian on my trail; not with Roth already gone. I had felt safer when Norbert was chasing me and I could outrun him. Now he could be anywhere, and so I didn't know whether to walk fast or slow, turn back, go forward, or stand still. Behind me was Roth's block and the river, so I walked forward.

FORBIDDEN LOVE

Morningside Coffee had just closed. I was standing in the bus shelter across the street, and, through the falling snow, I could see Joseph zeroing out the register, could see Faye actually mopping, doing some work for once in her life, and for probably the first time in my life, I longed to be back in there, back in time. How I wished I could walk into that coffee shop so that Joseph could ask me if I had sold any books and I could honestly tell him, "Hell, no."

Inside the café, the lights flickered, Joseph flipped the sign on the door from OPEN to CLOSED, and then he and Faye stepped outside and said good night. Joseph was twice Faye's size, yet he was the one bundled up—scarf, mittens, moon boots. He shuffled toward his Citroën, gave me an up-and-down glance, sighed, shook his head, and kept walking while Faye headed uptown, wearing her usual denim and baseball cap. By the time she reached the Columbia University gates, I was right behind her.

"Faye?"

She didn't seem to hear me the first time, but when I said her name again, she turned around. So much was different for me since the last time I saw her, when I'd tried to act so cocky. Just by looking into her eyes, I could see exactly how much had changed.

"What the hell happened to you?" she asked.

"I'm in trouble, Faye," I told her. I hadn't known how frightened I was until I heard my voice quiver, felt my hands and knees shake even as I tried to stand still. "Can you take me home?"

Faye inhaled sharply—I knew I was asking too much, but I persisted. "I just need somewhere to stay, Faye," I said. "Just a couple days. Somewhere no one knows me. I just need to figure some things out."

She said nothing, but when I told her that I truly had no one else, that she was the last person I could think of, that I was in real danger, like maybe even life-and-death danger, and that all I needed was a place to rest my head, and that she would never hear from me again afterward if she didn't want to, I thought I could see her weakening. I told her that I knew she had cared for me once, and I knew she didn't anymore; I knew that she thought I was a liar and a heel and I knew that she was right. But if she retained any of her prior affection, maybe she could find it in her heart to help me.

Faye took a long look at me. "You're sure you have nowhere else you can go?" she asked.

"If I did, I wouldn't be here," I said.

She raised an eyebrow and gave the hint of a smile. "All right, Sailor," she said.

We walked together down to the subway platform and got on a southbound highsmith. Never had I felt so glad to have someone I could sit beside.

I closed my eyes and put my head on Faye's shoulder as the subway doors closed and the train headed downtown. It all could have turned out so differently, I thought, had I always known how safe I would feel next to Faye in the subway car.

NAKED CAME THE STRANGER

I still felt too paranoid to tell Faye about everything that had happened, too obsessed with looking around to see if anyone was following, until we exited the Second Avenue subway station. By then, I finally felt confident that we were alone, so I let it all flow out. I told her that this was really all her fault; she was the one who had directed my attention to the Confident Man.

When I began telling Faye the story, she didn't seem all that interested, but once I got to the part about the Hooligan Librarian's strange tattoos, I thought I could see her getting hooked just as she always had when I told her stories about Blade or my "Lithuanian girl." I realized how much I missed talking to her, the way she listened without judging, laughed without mocking—even though now she didn't seem to care about me, she still seemed to think my story was worth hearing.

I was so thankful that Faye and I were together again, I almost didn't mind that she seemed to find my plight comic, as if my escape from Iola Jaffe and Norbert Piels was no more consequential than any of the stories I had told her before. She cracked up at the note Jed had left for me—"Perhaps we'll meet again after the last page"—for the corny line it was. As we walked, I reminded Faye of the conversation we had had at her gallery when I had asked if she would compromise her integrity for the sake of her art and she had asked if anyone would get hurt or killed in the process. How prophetic that conversation had been, I said; here I was, running for my life, just for the sake of some stories I had wanted to publish. Now all I wanted was to be back where I had been—no agent, no publisher, no prospects.

"But you wouldn't have the story," Faye said.

I told her I didn't want it, but she raised an eyebrow—I could tell that she didn't believe me.

Faye's apartment was an illegal conversion, a loft she had designed and wired herself atop an abandoned mechanic's garage behind a junkyard on Avenue D. I followed her through an obstacle course of hubcaps, stone statues, fountains, and vintage road signs, all of it covered by a thick layer of snow, until we reached her building's warped black front door. She opened the door with a jiggle of a key and a hard kick from one of her boots. Well, I thought, at least no one would ever find me here.

Inside, the wooden steps, dark blue and spattered with paint like a pair of Faye's jeans, creaked as we curved upward to the second floor, passing rusty shelves of random junk she must have been collecting for art projects—old model cars made of metal; dented cans of paint; dusty jars of brushes; hardcover books with big water stains on them. As we climbed, we could see our breath. Another turn of a key in a lock, another swift kick with the heel of a boot, and we were inside the apartment.

The place suited her. A long corridor, her workspace, led to closed doors, which led presumably to a bathroom I desperately needed to use, and her bedroom, which was sadly beside the point. In the narrow workspace, the windows were covered with sheets of opaque plastic held in place by lengths of duct tape to keep the heat in. The walls were strung with Christmas lights, and strewn about was a pleasing mishmash of vintage furniture—a lumpy maroon couch with its insides poking out of a rip in the middle cushion; red, green, and black barstools; a lopsided antique chest of drawers. Faye's approach to interior decoration seemed to be the opposite of mine, which was to take spaces as they were, then put the nicest stuff I could afford in them—she had reconfigured the whole space: dropped the ceilings, installed recessed lighting, fans to circulate the heat. What truly caught my eye, though, were Faye's paintings on the walls—seemingly perfect facsimiles of old master works but ripped apart, burned to cinders, revealing her whimsical line drawings and cartoons underneath. Real and fake, all mixed together.

"You make your bed, Sailor," Faye said as she nodded toward the couch. She opened a closet door, reached to a top shelf, and pulled down an old army sleeping bag and a mushy pillow sans pillowcase, and tossed them in my direction.

I tried finishing the story I had been trying to tell her, but she seemed too busy to listen now. She took out her cellphone to make a call, then turned up her thermostat; a little blue flame flickered on in the radiator as she walked briskly to the industrial metal sink in her kitchen. She poured herself a mug of water, drank it, poured herself another. I asked for the bathroom; she thumbed to a door.

In the bathroom was another window covered by a plastic sheet, held in place by duct tape. There was a wheezy toilet, a rusty sink, a sunken tub, and a dirt-speckled mirror. I looked in that mirror and saw the reflection of a weather-beaten man—shadows under my eyes, creases where I hadn't remembered seeing them before. I felt as though I were playing a game I used to play with myself when I was a kid—rubbing shaving cream in my hair, folding my cheeks, seeing what I would look like when I was old. I turned on the tap, looked in the cabinet for soap, couldn't find any, washed off the blood and dirt with brown water. I looked in vain for a towel, wiped my face with my shirttail, then exited the bathroom, face and hands still wet.

In the workspace, Faye was standing naked save for a pair of white briefs with Asian characters on them; her red hair was cascading down, and I could see the tattoo of the twilight flower on her right shoulder. I felt a pang of longing knife through my guts as I stood with my arms folded, body quivering. Faye acted as if she didn't notice me or the cold. She spoke on the phone as she stepped out of her underwear, then walked barefoot over the cement floor to the closet, where she grabbed another pair of underwear, jeans, a T-shirt, on it, the name of some seventies band.

Faye sounded as though she were speaking on the phone to a boyfriend, someone she would be meeting later, someone with whom she would probably be staying for a while, as evidenced by the fact that she was shoving pants, caps, and underwear into a backpack. I had been hoping she would stay here tonight.

She finished dressing, ended her phone conversation, put on her denim jacket and her black corduroy cap, stepped back into her boots.

"Can I stay here two nights?" I asked, and when Faye shrugged, then nodded, I wished I had asked for three, wished I had asked for a month or a year. I wouldn't even need the couch to help me fall asleep, I thought, the cement floor would serve me just fine.

Faye put her hand on her front doorknob.

"Back tonight?" I asked. She crinkled her nose.

"Going to your boyfriend's?" I asked.

"Something like that," said Faye.

"How long till you come back?"

"How long did you say you'd be here?"

"Three nights."

"Then not until after that," said Faye. When I called out to her and asked for a key, she only shrugged. "Nothing worth stealing in here, Sailor," she said, then added with a smirk, "Maybe I'll see you after the last page."

The door reverberated like a prison gate as she clanged it shut. I listened to her boots on the steps, the front door opening and closing, until all I could hear was the wind fluttering the plastic sheets covering the windows, and Faye whistling the song "Point of Know Return."

THE HEART IS DECEITFUL,
ABOVE ALL THINGS

I thought I'd fall asleep the moment my head touched the pillow, but I couldn't sleep at all. I rolled this way and that, scrunched my pillow, turned it to the cool side, fluffed it, scrunched it again, turned it some more. I was too warm and too cold. I couldn't sleep with the lights on, or with them off. I tried dimming the chandelier, smushing my head into the pillow, but I kept hearing my pulse resounding in my skull.

I felt as though I couldn't close my eyes all the way, as if they always remained open just a slit. I worried about who would find me while I was awake, about the dreams I might have if I fell asleep. I listened to the wind, fluttering plastic, distant traffic, the flame in the radiator erupting then diminishing, the heat knocking through the overhead pipes. Then, silence; the silence worst of all. I kept reaching instinctively for my phone, but I had no one to call; I had run out of people to trust. I pushed the OFF button, and the phone powered down.

I wasn't wearing a watch, all the windows were covered, so I wasn't sure what time it was when I finally gave up trying to sleep and turned the chandelier on all the way. I had to do something to calm myself. Maybe I could start writing down everything that had happened to me. If I got through all this, I would want to have the story on paper—who knew, there might be a book in it, another memoir, this time one that had actually happened to me. I started searching for paper and pen. On a warped easel was a single sheet of paper, but it was smeared with black paint. A pen was on the floor, but it was out of ink.

I went to the kitchen and turned on the cold water in the sink. I looked for a cup or glass in the dish rack, couldn't find one, didn't see one on the shelves either, so I drank from the one Faye had left; the water tasted like dirt. I shut off the tap and walked to the closed door at the back of the apartment. I reached for the doorknob, turned it, pushed, peered inside, and felt my heart plummet.

What I had thought was the bedroom was almost completely empty—sawdust on the cement floor, a grate in the center, a single lightbulb overhead, another duct-taped window, the plastic over it straining against the wind. I flicked the light switch. Maybe Faye had lived here once, but not anymore. Maybe this had just been her studio; maybe she had never lived here at all. Now all there was in this room was a wooden chair with two books on it and a little framed photograph on the wall above it. The cold from outside now seemed to be seeping through my skin; I saw the fog of my breaths hover, then dissipate in the harsh overhead light as my pulse lurched forward.

I stepped closer to the photo and to the plain wooden folding chair in front of it. On the chair was a paperback copy of *The Tale of Genji* and a little red artist's sketchbook. In the photo was a couple—a man who looked a little like me; he wore nice franzens and a light-colored linen gatsby. He had his arm around a red-haired woman wearing a Kansas concert jersey and a black baseball cap: Jed and Faye. The photo was wrinkled and faded, as if it had been taken some time ago, maybe ten years, maybe just one—I probably looked a lot younger one year ago too. In my mind, I replayed the past year in fast-forward, from the moment Faye had pointed Jed Roth out to me—"Too bad his taste in clothes doesn't match his taste in books"—to the moment tonight before she walked out the door: "Going to your boyfriend's?" "Something like that." So she was in on this plot too. Once when we were dating, I asked her why she never invited me over to her apartment—"I need my space, Sailor," she'd said. I remembered the night that Jed wouldn't let me into his place. Had Faye been there? How long had Faye known Jed? How long had the two of them been planning this, how long had they been setting me up? And setting me up for what?

I looked down at the red notebook. In *The Thieves of Manhattan,* the Girl in the Library had a red notebook too. I opened it and saw sketches from *The Tale of Genji*—page after page of Genji's life, his loves, his adventures, his exile, his return; page after page of Japanese characters, kimonos, parasols.

I kept turning pages, and saw sketches that looked more familiar to me—a copy of a Rembrandt, a Kandinsky, a Magritte, a prairie landscape that looked like the fake Wyeth in my apartment, the one that Faye had titled *No Place Like Home.* There was the country house, the vast meadow, the tiny graveyard, and a car on a distant road. I turned more pages. In medieval script, one word had been drawn: *FAKERY.*

On the next page, that word was split apart: *FA KERY.*

And, on the following page: *FAY KERY;* then, *FAYE KERY; FAYE KHOURI;* and finally, *FAYE CURRY.*

I turned a page and saw the sketch for the exhibition flyer at the Van Meegeren Gallery with the dates of Faye's show, which had opened almost exactly a year ago. *Faye Curry: Forged in Ink.*

I was still flipping through the red notebook when I heard the downstairs door open, then heavy footsteps on the stairs.

My heart racing, I ran to the window and ripped off the opaque plastic. Staples scattered to the ground. It was still night outside, snow was coming down hard, and, as I pulled the duct tape off the window locks, then threw open the window, I could feel that snow slap my face. Through the window, I could see two figures approaching—Norbert Piels in his black Rusty James jacket and tam-o'-shanter; Iola Jaffe in a frumpy tweed gogol and a gray felt Jane Marple hat. If they were outside, whose footsteps were those on the stairs?

"Faye?" I called out as I ran back to the front door. "Faye?"

A man's voice answered wearily: "No, it's not, Ian."

I shoved open the door as hard as I could, hoping it would slam whoever was there. When I heard the man's voice cry out, "Aww, goddamn," I didn't even look to see who it was. Not until I had scrambled halfway down the stairs and the voice said, "Aww, goddamn, Ian," did I look back up; Joseph was crumpled in a heap, holding his hands in front of his face.

"I'm here to help you, man," he said. "You gotta come with me."

THE NIGHT VISITOR

I had never trusted or particularly cared for Joseph. He'd always made jokes at my expense but couldn't stand when anyone said anything about him. But lately, I hadn't gotten very far with the people I had been trusting, myself most of all. In Faye's bitter-

cold stairwell, as Joseph grabbed hold of the banister and stumbled to his feet, the voice inside me told me to keep running, to
get away from Joseph. But I couldn't trust that voice anymore,
and so I decided I'd go with him.

Joseph drove an old black bathtub of a Citroën; he said it
was one of the only cars he'd been able to find with enough
head- and legroom for him. Once we were safely in the car, I
asked him why he had come here to help me when he'd never
really seemed to care for me. He told me that I was right, he had
never liked writers much in general and me in particular. He
didn't know what Faye had ever seen in me, couldn't understand what I had but he didn't; he thought I was probably the
most clueless employee he'd ever had. But still, he couldn't pass
up the opportunity to play the hero, a role in which no one had
ever seen fit to cast him. And besides, no matter what he might
have thought of me personally, I didn't deserve the fate Faye
and her friend seemed to have in mind. As we putt-putted and
skidded up Avenue A through the fog and snow, Joseph told me
that he knew most of what Faye and Jed had been up to, though
he didn't know where they were now.

As it turned out, I was right that Joseph had been untrustworthy; Faye had been wrong to trust him. She shouldn't have
spent so much time at Morningside Coffee detailing her and
Jed's plan on her computer, shouldn't have spent so much time
gabbing with her Confident Man when he came in for his tea,
shouldn't have kept from Joseph the fact that she was planning
to leave tonight with Roth, and that Joseph would have to find
someone to replace her after all the slack he'd cut her over the
years—not even two weeks' notice.

Joseph had read the diaries and notes Faye had kept on

her computer, and he had eavesdropped on conversations she had had with Jed. As Joseph drove uptown, he told me all he had learned: *The Thieves of Manhattan* was, if not a completely honest memoir, pretty close to the truth, albeit with some key details left out.

Jed Roth had indeed once been a young writer looking for a story when he'd stumbled upon the Blom Library and saw Faye in the reading room, admiring *The Tale of Genji* in its locked glass case. She was taking notes in her red book, and asking the librarian Norbert Piels about manuscripts, all of which he told her were unavailable. Faye's last name wasn't Curry then; it was Blom, and she was the sole surviving heir to the library's contents; she had just arrived in New York to begin her career as an artist and to inspect the books that her great-grandfather Chester Blom had collected on his travels and that Norbert Piels had been sneaking out one by one to his fence, Iola Jaffe.

The most intriguing volumes in the reading room—the personal letters and manuscripts of William Shakespeare and Christopher Marlowe, the original Emily Dickinson poems— seemed to have little in common, save for one key detail: they were fakes. Through his journeys, Chester Blom had amassed a history of literary forgeries and hoaxes of one kind or another that he had scattered throughout his reading room. There were the memoirs of Li-Hung Chang, which had really been written by an American army vet while serving time in a Hawaiian prison. Shakespeare's letters were the work of the eighteenth-century teenage forger William Henry Ireland. There were books written by fictional authors: Cleone Knox, whose eighteenth-century diary of a "lady of fashion" was penned by Magdalen King-Hall, who wrote the book in the 1920s at the age of nineteen; Emanuel Morgan and Anne Knish, phony poets who had pioneered a form of poetry called Spectrism; Ern Malley, the genius bard of Australia whose life was supposedly cut short at the age of twenty-five, but whose work was the brainchild of a pair of practical jokers who wrote all of Malley's poems in less than a day; Mario Benedetti, an Italian futurist who had briefly passed himself off as a time traveler from the twenty-first century in *The Golden State;* and there were volumes by Thomas Rowley, whose "medieval poems" had been written by Thomas Chatterton, who took his own life in 1770 at the age of seventeen.

Jed Roth had no idea that *The Tale of Genji* displayed under glass in the Blom reading room was a fake when he broke its case with the intention of stealing the book for his "Girl." But when he cautiously opened the book in a taxi speeding away from the library, he discovered that all but the first pages of the book were blank—the most prized item in the Blom collection was a phony too. Roth wondered what the *Genji* would be worth if it were real, and showed the cover and the first pages of the book to Iola Jaffe. When she told him how much it might fetch and asked to see the rest of it, he wished he could devise some way to make the book real, so much so that he risked his life escaping with the *Genji* after Jaffe pulled a gun on him and asked him to hand over the book.

On the day Jed returned to the Blom Library, it was gone. Shortly after Faye had fired Norbert for stealing books from the reading room, the man had sneaked back inside, taken all he could carry, then set the place ablaze. Faye was standing in the smoldering wreckage when Roth saw her and introduced himself. Despite the fact that Roth was more than ten years older than Faye and spoke in a far more elegant manner, they had a great deal in common—an illustrious family history, a fascination with art and fakes. They grew to be friends, then lovers. With his charm and intelligence, Jed had seduced her, much as he had seduced me; much as I had been seduced by Anya's stories and by Faye's art. After they woke up from their first night together, Jed asked if Faye would tell the police what had happened or press charges against the man who had apparently burned down the library. She said no; in fact, Norbert Piels had done her a favor. Now that the contents had been destroyed, no one could challenge their validity or worth. In burning the library, Norbert had allowed her to pursue a dream that had always consumed her—take something false and make it so real that no one could question its authenticity. She would create an entire eleventh-century illustrated manuscript of *The Tale of Genji,* a thousand pages of text and images; she would do the job so well that everyone would believe her when she presented her finished product and said that it had been rescued from the fire. She wasn't sure how she would be able to pull it off, but Roth was—he would write the story of the fire and the search for the *Genji;* the book he would write would attract so much attention that it would make Faye's *Tale of Genji* worth a fortune.

Jed and Faye spent nearly a decade on their respective projects. He wrote *A Thief in Manhattan;* Faye painstakingly forged the *Genji,* while they both managed to keep out of sight of Norbert Piels and Iola Jaffe. As Jed and Faye worked, their differences in manner and appearance proved useful—Roth knew that the best con-artist teams were made up of mismatched pairs, and people would find it hard to believe that this suave man and funky artist were actually working together. They found honest jobs—Faye pursued her art and worked in cafés;

Jed climbed the ladder in publishing, all the while looking for some poor sap to take the fall. I was the perfect mark—so desperate, I'd take any job that came along, so gullible I couldn't even recognize my girlfriend's phony Romanian accent. For a time, Faye felt conflicted about involving me in the plan, truly came to care for me, but after she witnessed my inconsiderate and self-involved behavior at the KGB Bar, she got out of Roth's way so that he could make me his partner and the plan could go forward. After Roth and I were finally done writing and editing our book, Roth made an anonymous call to Iola Jaffe, telling her where she and Norbert might find me. As for what I might say if I survived after those two got hold of me, the police wouldn't believe anything I told them; I'd already written a 250-page confession.

"If I hadn't shown up, you might already be one dead barista," Joseph said.

"Jesus," I said to Joseph as a chill shot up my spine. "All I wanted was to write a book and have some people read it, maybe sell enough copies so that I could convince someone to publish another. I didn't want to die for that."

Terrified as I may have felt, gullible as I have always been, I still wasn't willing to accept everything Joseph had told me. I believed what he said about Roth—I'd spent enough time listening to the man's bitter diatribes and reading his original *Thief* draft to believe that he didn't care much for his fellow human beings. I was sure he'd have little compunction about setting me up. I was less certain about Faye, though—had she really turned against me so drastically? When I had asked her why she had dated me when she had been dating someone else, whom I now knew was Roth, she said she had liked my stories better than his.

It was hard for me to believe that she had changed her mind about that. And why had she laid out her notebook, her picture, and the paperback *Tale of Genji* in her apartment as if on exhibit for me? Maybe she was leaving clues, I hoped, assuring me that somehow she would be watching out for me. Maybe she'd been leaving clues for Joseph, too, giving him his chance to play the hero, knowing that he'd come to my aid. Hadn't she been the one to tell me that Joseph wasn't such a bad guy and that if anyone ever gave him the chance, he'd come through? Or maybe all this was just wishful thinking on my part. For the time being, I knew I had to stop imputing motives to people I had so obviously misjudged. The wind was howling outside, the snow coming down hard, I was so tired and cold and Joseph's car was so warm.

I was fast asleep, my head against the fogged-up window of the Citroën, when Joseph shoved me. "We're here," he said, and when I looked out the window I could see that dawn was upon us, and once again, I was in front of Morningside Coffee. The sign on the door read CLOSED.

LIKE A GIANT REFRESHED

The last time I slept in the basement of the coffee shop, the cement floor had been my proust and bags of coffee beans had served as my pillows. But this time, Joseph had already prepared for my stay. There was a tall lamp, a desk, and a cot with space heaters on either side of it. In the refrigerator were day-old pastries and cartons of juice—take as much as you want, Joseph said. No one would think to look for me here; the only person who might consider it was Faye, but she was already gone, and he said that she would probably never imagine that he would go out of his way to help me.

I still vowed that I would not trust Joseph, but moments after he galumphed up the steps—to fix me a cup of coffee, he said—the cot and pillow looked so inviting that I thought I'd just rest my head for a minute. The next thing I knew, half a day must have passed because I could hear the coffee shop in full swing—the steamer, footsteps, cash register, front door opening, closing. I considered getting up but closed my eyes again, and when I opened them, it seemed like evening—Joseph, wearily gossiping with customers, less rush to their voices. I closed my eyes again, and when I opened them, I heard dishes being washed, Joseph singing along with the radio, locking the front door; he must have been closing for the night. When I awoke again, Joseph was coming downstairs, carrying fresh towels, soap, a toothbrush, and toothpaste.

"Trust me yet?" he asked.

Trusting Joseph went directly counter to my lousy instincts, which was why I tried to keep doing it. I gave him tasks—asked him to stop by my apartment, bring me clothes and my mail, and when he'd done that, I asked him to bring my laptop and printer. When he had done that, too—in a pissy, world-weary mood perhaps, but when he had done it nonetheless—I developed a plan: stay here in Joseph's basement and write down everything that had happened to me. I sensed that writing the truth could protect me. Stay as long as you want, Joseph said; he liked having a person down here—maybe I would keep away the mice.

The mail Joseph brought to me offered hints of the life I could have been enjoying if I hadn't been here at Morningside Coffee with Joseph playing Man Friday to my Robinson Crusoe. There was a check from Geoff Olden's office, a pair of letters from editors at other publishing houses, asking if I'd consider providing a blurb for this or that debut memoir. There was a copy of *Poets and Writers* magazine with my picture on the cover, and a final expiration notice from *Writer's Digest,* a publication I felt I no longer needed to read.

Still, I stayed in the basement eating café food—wraps, smoothies, old pastries; I drank coffee, tea, and steamed milk. Before the café opened, I would tumble out of my makeshift proust, wash up in the industrial sink, settle down at my laptop, and type everything I could remember, starting from the time that Faye had pointed the Confident Man out to me. And when I was done, I would eat my spinach-and-feta croissant or my tuna wrap, glug my caramel apple cider, print out what I had written, then read it to make sure that everything was accurate and true.

After closing for the night, Joseph would come down and bitch about the day he'd had—the pastry deliverers had been late again; college kids spending their parents' money still didn't tip; the new employee he had hired to replace Faye was already giving him guff. Joseph described him as "an arrogant writer type," some "sullen dumb-ass with hipster glasses," who was always late and was rude to customers. In fact, Joseph said, the guy reminded him of me, though Jens was already a published author.

"Von Bretzel?" I asked.

"That's him." Apparently, Joseph said, Von Bretzel's debut

novel, *The Counter Life,* hadn't sold well, his editor had been laid off, and now his agent was having trouble getting a decent frazier for his follow-up, which he was calling *Java Man.* Von Bretzel needed a job to tide him over—he'd been fired by the Williamsburg Starbucks that he'd written about in his first book. I felt a little bad for Von Bretzel—if I hadn't stopped writing quiet, small stories about café life, I'd be in just about the same position as the one in which he found himself now.

While I worked in the Morningside Coffee basement, I never turned on my phone, didn't return any emails from Geoff Olden or anybody else. I didn't want anyone to know where I was, and I figured anyway that a bit of mystery never hurt an author's reputation.

Despite the fact that Joseph had always acted as if I owed him something, he never asked for money—he flashed me dirty looks the few times I mentioned it. But the more time we spent in late-night conversation, the more he opened up. I began writing about Joseph, too, and as I did, I began to sympathize with him more. I felt angry with all the casting directors who'd overlooked him; why couldn't a morbidly obese café manager play a hero?

Before I went to sleep, I put my pages in plain view for Joseph to read. I was happy to let him snoop through my life, learn my secrets, just as he'd learned about Faye's. I wanted him to know that I thought he was worth writing about. And I always made sure to end the day's writing on a suspenseful scheherazade so that he'd have something to look forward to reading the next night.

ZERO NINETY-EIGHT

I kept writing. I had a story to tell, and I wanted to get all of it down. I typed so hard and fast that I wore out letters on my keyboard. I couldn't see the E, the T, or the DELETE keys anymore, and half my punctuation marks stopped working altogether, which didn't really matter because the story was woolfing out of me in one long, unpunctuated stream. Some nights I fell asleep with my head on the keyboard, which repeated whatever letter my nose or ear rested upon. I could measure how long I had slept by the number of letters or symbols on my screen. My fingers hurt, my wrists ached, my eyes could barely focus, and I felt dazed, but I kept typing as if somehow my life depended on it. I felt certain that it did.

And then I was done.

Never had I written anything so quickly or intensely. I had no idea what to call the story I had written, I knew only where it would be shelved in a library according to the Dewey decimal system, so I called it *Zero Ninety-eight*. I fell asleep to the sound of the printer spitting out pages, and when I woke up, Joseph was sitting at the desk beside my proust, reading the last page.

"I started a diet," Joseph said when I opened my eyes. "Can you change my weight in the next draft?"

I said I'd try.

"And can you give me more lines?" he asked. "I don't say all that much."

I said I would do my best, then asked if he would do one final favor for me. I had printed two copies of the manuscript. I asked Joseph to take a copy to Geoff Olden with a note I had written, telling Geoff to sell the book if he learned that anything bad had happened to me. I told Joseph to keep the original for himself, and I kept my own copy on my thumb drive.

I then asked if Joseph would drive me to JFK Airport tonight after the café closed. I didn't yet know where I was going, but didn't really care as long as it was far away. If he helped me with all that, I would dedicate the book to him. Joseph agreed, and when I reached in my wallet for cash, he shook his head; the dedication would be better than money, he said, and maybe if someone made a movie out of my story, he could play himself—though he'd have to lose some weight for the role.

I packed my clothes in two big empty burlap coffee bags, shut down my computer and put it back in its case, then lay back on the cot, too awake to even close my eyes. While I waited for the day to pass, I started to read the paperback *Tale of Genji,* which I had grabbed from Faye's apartment, the epic story of the life of the titular son of an emperor. Though I could relate to Genji's uncertain status, to the way he drifted between the realms of the nobility and the commoner yet never felt that he was really a part of either, I liked the book less than I had anticipated. There wasn't enough plot, there was too much aimless dialogue, and I couldn't get a strong sense of any of the characters. Genji was too much of a reactor, I thought, not enough of an actor. Two hundred and fifty pages was plenty for a book, I thought, and by the time I'd read that much, I put down the book and conked out.

I had been sleeping for some time when I heard the front door open and close, then Joseph's voice calling my name. I rose to my feet, picked up my bags and my laptop, shut off the bed-side lamp, and called back up, but no one answered. I heard footsteps, then something landing hard against the counter.

"Joseph?"

I mounted the steps toward the dark café. I had barely seen the outside world since I had begun writing *Zero Ninety-eight;* Joseph had always advised me to keep out of sight.

"Joseph?" I called again.

No response.

I stood on the top step and looked into the café, then up at the counter. In the white-and-red glow of the exit sign, I could see Joseph's body slumped over a stool, his arms outstretched. One of his hands was clutching the copies of *Zero Ninety-eight*. His head was on the counter, his eyes were closed. Two figures were standing above him. As my eyes grew accustomed to the dark, I could make out the bald, tattooed man with the black Rusty James jacket clutching a .38-caliber canino and the woman in the tweed overcoat, dull brown shoes, and gray felt marple. She was holding a copy of the Riverside edition of Shakespeare's complete works. And then the stool slipped out from under Joseph, and his body hit the floor. I heard him give out a low gasp.

I crouched at the top of the stairs, my heart pounding. I prayed they would leave without noticing me, but then the Hooligan Librarian began lumbering toward me, and Iola Jaffe followed right behind him. I tried to dash for the door, but Norbert Piels grabbed me and brought his gun down fast against my skull.

"I've always wanted readers to feel the full impact of Shake-speare," I heard Iola Jaffe say as she raised her book, then hit me hard across the face.

A ROCK AND A HARD PLACE

I awoke slowly in an initially unfamiliar place, with an oddly acute awareness of my elbows; they seemed to be the only part of my body that wasn't feeling either a sharp pain or a persistent ache. My face burned, and I felt bruises on my knees. My wrists were bound together with ropes and my ankles were tied to the chair's legs. My palms and fingertips had already felt tingly and weary from typing before Iola Jaffe and Norbert Piels arrived at Morningside Coffee, knocked Joseph out, then did the same to me before apparently lugging me into their car and bringing me here. Now when I inhaled, I smelled the musty, airless, vaguely fetid office in which I was sitting, a room whose windows seemed as if they had never been opened; when I tried to breathe through my mouth, I felt something stabbing my ribs. I was nauseated yet famished, tired yet well beyond the point of sleep; I felt so thirsty and parched that I could detect each crack in my lips. When I tried to swallow, I tasted sawdust and blood.

I opened my eyes onto the room. Atop a long, unfinished wooden table were jewelers' loupes, magnifying glasses, over-sized leather-bound books that looked like ledgers. On the walls on either side of me were long, warped shelves sagging under the weight of stacks of reference books. I didn't need to look any closer at the table to recognize the woman seated at it, paging through a galley of *The Thieves of Manhattan*. "A diminutive, silver-haired, beak-nosed woman with her lips pursed as if she had just tasted something foul" was how Roth had described Iola. So this had to be 129 Delancey Street, Iola Jaffe, Rare Manuscripts and Appraisal Services, "a musty, unrenovated office four flights up from an infested bodega." I didn't need to look up from the scuffed, steel-toed boots tapping in front of me to know that Norbert Piels was here too, that he was holding a canino, and that this time, I couldn't knock it away.

" 'E's wikin' oop," Norbert Piels said.

Skinny cats lurked about, skulking in and out of the office as Iola Jaffe's eyes scanned *Thieves,* searching for information. She read fast, slapped at pages, angrily cursing to herself as she did so, seemingly unable to find what she was looking for. I knew what she was after, but no matter how clever a reader she was, she would never find *The Tale of Genji* by reading the book Roth and I had written.

"I say *'e's wikin' oop,*" Piels said. His eyes seemed as dull as Iola's were intense as he smoked a vonnegut down to its butt. I tried to speak, but my throat was so dry that all I could do was let out a small, pathetic rattle.

"Where's Joseph?" I finally gasped.

" 'E'll be all right," Piels said. "More than I can say for you."

I tried again to swallow, still couldn't do it.

"Water," I said meekly. Piels looked to Iola Jaffe, who nodded tightly. Piels fetched me a jam jar half full of gray water. I drank it down fast, then held the jar out toward him.

"More?" I asked. Piels took the jar and shook his head. I looked to Iola, but she didn't return my glance. "Can you please fill it up?" I asked. Piels took the jar to the sink and left it there.

What did they want from me, I finally said. Why didn't they just ask? I wasn't a tough guy; I'd tell them whatever they wanted—they didn't need to subject me to this medieval torture.

"Medieval?" Iola snapped shut *The Thieves of Manhattan.* "Me-die-val?" She lingered on each syllable, then rose to her feet and stood beside her desk, hands folded in front of her like some child's nightmare vision of a seventeenth-century Pilgrim schoolteacher ready to rap knuckles with a yardstick.

Iola's body was framed by shelves of old books. Her flat brown shoes click-clacked as she paced before me. Exactly what did I know about the Middle Ages, she wanted to know, and when I said honestly not all that much, she said, well, that was the trouble with people these days, using words yet not having the slightest idea of their meaning. Medieval? Why, she'd written her graduate thesis about the Middle Ages, gotten her useless graduate degree on that very topic, spent years studying illuminated manuscripts, teaching them at university, the origins of the novel as exemplified by illustrated versions of the *Chanson du Fucking Roland,* if I really wanted to hear about it.

In *The Thieves of Manhattan,* Iola had been a gifted scholar, but she had turned to crime when she'd failed to get tenure or publish her work. Norbert had been her finest research assistant, a brilliant ex-con with a photographic memory who could remember just about everything he'd ever read. But he'd lost a good deal of his mental faculties when he'd been injured during one of the many accidents that had befallen the Blom Library. I thought I had made all that up, but now I suspected that Jed Roth had led me to those stories too. I shuddered as I thought of the shootout that Roth had written at the end of the book but I had insisted we eliminate; I hoped that part wouldn't turn out to be true as well.

"Where did you get that galley?" I asked. I tried to gesture

"Not that Roth," I said.

Another memory seemed to ripple across Norbert's face followed by another look of disgust. "He wrote filth too."

Which Roth was he thinking of? Henry? Philip? "No," I said, trying to sound as polite as possible, "not that one either. Jed Roth."

Norbert's eyes fluttered briefly as if he was trying to place Jed Roth's name but couldn't. His eyes turned dull again. "*Wot* you said?" he demanded, but before I could speak, he hit me with the gun again, and I collapsed into the shelves. Books scattered around and on top of me. The cat scampered out of the room as I felt my eyelids flutter.

When I awoke again, I no longer felt individual aches as much as a general sense of woe. My entire body had become one giant bruise. Now I was sitting on a wooden chair across the table from Iola while Norbert stood, aiming his canino at me. In front of me were a full glass of water and a bag of stale pretzels. I would have chosen anything to eat before pretzels; their dust dried my throat even more and the salt burned my lips, but I ate fistfuls anyway.

Norbert interrogated me while Iola scanned my face as if it were a book that held a secret she could divine.

"Just tell us where the book is," Norbert said. "How's that soun' like a good idea?"

"Beneath a golden cross in a desolate field," I said, slowly, so that Norbert would understand each word.

Norbert looked at Iola, seeking permission to strike me again, I assumed, but she shook her head.

"Tell us where the desolate field is," Norbert said. "How's 'at soun' li' a goo' idea?"

"Outside Manhattan."

"*Maw* details," said Norbert.

"It's all made up anyway," I said.

"Tell us where."

Listening to Norbert repeat his question was nearly as torturous as his slaps, punches, and kicks. "I'm telling you the truth," I said, desperate now. "I've told you everything I know. Come on, don't you think if I were lying, I'd at least have made up something a little better than just some random desolate field? Something more specific maybe? Some safe-deposit box? Some road marker? Some longitude or latitude?"

Norbert raised his canino, but I held out my hands; a memory was returning to me. "Wait," I shouted as my eyes pleaded with Norbert, then Iola, then Norbert again. He held the gun high, his face lined with the strain of unexpended energy. I could see a glint in his eyes; they betrayed a hint of life in that weary, tattooed mask of a face.

"Wait!" My mind swirled back to Roth's apartment, back when I was editing the book, lishing adjectives, metaphors, digressions, everything that got in the way of the story. Roth had told me to hang on to the original he had written, said that someday I would find that his worked better. Maybe he didn't mean it worked better in the story; maybe he meant in real life. In Roth's original, he had indicated the supposed location of the buried *Genji,* had given a longitude and latitude: -096.571, a number that corresponded to the Dewey decimal code for illustrated manuscripts; 039.183, a Dewey code that indicated where foreign reference works were shelved. I had always assumed it to be just another of Roth's distracting and gratuitous details.

"Check the original manuscript," I said. "In my apartment."

"The original," Iola repeated. The word had gotten her attention, as if the book she was reading had finally offered up its secret. She sprang up and started walking quickly to the door.

SHALL I DIE, SHALL I FLY?

My apartment was neater than the last time I saw it, back when Iola Jaffe was hurling my belongings to the floor, muttering and swearing as she searched for *The Tale of Genji*. In fact, it was probably neater and cleaner than it had been since I moved in. Maybe Iola had cleaned up after rummaging, I thought, but deep down, I knew that Joseph had done it. I felt sorry that I had misjudged him. If I did survive this, I vowed that I would hold true to my promise; if I ever published this story, I would dedicate it to him. And if I had a say in the movie, he could play any part he wanted in it.

As the three of us entered, I looked longingly at my proust, at my desk, at the view from my windows. But Norbert was holding the canino and I didn't want to get "pulped" or "remaindered" or whatever else Norbert might threaten me with, so I limped over to my file cabinets. I had misjudged him and Iola, too; I had thought they were fictional.

Jed Roth's first draft was in a drawer labeled MANUSCRIPTS. There were only two file folders in there—one marked *Thieves*, another marked *Myself When I Am Real*. My only copy of *Zero Ninety-eight* was on my key chain's thumb drive, but apparently I wasn't done writing that book yet—unfortunately, I had to live it first.

The passage in the manuscript of Jed Roth's *A Thief in Manhattan* was easy to find—I had struck a red line through it, but the latitude and longitude numbers were visible. I still felt certain that it was all some kind of joke. Sure, I could now believe that Faye had forged a *Tale of Genji* that she and Jed would try to pass off as real, but no way would they have buried it anywhere. Nevertheless, Iola vigorously copied down the numbers in a little notebook and I could see her muttering those numbers to herself, trying to figure out what they might mean.

We stepped out of my apartment and into the hallway, Iola walking briskly in front of me, Norbert behind with his gun. I suggested hopefully that they could leave me alone since they had found what they wanted, knew where the manuscript was and how to track me down if something went wrong. But Iola just walked ahead, while Norbert urged me onward.

Iola's olive green Opel Manta was parked outside my building. She popped open the trunk; a shovel was lying atop piles of old reference books. Norbert reached in, pulled out a dusty and creased book of maps bound in black leather, and handed it to Iola, who nodded, then slammed shut the trunk. She carried the book to the hood of the car, where she began thumbing through it.

When she reached the middle of the book, she began to turn pages more slowly until she found the map she was looking for. She smoothed out the page with her palms, using a handle of her glasses to follow the lines demarking latitude and longitude, then stopped on what appeared to be an empty field. The field was in the state of Kansas, north of Climax, near Lake Eureka, outside a town called *Manhattan*.

"Book people don't know much about the lives real people

live. They think the only Manhattan is the one they live in," Roth had told me.

" 'Carry on my wayward son,' " Faye had said to me, quoting a Kansas lyric. She had always liked to listen to that band's song "Dust in the Wind."

Manhattan, Kansas.

Iola snapped the book shut, carried it under an arm, then walked around to the driver's side door, and opened it. Norbert told me to get in.

POSITION UNKNOWN

Iola told me that I would be the driver. So I sat at the wheel of the Opel and started the engine as Iola mapped our route out of New York across the George Washington Bridge, then onto I-80 heading west—destination: Kansas.

The car was as cluttered and musty as Iola's manuscript appraisal office. There was barely enough room for Norbert to sit with all the old books piled in the back. They were on the passenger-side floor, too, piled atop the parking brake, wedged between my seat and Iola's. With the exception of the galley of *The Thieves of Manhattan* that Iola had placed on the dashboard, they were mostly reference books or literary anthologies. There must have been more than a hundred, plus all the ones I could hear shifting around in the trunk.

I couldn't see any order to the arrangement of books in the Opel, but whenever Iola would call out the title of one, say, a thesaurus or a poetry collection, Norbert would locate the book in an instant and either point to it or flip to a key passage and hand it forward with an expectant expression, seeking approval; in his own way, he was still talented at his job, still seemed to be able to remember any book, no matter how obscure.

Iola would snatch the volume from Norbert and start whipping through it, moving her lips as quickly as she shifted her eyes back and forth across the pages, muttering the words that described the supposed location of *The Tale of Genji:* "Outside Manhattan in a desolate field beneath a golden cross." I gradually came to understand that she seemed to think those words contained some code. She searched religious texts with crosses in their titles, books of quotations that she scoured for references to desolate fields, antique atlases with maps of Manhattan, Kansas. She and Norbert may have been criminals, but she was still a scholar and he was still a librarian; both thought that they could find the solution to any mystery by discovering the right page in a book. As Iola searched for clues, Norbert awaited Iola's next instructions, occupying himself by savagely attacking books of crossword puzzles. I'd never seen anyone work crosswords so fast.

At first, it felt good to drive; for the first hour or so, I could almost forget about the man with the gun and the puzzles in the backseat, the woman speed-reading reference works in front, the bruises on my body. But then the fatigue set in at almost the same time as the bad weather. I hadn't driven a car in years, not since I'd gotten to New York. Even with the wipers going and the defrost on full blast, I could barely see the road in front of me, and I'd forgotten the faith that driving sometimes requires, the faith that there will be more straight highway beyond that hill before you, that the pickup truck ahead won't lead you over a cliff. Jed Roth had told me that writing was like stepping on the gas and never looking back; the way I used to write before teaming up with Roth had a lot in common with the way I was driving now. Whenever I could finally see clearly through the windshield, some truck would pass, horn blaring, and splatter our car with filthy water. I'd have to slam on the brakes and wait for my heart to slow down before I could speed back up.

Interstate 80 was treacherous, icy, shrouded in fog, and I hardly ever exceeded forty miles per hour on it. I sputtered in and out of black-and-white winter landscapes, stretches of asphalt bordered by snow-covered fields. The country never seems as big as it does when you're driving through whiteout weather with a gun pointed at your skull. Along our way, Iola would occasionally look up from her books and point out road signs that indicated the routes to writers' birthplaces—Norman Mailer's Newark; John Updike's slice of Pennsylvania; Zane Grey's Ohio. Whenever she'd utter a writer's name, I could see a glint of memory flicker across Norbert's face, then extinguish itself. Somewhere, in the deep recesses of his mind, he still remembered.

When my sharp pains resolved themselves into nagging aches and the roads became more passable, I began plotting escapes. I felt that I would soon be able to run again. Still, every time I began to reach for the door handle, Norbert looked up from his puzzles. Whenever I considered jerking the steering wheel, driving off the road or into oncoming traffic, I lost nerve. Upon entering the Hoosier State, where I and, Iola informed me, Kurt Vonnegut had been born, I thought Norbert had finally fallen asleep. I quietly turned on my cellphone, but Norbert's eyes popped open; he asked if I knew what happened to writers who disobeyed him, and when I said I didn't, he snarled, "They get taken out of circulation." He reached forward, grabbed the phone, and flung it out the window.

A lifetime ago, I could have used that phone to call someone who lived nearby and who might have helped me—my dad or some of his colleagues at the university, my high school buddies from our little writing club, our next-door neighbors, who watched our house whenever I had to stay overnight at the hospital with my dad. But tonight, my home state was every bit as strange and desolate as the others through which we had already passed.

As a teenager in Indiana, I had read and reread *On the Road, The Subterraneans,* and *The Dharma Bums* and fantasized about kerouacking my way across America, getting onto the highway and seeking the promise of the undiscovered country. But now my life had become the opposite of a road novel—the end of my odyssey loomed before me not as a promise but as a threat.

Along our route, I paid for everything with my credit cards, hoping to create some trail. Maybe if this ordeal lasted a month, American Express or MasterCard would send some bounty hunter after me. I bought gas for Iola's Opel at Texacos, meals at McDonald's and Ponderosa—my companions never offered to pay and never let me out of their sight. Iola pumped the gas, Norbert always stood behind me on line for food, took the urinal next to mine in the john. And when I was too bleary to drive anymore and I turned off I-70 and paid for a night in a Red Roof Inn, Iola and Norbert insisted that we share a room, a smoker's double with a radiator that exhaled heat that smelled like a locker room. There, Iola slept on a proust in front of the door, Norbert on one against the locked windows, while I took the floor between them, wondering when someone might find me and how, wondering if I would ever be able to sleep at all, then waking up to find that the night had passed far too quickly, and that it was time to get back in the car.

Across the Missouri-Kansas border, I began driving slower and made more frequent stops. I kept hoping Iola and Norbert would falter, let me out of their sight, make the mistake of trusting me. Just one slip, and I could run. By now, I had regained more of my strength, but I also found myself again succumbing to one of my worst tendencies—distrusting people at a distance while sympathizing with them up close. Even with a canino pointed at me, even with my shoulders still aching and my palms sweating as I gripped the steering wheel, I couldn't help but feel a little sorry for Iola and Norbert, hoodwinked by a con to which I was already wise.

Past Topeka, the sun began to dip before us. I could now identify each of the parts of my body that did and did not feel pain. My back was still sore, my wrists and ankles, too. But my legs and arms felt stronger. We were driving along Route 177 when the sun finally disappeared beneath the horizon, and signs began to appear ahead for Lake Eureka, Climax, and Manhattan. Iola reached over, flicked the turn signal, tugged at the steering wheel, and pulled a hard right to exit the highway.

A DESOLATE FIELD

Iola Jaffe had scanned every reference volume and anthology that Norbert had handed to her in the Opel, but she still seemed no closer to finding *The Tale of Genji*. Now, as we stood outside the car, she held her book of maps. Norbert held his gun. In a back pocket, I carried a flashlight Iola had given me, and in my right hand, I held the shovel that had been lying in the trunk. The shovel had a rusted metal blade and a thick, dark green handle. Our car was parked at the side of the two-lane road, and we were now walking alongside it underneath the darkening skies. Our footsteps crunched frozen grass as we passed old silos and barns. Desolate soybean fields were easy to find; not so, a golden cross.

I walked slowly, pretending to limp, and used the shovel as a cane even though I was fairly sure I could run now. But I couldn't see anywhere to run to; there were no cars on the road, and only the occasional truck passing some distance away on Route 177. I knew that route number was the Dewey code assigned to books about social ethics, but if there was a joke or clue in there, I wasn't getting it.

Iola studied her map, then pivoted sharply to the right and began to walk away from the road and onto a vast, snowy field. The night was dark and blue; the half-moon and the halo around it were becoming more distinct. The winds were beginning to pick up. I kept one hand in my pocket, the other on my shovel-cane, my eyes focused on Iola Jaffe's shoes. Norbert stopped to light a vonnegut, throw down a match, and take a drag, but he was still holding his gun and was far too close for me to consider running.

Iola was no longer muttering or soliloquizing. She walked faster over the white field. Still no crosses in sight, golden or otherwise—only snow, dead crops, grass. Soon we were walking in single file—Iola in front, Norbert behind, me in between—moving almost in unison.

With the flashlight, I kept sweeping the barren landscape in search of a road with a police car to flag down, a trucker to befriend, a charming old farmhouse where I could hide. Nothing. No sounds save for wind, footsteps, breaths, and, once, a lonely saramago dog howling far away.

Venus and Jupiter had become visible overhead when I began to discern something white and glowing way off in the distance. And as we continued to walk, that bright whiteness began to resolve itself into individual balls and beams of light shining down upon something enormous, enough light for a stadium.

The faster Norbert and I walked, trying to keep pace with Iola, who had seen the light and was now running toward it, the clearer the image became. The balls of light became blindingly bright bulbs illuminating low, boxy brick buildings and a parking lot. We seemed to be approaching a shopping mall or a highway rest stop, but I couldn't say for sure because, when we finally stopped, we were standing behind whatever it was, and I could see only light brown bricks, slate-colored doors, and a half-dozen snow-covered stone steps that led down to black dumpsters. Iola was no longer consulting her map. Gesturing to the building, she gleefully exclaimed, "We're going in there, lads!" Then she led the way around to the front.

ILLUMINATION

Probably some time in the past, this too had been an empty field, certainly when Iola Jaffe's book of maps had been published, maybe even when Jed and Faye had hatched their plan. Maybe there had even been a golden cross here, whole fields of them. Tonight, though, this was a shopping mall.

On our drive, we had passed scads of malls just like this one, each with their chain fast-food and sit-down restaurants, electronics and clothing stores, and cineplexes. The only difference was that this one was empty—no cars in the parking lot, not even a single security vehicle. The lot was awash in light, but the stores themselves looked dark inside. The numbers 1 through 12 were visible on the cineplex marquee, but there were blank spaces where titles ought to have been.

To our right was a shuttered Best Buy; across a service road, a dark Potbelly Deli Sandwich Works; and before us was the entrance to 3B: Big Box Books. The company had gone into receivership, and the two other big chains were vying to take it over; this particular 3B was going or had already gone out of business. In front of the locked doors were shelves of remaindered hardcovers—travel guides, children's story collections, an atlas of the moon. Anyone could have taken the books, but no one else was here. Snow had flecked onto the frozen book spines.

The doors were locked, but Norbert jimmied them open with the sharp blade of the jackknife he took out of a pants pocket. A sign in the vestibule read NO SMOKING, but Norbert lit another vonnegut anyway, and threw down his match. The red light on the security camera above wasn't flashing; no alarm sounded when we entered the store.

Flashlight in one hand, I pointed out a path over the speckled gray carpet and down the main aisle as I limped along with the shovel. The store was indistinguishable from every other 3B in which I'd attended author readings then departed halfway through in a dark, envious mood, flipped through magazines and books without ever considering buying them, or wandered about, grousing that my work was still unpublished while this joker's was on sale for $24.95. The café and magazines were up front; the music section was in back; the nonfiction books were up and to the left, the fiction up and to the right. An information kiosk at the back of the main aisle had a computer monitor flashing the 3B logo.

As we walked, I swept the flashlight over the front sale tables, picking out books: stacks of Blade Markham paperbacks—"Soon to be a major motion picture." On the bestseller table was *We Never Talked About Ceaușescu;* Jens Von Bretzel's *Counter Life* was on the BUY TWO GET ONE FREE grab table. I wondered where *The Thieves of Manhattan* would wind up, then decided it wouldn't matter much; Norbert could tell me where all this store's merchandise was headed—out of circulation, then off to the pulping mill.

I began approaching the aisles on the right when Iola said, "Give me that damn torch," then snatched the flashlight from me. She pointed it directly in front of her as she stepped purposefully to the fiction shelves, passing the beam of light over one row of books and then the next, muttering with what sounded like anticipation.

From what I could see in the illumination provided by her flashlight, she was continuing to seek out books with crosses in their titles, poems with references to bleak or desolate fields. She found the complete works of G. K. Chesterton, which included the short story "A Golden Cross," and a collection of poetry containing William Carlos Williams's "A Desolate Field," but nothing seemed unusual about those books. She kept looking.

Norbert grabbed hold of a sleeve of my gogol and led me away from Iola, pulling me across the aisle to Nonfiction. "This *wigh*," he said, for an idea seemed to have occurred to him.

"Wot useta be your name was again?" he asked.

"Ian Minot," I said.

Not the answer he was looking for; he shoved his canino against my chest. "Wot useta be the name of the man you said you wasn't?"

"The man who I told you wrote the book?" I asked. "Roth. Jed Roth."

Norbert shuddered, then shook off his disgust and nodded. He led me onward fast, a fierce and purposeful expression on his face. When we got to the nonfiction shelves, he pressed his canino against my back; with his other hand, he dragged on a vonnegut. Then he put the vonnegut between his lips and struck a match to light up the books on the shelves in front of us. I wanted to ask what he could possibly be looking for, but the more attention he paid to the books, the less he paid to me, and the better chance I might have to run.

Across the main aisle, Iola was walking back and forth, holding the flashlight steady, as if painting a long wall with it. She muttered aloud names of authors and titles of books that she apparently could see in the beam of light. It sounded as if she were casting some spell: "Ambler, Borges, Calvino"; "Chandler, Christie, Conan Doyle." Every time she said an author's name, Norbert's eyes flickered in recognition, but I could sense Iola's frustration growing—all this time, all these years; still she had nothing—all these clues for a mystery that she still couldn't solve.

When Norbert and I reached the reference section, I began muttering aloud book titles and author names too. I pulled down books and pretended to study them as if they might hold some secret, but Norbert seemed to understand I was faking it and knocked down whatever book I was holding with the nose of his gun. Maybe he'd take his eyes off me, I thought; if I could run away fast enough, he'd have a hard time finding me in the store. I started looking for a particularly heavy and thick book, one I could bring down hard on Norbert's skull.

In the light of one of Norbert's matches, I could see a copy of *Books in Print* on a low shelf—that book looked like it could inflict some serious harm, I thought. But before I could reach for it, Norbert grabbed the book and grinned. "There's the bloke," he said. He tossed down his vonnegut, then dragged me toward the information kiosk, where he began roughly flipping through the book in the glow of the 3B computer monitor.

When he got to the R's, Norbert stopped flipping. And then his eyes lit up again, even more so than they did when he had filled in the last word of a puzzle, when Iola mentioned the name of an author he seemed to recall, or when he was beating me with his gun. He shoved me toward the literary anthologies section, where Iola was already standing, passing her flashlight over book spines. Norbert reached down and grabbed a slender volume, a collection of contemporary adventure stories. The title was printed in white type on a black background: *Unknown Tales*. I remembered that title; it was one of the few anthologies to which Jed Roth had contributed before he had given up writing.

Norbert handed the book to Iola and looked at her, seeking approval. And when Iola turned to the table of contents, her lips formed a small, craggy cheshire. She thrust the flashlight into my hands, then turned to a story near the back of the book: " 'A Desolate Field, Beneath a Golden Cross,' a short story by Jed Roth." There was a biography of the author at the bottom of the first page: "Jed Roth is an editorial assistant in Manhattan, where he is also working on his first novel, *A Thief in Manhattan.*"

I was just beginning to try to figure out how this book had gotten here, when Iola shouted "Eureka!" A slip of paper had been folded into quarters and inserted between the pages of Roth's story. Iola removed the folded sheet, then handed me the book, which I stuffed into a pocket of my gogol.

"*Wot* that is?" Norbert asked, squinting at the paper Iola was holding.

Iola patted Norbert on the shoulder. "The stuff dreams are fucking made of, Norbert," she said. "A treasure map."

ON A DARKLING PLAIN

Jed Roth told me he had always liked treasure maps; he put one in just about every story he wrote, said that all good adventures should have at least one, preferably yellowed and blackened with burn marks, with generous use of the word *ye,* and evocative place-names, such as Dead Man's Cove, the Sea of Serenity, or Smuggler's Lair. He liked terrifying warnings marked with skulls and crossbones—Here Be Dragons.

The map that had been hidden "outside Manhattan" in "A Desolate Field, Beneath a Golden Cross" looked like an antique—brittle, yellow paper; charred edges—but the writing on it suggested it was a recent work: "Ye Olde Potbelly Sandwich Works," "Lair of the Circuit City," "Target's Cove." The Game Zone and Hot Topic stores were labeled with shaky capital letters—"Here Be Mall Rats!" Clearly, this was Faye's work; she was leading us onward.

Iola held the flashlight with one hand while she traced the route on the map with a slender finger and nimbly made her way to 3B's main corridor between Fiction and Nonfiction. Beneath the NO SMOKING sign at the front of the store, Norbert paused to light another vonnegut before we stepped out into the white-bright parking lot underneath the cold black Kansas sky.

Past Old Navy Reef we walked, out of the mall, farther and farther away from Ye Olde Route 177. Wind howled, leaves crackled as Iola counted off the paces indicated on the map. I trudged behind her. We approached another expanse of frozen field, even darker than the one we had traversed before; by now, the moon had disappeared behind a low, purple-gray cloud that was speeding through the sky.

As the mall receded behind us, there was no sign of any town, none of any civilization save for the mall itself, which seemed as if it had been built in the hopes that a population might grow around it. But the mall had come and gone, and the town had never arrived. The air smelled clean but with a hint of smoke—I turned around to see Norbert drag on his cigarette as the air grew foggier.

"Straight ahead, ay," Norbert said. His voice sounded gentler now—he had discovered something that met with Iola's approval, and now he, too, was succumbing to the excitement.

As for me, I knew that I was running out of time. Whose fault would it be when they learned that no *Tale of Genji* was here, that everything I had told them before was true? Upon whom would they take out their frustrations and their disappointment? In Roth's manuscript, his hero shot Iola and Norbert dead, then buried them in the desolate field. But I had cut that scene, and anyway, I wasn't the one with the canino. In the book, I managed to "wrest the gun away" from Norbert, but exactly how was that supposed to work? I might have put up a good fight against some of the men I'd met when my dad took me along to librarians' conferences, but Norbert was no typical librarian. The directions on the map were leading us farther into darkness, and the fog was growing thicker.

This was a hell of a place for an adventure to end, I thought, on some futile march through this dark and cold. As we walked, I cursed everyone who had brought me here—my mother, who had given birth to me and died before I knew her; my father, who had given me faith in stories and dreams, but left me too soon to know where that faith would lead; I cursed the Confident Man and I cursed Faye for pointing him out to me; I cursed Anya and Anna Petrescu, and I cursed Blade Markham; I cursed Geoff Olden, and I cursed Jim Merrill, Jr. I cursed Norbert Piels, and I cursed Iola Jaffe; most of all, I cursed myself: I cursed the author of *The Thieves of Manhattan,* who had led me to this fate, and I cursed Ian Minot, who had been too stupid and naïve to anticipate it.

And then, when Iola stopped walking, I cursed the crosses that I saw before us in the middle of a little Kansas family plot, in which every headstone displayed the name Blom. I cursed Faye's painting that was still hanging in my apartment with its country house, its gleaming white car, its meadow, its graveyard, and its title, *No Place Like Home*. I cursed the freshly turned grave that had no headstone and was marked only by a golden cross. I cursed the man whose eyes ignited as he said, "That's it, is it?" I cursed the woman who took a deep breath, then said, "At long fucking last." I cursed the thick, smoky air as I pulled out the cross. It wasn't a cross for Christ; it was a T for Truth, I told myself, and now that truth—either an empty grave or a forged manuscript—would finally be revealed. I tossed the cross onto the earth, then began to dig.

MY SWEET LORD

Two feet down, mounds of black earth atop the snow on either side of me, there was still no sign of any book, but Norbert urged me to *keep at it, ay,* while Iola anxiously muttered Shakespeare soliloquies and swearwords. My hands were cold; they ached as they clutched the shovel handle, and I could feel pain in my shoulders and back with each plunge into the earth. But I kept digging; at least, the deeper I stood in the ditch, the less I could feel the snow and wind.

When the hole was waist-deep, I could feel the dirt in my

nostrils, taste it on my tongue. Another foot of earth, another mound; the ground was getting rockier, harder to dig. I was growing woozy and delirious, and the wearier I felt, the more I considered just surrendering. I could lie down, hands across my chest; the grave was ready-made. I sank the shovel into the earth one more time. And then I heard a clang as it hit something hard and metal.

"Wha's tha'?" Norbert asked.

Five feet above me, Iola sprang to attention, and now so did I. Norbert threw down his vonnegut and lit another. I dug once more, heard a louder clang.

"Wha'sat?"

I stopped digging and cleared away the dirt. Iola pointed her flashlight into the hole, and I could see what appeared to be a metal case with a dull red handle. Iola's hands shook, her eyes sparkled; she looked ten years younger. Norbert panted as he bent his knees, desperate to learn what I'd found.

I pulled the case out of the earth. Something inside seemed to shift. It felt like a manuscript, maybe a book. I remembered how Roth and I had described *The Tale of Genji,* and now I could picture it: the shimmering gold Japanese characters on the black leather cover, the lovely, intricate illustrations.

"Don't you dare jiggle it," said Iola.

I laid the case on the ground above me, then climbed out of the grave. Iola crouched over the case. From her pocketbook, she removed a pair of thin white cotton gloves, and put them on. She flicked aside the few remaining particles of dirt. Norbert was watching me closely, but I could see him beginning to shift his weight, lick his lips, bob his head. I held on tightly to my shovel, my pulse accelerating.

Iola put her ear to the combination; she twirled one dial, then another, and a third. There was a click, a clunk, then another click, and I couldn't tell whether that click was the hammer of Norbert's gun or the cylinders of the lock engaging. I couldn't run now, even if I wanted to—not until I learned what was inside.

Iola opened the case. "Jesus," she said as she eyed its contents. *"Jee-hee-zus."*

THE TREASURE OF THE *GENJI*

I didn't know whether "Jesus" meant good or bad. I wasn't looking at Iola or at the case yet; I just kept looking at Norbert.

"Jesus," Iola said again, and when she said it one more time, Norbert took his eyes off me. He looked over to Iola, then down to the case. His eyes opened wide as he mouthed the words, *"Wot that is?"* And in that moment, I raised the shovel high and brought its blade down hard on his hand, right on one of his tattoos. Norbert yelled, his hand opened, and his gun fell onto the snow. When he reached for it, I thrust the shovel handle hard into his guts. He doubled over. I lunged for the gun, and grabbed it.

I pointed the canino at Iola and Norbert, no longer feeling any pain. Norbert made as if to speak. "Quiet," I said and pulled back the hammer. I told both of them to stay still, and how did that sound like a good idea?

Norbert shuddered, clearly expecting me to show no mercy. He put his hands over his head, stepped backward toward the edge of the hole I had dug, and quietly asked me to put the gun down, *put it down, ay.* I told him to keep his mouth shut. Iola was still staring at the case, inside of which was not *The Tale of Genji,* but a 250-page manuscript; on the title page—*Zero Ninety-eight, A Memoir by Ian Minot.* Someone had brought my book here, buried it right in time for me to save myself, the same person who had put Faye's map in 3B's copy of *Unknown Tales.* Maybe Joseph, I thought, maybe Roth, but I was hoping that Faye had done it, that she had stopped at Morningside Coffee, found Joseph, and gotten the manuscript from him.

Iola's voice trembled as if she was finally feeling the chill of the winter air. She picked up *Zero Ninety-eight* and somberly paged through it—*what the hell was this shit,* she asked; this couldn't have been what she had spent so many years searching for.

I kept my index finger on the gun's trigger as Norbert teetered at the grave's precipice. Now all it would take would be two squeezes of the trigger, and down both Iola and Norbert would fall, just as in Roth's original draft, in which his hero shot the pair of them without even a hint of remorse, an act that took him little more than a sentence to describe. Iola and Norbert had thought I was digging to find *The Tale of Genji,* but now it must have appeared to them as if I had been digging their grave. The buried manuscript of *Zero Ninety-eight* was a nice touch, a little turn of the screw, as Jed would have said, enough to distract Iola and Norbert and give me time to make my move.

Iola's face was ashen and Norbert was now a fearful, faceless creature, preparing to tumble into the abyss that awaited. He knew all too well what happened to men in his situation—they got shelved, remaindered, pulped. I could see his pulse beating against the tattoos upon his temples, making them dance. And it would be so easy, I felt now, just like in a book—*click* and *bang*. They would fall, I would shovel the dirt over them, then run back for the Opel and drive east—on to the next chapter. I was sure I could get away with it too. Interviewers would ask the same question they asked of Blade Markham: Wouldn't I feel afraid that the people I wrote about would try to *take me out*? "Nah," I'd say, "those punks I wrote about, they all dead, yo." Yes, I could almost do it now. For a moment, I didn't give a damn about Iola or Norbert or anyone else. How much mercy had they shown me, after all?

I studied Norbert's face, and for the first time I began to look closely at the swirls and crisscrosses of his tattoos. The raised lines still seemed to have no clear pattern; they now reminded me of bursts of lightning, or cuts on a shattered mirror. Or, more probably, I thought as I stepped closer to him, bruises from an accident and scars left by fire—like scars left after running through a burning library, still looking in vain for a book that was already gone.

In those tattoos—those scars and bruises—and in the creases on Iola's face, I could imagine all that this pair had been through to find *The Tale of Genji,* the most valuable document that either thought they had ever seen. I considered the chases, the struggles, the fire, finally the glimmer of hope, but now, at last, the defeat. In their faces, I could see how what they had experienced could drive them to want to kill. I understood that feeling, had the canino in my hand and my finger on its trigger to prove it. But that old fault of mine was emerging big-time— loathing at a distance; sympathizing up close. Empathy might be a good quality for a writer, but it's not very useful to a man holding a gun. Looking at Iola and Norbert, I thought about the lives Roth and I had written for them, the ones I thought we had invented but now I understood were true, the ones that Roth had left out of his draft, which made killing the pair of them seem easy. I imagined Iola whiling away thankless hours in dim libraries and classrooms, working on a book she would never finish, articles she would never publish, losing her job at the university where she taught, and growing more bitter with each passing year. I imagined who Norbert had been before the accidents and the fire—the promising scholar, the best research assistant Iola had ever had, the one who could instantly recall nearly everything he had ever read. I imagined the *Genji,* how much it would have been worth to Iola and Norbert had it been real—not only the money it could bring, but the notoriety and perhaps even a chance at redemption. And all they had gotten for their troubles was the shame of learning that they had been fools to believe they would ever find it. I knew all too well what it felt like to be taken for a fool. I played out Roth's ending over and over in my mind—Norbert first, down he'd go, then Iola. Shovel the dirt, grab the manuscript, run. Life can be cheap in a novel; but in a memoir, it's harder to kill.

And so instead of shooting Iola and Norbert, I lowered the canino and told them the whole story, everything that had really happened as far as I knew, from the time I met Jed Roth to the way we ended up here. I told them that it was all written in the manuscript I'd unearthed. And when I was through, Norbert quietly and resignedly asked what I would do with them; he still seemed to expect that I would shoot them dead like all good villains do after they've told their stories to their victims. But I was feeling better than I had in weeks—alive, in control, and even a bit giddy. I pulled my wallet out of my back pocket and took out a business card from the Olden Literary Agency—"in case you meet someone else with a great story to tell," Geoff liked to say. I suggested that Norbert and Iola go back to New York, lie low, write their story, and when they were done, find Geoff; he'd know what to do with it—after everything Jed and I had written about them, allowing them the chance to tell their side of the story seemed only fair. I told Norbert and Iola to get moving fast before I changed my mind.

When I heard the chugging of an approaching highsmith, I tossed down the shovel, picked up my manuscript, put it in the metal case, closed it, and started running with the case and the gun. I had no phone or watch to tell me what time it was, but I had a pretty good feeling that it was the same number as the combination for the metal case: 8-1-3.

As I ran for a black freight car with a wide-open door, I could glimpse Iola and Norbert. They were running through the graveyard back toward the highway and the deserted mall. Iola was holding the flashlight; Norbert was holding the most valuable item he'd been able to find: the golden cross. In some strange way, I wished them well. But now the air behind me was getting even thicker, the clouds in front of the moon were moving faster, and as I made out the tiny glint of Norbert's cigarette tip fading into the night, I could see that smoke was coming from the mall: Big Box Books was on fire.

THE HAND THAT SIGNED THE PAPER

Growing up in small-town Indiana, I learned early on that hopping onto freight cars is much easier than jumping off them. Once you grab hold, the train practically lifts you all by itself. And tonight, when I saw the hand reach out toward me from the darkness inside the car, I knew I could get on board without even losing balance or breaking stride, just as the hero of *The Thieves of Manhattan* had done. So when I found myself lying on my back on the floor of the car with the metal case and the canino at my side instead of in my hands, I knew the person who had pulled me up had tripped me. I had hoped that Faye might be on board the train, but when a green light along the tracks shone into the car, it lit up the face of Jed Roth, who was wearing his black gogol and matching capote. He helped me to my feet, shook my hand, and smiled. But he was holding the canino now, and though he wasn't pointing it at me, he didn't look as though he was planning to return it.

"Dead, are they?" he asked, and when I didn't say anything, he asked if I had checked Iola's and Norbert's pulses. As always, there was a rote expectancy to his questions, the unflappability and confidence that had always alternately charmed and annoyed me, as if he assumed I was still acting a part in his story. But there was a new bitterness to his demeanor. I brushed dust and dirt off my pants, then sat atop the metal case, while he sipped tea from a thermos cup.

The inside of the train car was dark, and so I could see Roth's face only in flashes provided by white and amber high-

way lights; by the pale half-moon when it emerged from behind
the clouds; or by the pulsing reds of fire trucks rushing to Big
Box Books. Roth looked even older and more severe than when
I had last seen him. Once, he had looked like the man I hoped I
might become; now like a man I hoped I would never turn into.

"Dead, are they?" he asked again. His voice was cold and
authoritative, his eyes dark and fierce, as if he had stopped playing a game, or as if he was now revealing that he had never been
playing a game at all. It seemed clear what he thought had
happened—Iola and Norbert were dead, just as he had written
in his original draft; I was still alive, so I must have managed to
"wrest the gun away," shoot them, bury them there in the frozen
ground, and run for the train. Now Roth was pointing the
canino at me, looking as blank and unsympathetic as a character
in a story he had written.

The moon peeked out from behind a cloud, for a moment
revealing the intensity in Roth's eyes, the mad rage and hatred
that he apparently felt no more need to conceal. But I met them
with the same intensity with which they regarded me. I
wouldn't answer yes, because that would mean moving on to
what I imagined would be the next part of Roth's plot—me with
a hammett in my guts, flying backward out of the train, rolling
down into an empty field, while he would go off to find the
girl. In Roth's story, only one man was on board the highsmith
heading away from that field outside Manhattan, and his name
was Roth. I should have known not to trust him the minute I'd
finished reading his manuscript for the first time; he was an
amoral writer, cold and unfeeling, didn't give a damn about his
characters—all he cared about was getting on with the plot.

"You checked the pulses?"

"I didn't," I said, trying to speak in the same concise and self-assured manner that Roth had when he was pulling me into his story.

"What?" he asked.

Roth tried to maintain his characteristically confident look, but in the twirling orange light of a tow truck stalled at a crossing, I could see it fading. He asked his question again.

"Dead, are they?"

"No, they're not, Jed."

Roth was silent for a moment.

"What happened after they found out the case was empty?" he asked. "What did you do, Ian?"

I could now hear an unfamiliar tremor in his voice as our train passed beneath a highway. We had both emerged into uncertain territory; I could see that he had no idea that the case had not been empty, that it had contained my manuscript of *Zero Ninety-eight*. He had no idea that I had even written it. That had not been a part of our story. Jed hadn't buried the manuscript beneath the golden cross, that was for sure; either Joseph or Faye had done it, and had helped to change the plot Jed thought he had planned so well.

"The case wasn't empty, Jed."

"What happened?" Roth asked, for apparently he couldn't come up with his own answer—he had forgotten what it was like to have to wonder *What if*. I now thought of what Roth had told me when we were discussing strategies for getting our book published—the smarter and more powerful a person is, the easier it is to trick him; find the cockiest man you can—taking him down is as easy as swatting a fly. It's the inexperienced guy you have to watch out for. I opened the metal case and took out the manuscript of *Zero Ninety-eight*. I thrust the pages at him, and as the train slowed in a pale yellow caution light's glow, I instructed him to read.

"Why should I?" asked Roth.

"Read it and I'll tell you."

"What for?"

"Read it and you'll know."

Warily, Roth took the pages from me and put the gun down at his side. The manuscript wasn't long; even a slow reader could have made his way through it in an evening. But Roth could only steal glimpses through the lights we passed, and so I closed my eyes and slept soundly for the first time in weeks, confident that, even though he still had the canino, even though I was sure that he still wanted to use it on me, he wouldn't do anything to me before he had finished the book.

LOVE AND CONSEQUENCES

By the time Roth reached the last page of *Zero Ninety-eight*, dawn had broken, casting his face and my manuscript in a deep blue glow. I had been awake for about half an hour. I discovered that the *Unknown Tales* anthology was still in my gogol pocket, and I spent a few minutes reading Roth's story, "A Desolate Field, Beneath a Golden Cross." It was a diverting little sketch, one that had formed the basis for the shootout scene in *A Thief in Manhattan*. But since the characters were thin, the violence seemed gratuitous, and the story felt trivial and recycled. I could have helped Roth develop his characters, make them more sympathetic and their dialogue more believable, but as it stood, the story would have been a whole lot more compelling had any of it been true.

I was admiring the glacial and conical shapes that ice and snow had made atop the rusted cars in the junkyards we passed when Roth finished reading *Zero Ninety-eight*. He could have pretended that he didn't care I had written everything I had learned about him and the plan he and Faye had hatched, but the hand that held my manuscript was quivering, and when he had read the last page, his face had gone pale. He put down the manuscript, took a breath, and looked up. He didn't have to ask what had happened or what might happen next—I knew that's what he wanted to know. And because Roth had taught me that the best lies are always intertwined with facts, I began by telling him I had made copies of the book he had just finished reading. And then I told him I had sent one copy to Geoff Olden with clear instructions about what he should do with it if anything happened to me, conveniently leaving out the fact that Iola and Norbert had gotten to Morningside Coffee and knocked out Joseph, and that as far as I knew, Joseph hadn't been able to deliver *Zero Ninety-eight* to Geoff.

I told Roth that if he left me alone, I would continue to act out the whole scenario just as we had discussed. He could sell *The Tale of Genji* as he and Faye had planned, and when I felt the moment was right, I would do exactly as Roth and I had agreed, reveal that *The Thieves of Manhattan* was a lie so that he could have his revenge. As for *Zero Ninety-eight,* I would promise never to publish it unless anything happened to me, in which case the whole story would be revealed.

I put out my hand for Roth to shake.

Roth regarded the manuscript on the floor beside him, then my hand; he searched my eyes as if wondering whether I might prove more trustworthy than he had ever been. It was a rotten bet for him to make, considering all he'd taught me, but it really was the only one he had. Kill me, and he risked blowing the whole plot; let me live, he might still get away with it. Slowly, he reached out to grasp my hand, even though I could see that it was just about the last thing he wanted to do.

"Now, the canino," I said.

Roth's facial expression was becoming one I no longer recognized—part admiration, part envy, part nostalgia, as if I were now something he had only dreamed of, as if he were a Geppetto whose Pinocchio had slipped his strings and become real. There was something he didn't understand about people in books and in real life—they didn't always do what you wanted or expected them to or what you thought your plot required; sometimes, they took on lives of their own.

Roth handed the gun to me; I took it, then threw it out the open door. I didn't need it anymore; I had *Zero Ninety-eight* on my thumb drive and that was enough protection for me. A gun might not wound Jed. He could even wrest it away from me, but the knowledge contained in *Zero Ninety-eight* could derail his plot. I picked up the copy of the manuscript that Roth had read, skimmed it, glanced at the last page, then tossed it out of the train, one page after another, as if to symbolize to Roth that I meant to keep the promise I had made to him. I sat back down upon the empty case and asked Jed where the forged *Genji* was really hidden.

"In a safe-deposit box," Roth said. For once, his voice sounded almost humble.

We sat in the train, me on the metal case, him on the floor, watching the fleeting American landscape—flatlands giving way to hills; empty fields becoming housing tracts, malls being built or going out of business. For a long time, Roth said nothing, but I could see him thinking, wondering, trying to figure out how the tables had turned so quickly. He liked stories that ended well, ones in which heroes got what they wanted. But now I knew he couldn't say for sure which of us was the hero.

Roth sighed. In some adventure novels, he said as he gazed out the door, this might be the time to tie up loose ends, to tell me more about Faye's childhood as heir to the Blom family, about what he and Faye had in common. He would describe the old Blom family home, which had been leveled to make way for a shopping mall; then he'd make wistful observations about old worlds that were disappearing. But he said he always skimmed long speeches in books, and he never cared for the surprise revelations that tended to pop up toward the end of mysteries. All I really needed to know was that once, he had seen a girl in a strange, doomed library, and had risked his life to bring her something he thought she wanted. In return, she had given him an idea for a story he hadn't known how to finish. And now, even though he understood that their story wasn't over, and that it might not turn out the way he had written it, he knew that the only choice he had was to still trust it. He had to have faith that she would be waiting for him, just as the story promised she would, and that they would escape together.

But I wasn't so sure about that. For I had recognized Faye's handwriting at the bottom of the last page of *Zero Ninety-eight,* the page Roth had been reading when his face went white. And the words she had written there had convinced me that she was in charge of this story now, that she was helping to create it even as Jed and I spoke, that she had managed to get *Zero Ninety-eight* from Joseph, then bury it in the empty field, knowing that I could use it to save myself. She was doing the same thing she did in her art—taking a story she knew, and making it her own. She had written the same basic message that Jed had left for me in his apartment: "Maybe I'll see you after the last page." I felt pretty sure now that Faye intended that message for me.

I asked Roth what he would do with the money from the sale of the *Genji*. He paused a moment and considered.

"We'll build another library," he said. "We'll fill it full of fakes. We'll write another story. And then another. Fool as many people as we can."

But I wasn't sure about that either. Faye had told me she didn't like sequels, and I figured she probably didn't much care for the sorts of stories Jed invented—too violent, too many people getting hurt. Maybe that was one of the reasons why she might have hidden my manuscript in the desolate field—not only to let me show Iola and Norbert that I'd been telling the truth, and Roth that I knew all about his plot, but also to show me that she understood the difference between the sorts of stories that each of us wrote. I knew that she preferred my stories, ones that may have been quiet and uneventful, but everything in them felt true. The question that neither Roth nor I could answer was whether she preferred me or him.

"Do you even love her?" I asked Roth.

"There is an inseparable bond between her and me," he began. But I recognized that quote—it came from *The Tale of Genji*. It had been borrowed just like the plots of Jed's stories. Faye wasn't real to him—he didn't love her for her art or for who she was, only for what she could do for him. We were both just characters in a book to Roth, useful devices who could help get him his money and his revenge.

When I finally saw her, she was leaning against the hood of a gleaming white car stalled at a railroad crossing. She was wearing a sky blue Kansas concert jersey, and her red hair was flying out from beneath a black corduroy baseball cap.

Roth stood in the doorway of our train car. He shook my hand once more, took a breath, then leaped from the train. He leaped as if he understood the speed of railroad cars and knew how quickly the ground would come up to meet him, for that's the way it had happened in a book; as he touched the grass, he didn't even break his stride. He held one hand atop his capote, and the tails of his black gogol seemed to fly as he ran through the snow toward Faye, but she was smiling at me as my highsmith sped east toward Manhattan, New York, and the rising sun.

FAMOUS ALL OVER TOWN

The Thieves of Manhattan had been out for nearly three weeks. I had completed the first leg of my author tour with a standing-room-only gig in Coral Gables, Florida, and had just gotten back to New York for the celebration at Geoff Olden's. Everything was going according to the original plan. Though the booksellers I'd been meeting around the country had told me horror stories—publishers consolidating; regional sales reps losing their jobs; independent bookstores shutting down; publicists canceling author tours; Miri Lippman turning *The Stimulator* into an online-only journal—none of this seemed to be affecting *Thieves*.

My schedule was booked solid, the film was in production, *Myself When I Am Real* was being hurried into the Merrill pipeline. There was a global recession on, and it was apparently the perfect time for a story of riches, thievery, and a rogue who was willing to risk his life to give a girl he loved something precious and rare. I was even featured in *U.S. News & World Report,* interviewed by the real Simian Gold. Best of all, neither Gold, nor any other reporter or feature writer who interviewed me, ever asked whether my story was true. No journalist had been enterprising or curious enough to try to track down Iola and Norbert to learn what had happened to them. I didn't breathe a word about the provenance of *The Tale of Genji* or about *Zero Ninety-eight.* As for my readers, when they asked how I'd managed to lead such an eventful life and I smiled and told them I had made everything up, they seemed to think I was joking or acting modest. When they asked if I had any tips for writing memoirs, I told them to steal someone else's. What Roth had told me was right—truth can be the best kind of lie; what makes it false is why you're telling it—say, for instance, telling the story of your father's illness or your mother's tragic death to gain a reader's sympathy and trust.

Geoff Olden's townhouse was as opulently appointed as ever; yet on the night I was the guest of honor, it seemed smaller than the last time I was there, when Blade Markham had threatened to take my life but took my girl instead. Jim Merrill, Jr., was popping hors d'oeuvres into his mouth; Rowell Templen was on the back deck, drinking a fitzgerald and holding forth to a pair of editorial assistants, both of whom were awaiting the right time to tell Rowell that they had story collections they were looking to sell; Isabelle DuPom had moved on to form her own literary agency, and Geoff Olden had replaced her with another black-clad knockout with an accent. Olden was holding court and cackling; Pam Layne and her assistant, Mabel Foy, were pretending to keep a low profile as they spoke to me quietly and told me to expect an important phone call soon. Joseph, who had lost weight as he prepared to take a role in the film of *The Thieves of Manhattan,* was chatting up a pair of ICM agents, trying to interest them in a diet-and-recipe book that he said he wanted to write for JMJ Publishers. Perhaps Olden's place seemed smaller because Blade Markham wasn't here—even though I now wore a trust cross around my neck and black boots just like his, my personality seemed to occupy less space than his did. Jens Von Bretzel was here too, flipping through a copy of *Thieves,* snorting at it; I could have threatened to roll him—*Something funny 'bout what yer readin', Barista Boy?*—but that still wasn't my style.

My role here was completely reversed from the one I had played at Blade's party—and yet I felt nearly as out of place as I had then. Before, I hadn't been able to tell anybody who I was or what I did because I didn't feel myself worthy of anyone's attention; now I couldn't tell the whole truth because I wouldn't have wanted anyone to know it. I had grown so tired of my spiel— "With a story like this, you don't really write it, man; you gotta live it"—and yet I had no new spiel to offer. I wandered from room to room, snacking on appetizers, drinking cocktails, greeting fans, cutting off conversations early, and listening to snippets of other people's grim dialogue—*film got stuck in turn-*

around; failed to earn out; defaulted on the mortgage; got slammed by Michiko; canceled the paperback; shut down its books section; got gonged by the NEA; had to buy my own lunch at Yaddo; thinking about going back to business school. I was considering asking Joseph if he wanted to leave and get a drink somewhere else when I heard a voice cry out:

Ee-yen!

I hadn't realized how much I missed Anya Petrescu until that moment; when she smiled, dropped the accent, and called me Ian, I was struck by how ordinary my name sounded, how dull both of our own lives must have seemed to us before we started making up stories. Her name was Anna now, and she was holding a bottle of Budweiser and a copy of *Thieves* as she ran from the bar to embrace me, kiss my cheek, and tell me how happy she was for me, how much she loved my book, how much she admired my ability to keep my real life secret from her for so long.

She wasn't wearing one of her usual slim, elegant golightlys, just a black T-shirt, jeans, and boots. I didn't mind the new look; what I truly missed was the way she used to say my name.

"Is that how you really talk?" I asked.

She kept smiling but looked as though she might burst into tears. She said she didn't know; she had spent so much time being Anya, she had forgotten who Anna was. Everything she used to be and wear seemed fake to her now. Anya Petrescu's life, one she had invented from stories she had heard from her friends and relatives, and even from stories I had told her about my parents, seemed too ridiculous to be true, while Anna's seemed too dull to commit to print. Her memoir was going poorly, she added; she hadn't written a word in months.

As I kept listening to Anya, I noticed that she was no longer wearing the engagement ring Blade had given her. When she saw me looking at her left hand, she rubbed the spot where the ring had been.

"He dumped me," she said.

Blade had ended the relationship in the greenroom backstage at *The Pam Layne Show,* just minutes after he learned that she was a fraud, Anna said. He was crushed, couldn't stop crying, kept saying that he couldn't understand why anyone would make up a life she never had, said he would've paid a whole pile of dough to have had an ordinary life like hers. Anya told him she didn't understand why he was so upset; hadn't he invented some parts of his life? Changed some things around? Wasn't that what writers did, what he had done in *Blade by Blade*? Blade had stared at her in disbelief. How could she even think that, he asked. And then he lost it, called her a "low-ass hoodrat," said it was bad enough that she had made up her own life, but what kind of lying buster did she think he was?

That was the last time Anna had seen Blade, she said. Now Anna stepped closer to me and confided that she had never felt as real as she had when she had been with me—being Anya had freed her, made her feel less inhibited, more like who she really was. She sighed and took a breath, reminded me of what she'd said on our last night together: that we should have met earlier, when both of us were different *pipples.*

I felt a pang in my heart as Anna took me by the hand and led me to the back deck, where she told me that she was single and hadn't dated anyone since Blade. For a moment, I thought about pulling her to me, then asking her to sneak upstairs. But I knew that I couldn't trust Jersey Anna any more than I could trust Bucharest Anya, and besides, I didn't want Faye to have been right when she said that my Ukrainian and I deserved each other. So before I went back inside to find Joseph, I just kissed Anna on the cheek, and for the first time in my life, I wished her *goot lock;* I figured that now she could probably use some.

GIRL, YOU KNOW IT'S TRUE

I had promised Jed Roth that I would never publish *Zero Ninety-eight.* I didn't think I would have any trouble keeping my word. I didn't need the money—*The Thieves of Manhattan* was still on the *Times* and IndieBound hardcover bestseller lists; the paperback hadn't even been released yet. *Myself When I Am Real,* my collection of stories, probably wouldn't do as well, but breaking my promise to Jed to bolster my book sales seemed too mercenary, particularly since Geoff Olden had assured me that I could choose just about any topic for my third book and get a whopping frazier for it.

But I still hadn't seen any trace of Faye, no matter how many notes I left at Morningside Coffee with Joseph, who always told me he hadn't seen her, no matter how many letters I sent to the London auction house that had sold *The Tale of Genji* to an anonymous collector for $8.13 million. And the more I thought about it, the more I figured that Faye had meant it when she said I wouldn't see her until "after the last page," until after I'd written the rest of *Zero Ninety-eight* and recounted everything that had happened to me after Norbert and Iola had caught up to me at the coffee shop. I kept wondering if Faye would stay with Roth, or if she would come back to me; if she liked me better or only my stories; if she had truly been the one who had helped to save me as I had suspected or whether I had made all that up. Finishing the book was the only way I could think of to find out.

I spent almost a year writing the rest of *Zero Ninety-eight* while sitting at a window table at Morningside Coffee, drinking tea, and chatting with Joseph, who was usually in far better spirits than he had ever been when I'd worked there. At that table, I wrote about my trip to Manhattan, Kansas, about the desolate field, the fire at Big Box Books, the ride aboard an eastbound train, the night I met Anya again. I suppose I could have left Jed's and Faye's names out of the story, could have written that Faye had forged some book other than *The Tale of Genji*. But I wanted to tell my tale as honestly as I knew how, because I thought Faye would never come back to me if she read my story and saw that I was still telling lies. I figured that any future I might have with her depended on my telling the truth. Jed Roth had told me that a time would come when I would reveal that *The Thieves of Manhattan* was a lie so that he could have his revenge, and now I was revealing the story just as he told me I would. But he hadn't wanted me to tell the whole truth, so I doubted that this book I was writing was what he had in mind.

Completing *Zero Ninety-eight* took far longer than I anticipated, for I wanted to get every detail right. I was writing for different reasons than I ever had—not to escape my loneliness as I used to; not to try to make my rent; not to save my skin; not to play a trick or get revenge or draw attention to my fiction. I was writing to explain to another person who I was now and how much I had come to realize she meant to me; she had given me not only this story, but the chance to tell it and make it true. And as I wrote, I vowed to myself that this would be why I always would write—to tell another human being a story, one that felt meaningful to me, whether it actually happened or I had just made it up—and I sensed that, now that I had lived a true adventure, I knew how to make one up pretty well.

Thieves had ended just as Roth had wanted it to—with a romantic embrace between the hero and the Girl in the Library, who takes the manuscript that he has brought her and melodramatically tells him that true love never has to end, that it should live on "even after the last page." But, though Roth was a decent storyteller, he didn't know too much about how people spoke and acted in real life; he'd read too much, lived too little. I had no priceless manuscript to give the woman I loved, just a story that was as true as I knew how to write it. On the autumn day that I sat in the café with my laptop and approached the end of my story, no one leaped into my arms for a passionate embrace; instead, I just felt a hand on my shoulder. And after I started writing my last page and I heard a woman's voice behind me, it didn't say anything profound or romantic; it just said, "I thought you'd never finish, Sailor." When I looked up, and saw Faye standing there, a cheshire on her face, the moment felt so perfect that I wished it could really be happening. And then I realized it was.

GLOSSARY OF SELECTED TERMS

atwood *n.* A mane of curls as sported by the author Margaret Atwood.

canino *n.* A gun, from Lash Canino, the gambler Eddie Mars's menacing hired hit man in Raymond Chandler's *The Big Sleep.*

capote *n.* A broad-brimmed hat of the sort favored by the author Truman Capote. The hat is often worn to best effect at a rakish angle.

chabon *n.* A wavy mane like the one worn by the author Michael Chabon.

cheshire *n.* A gleeful, mischievous smile that seems to conceal a secret, from the grinning Cheshire Cat in Lewis Carroll's *Alice's Adventures in Wonderland.*

chinaski *n.* The sex act, usually divorced from any pretense of romance, from Charles Bukowski's alter ego Henry Chinaski, who observes in *Notes of a Dirty Old Man,* "Love is a way with some meaning; sex is meaning enough." *Vulgar.*

daisies *n.* Dollars, from Daisy Buchanan, a character in F. Scott Fitzgerald's *The Great Gatsby,* about whom Jay Gatsby remarks, "Her voice is full of money."

droog *n.* A friend or henchman, taken from the Nadsat language invented by the author Anthony Burgess in his novel *A Clockwork Orange.*

eckleburgs *n.* Yellow-framed eyeglasses reminiscent of those that appear on an advertising billboard for the oculist T. J. Eckleburg in F. Scott Fitzgerald's *The Great Gatsby.*

faulkner *n.* Whiskey, from the author William Faulkner, who once observed, "There is no such thing as bad whiskey. Some whiskeys just happen to be better than others."

fitzgerald *n.* A gin rickey, which was said to be F. Scott Fitzgerald's favorite drink.

franzens *n.* The sort of stylish eyeglasses favored by the author Jonathan Franzen.

frazier *n.* A particularly large advance for a book, from Charles Frazier, author of *Cold Mountain,* who was rumored to have received a healthy seven-figure advance for his follow-up novel, *Thirteen Moons.*

gatsby *n.* A stylish men's sport coat or suit jacket that might have been worn by F. Scott Fitzgerald's Jay Gatsby.

ginsberg *n.* A somewhat unruly beard of the sort favored by the Beat poet Allen Ginsberg.

galumph *v.* To move in a decidedly ungraceful manner, coined by Lewis Carroll in his poem "Jabberwocky" in *Through the Looking-Glass.*

gogol *n.* An overcoat, from Nikolai Gogol's "The Overcoat."

golightly *n.* A slim, elegant cocktail dress of the sort favored by the character Holly Golightly in Truman Capote's *Breakfast at Tiffany's.*

hammett *n*. A bullet, from the crime writer Dashiell Hammett, in whose books it is frequently featured, e.g., *Red Harvest:* "The bullet smacked blondy under the right eye, spun him around, and dropped him backwards . . ."

hemingway *n*. A particularly well-constructed and honest sentence, from the author Ernest Hemingway, who once advised himself, "All you have to do is write one true sentence. Write the truest sentence you know."

highsmith *n*. A train, the sort of vehicle that plays key roles in novels such as *Ripley's Game* and *Strangers on a Train,* both by Patricia Highsmith.

humbert *n*. A sexual deviant, from the character of Humbert Humbert, who embarks upon an obsessive sexual relationship with his fourteen-year-old stepdaughter, Dolores Haze, in Vladimir Nabokov's *Lolita.*

kerouac *v*. To take a cross-country road trip, from Jack Kerouac, whose alter ego Sal Paradise journeys from the East Coast to the West and back again in *On the Road.*

kowalski *n*. A sleeveless white T-shirt of the sort favored by the character Stanley Kowalski in Tennessee Williams's *A Streetcar Named Desire,* in which he is depicted by the playwright in one instance as wearing "an undershirt and grease-stained seersucker pants."

lish *v*. To savagely and mercilessly edit, from Gordon Lish, the legendary editor at *Esquire* and Knopf, who is particularly known for the influence he had on the unadorned style of Raymond Carver.

marple *n*. A sensible and decidedly unstylish felt hat of the sort worn by the detective Jane Marple in the works of Agatha Christie.

murasaki *n*. A kimono such as the one worn by the character Murasaki in Murasaki Shikibu's *The Tale of Genji*.

palahniuk *v*. To vomit, taken from the name of the author Chuck Palahniuk, whose works are often said to have a particularly visceral effect on sensitive readers.

panza *n*. An underling, named after the subservient character of Sancho Panza, who plays servant to Don Quixote in the epic by Miguel de Cervantes.

poppins *n*. A graceful, and occasionally parrot-headed, umbrella that seems as if it might possess the ability to fly, the sort favored by the character of Mary Poppins, P. L. Travers's eponymous heroine.

portnoy *n*. The male sex organ, from the titular character in Philip Roth's *Portnoy's Complaint*, who is rather obsessed with this body part. *Vulgar.*

proust *n*. A bed, particularly when used as the locus of inspiration, taken from the favored location of the author Marcel Proust.

Rusty James *n*. A leather jacket of the type worn by Rusty James, narrator of *Rumble Fish*, by S. E. Hinton.

salinger *v*. To live in seclusion, after the reclusive author J. D. Salinger.

saramago dog *n*. A stray mongrel of the sort featured in just about every novel José Saramago has written, particularly in *Blindness* and *The Cave*.

scheherazade *n*. A cliff-hanger so suspenseful that it will keep the reader involved in a story until the next night, from *The Arabian Nights'* Scheherazade, who manages to prevent her execution by telling King Shahryar stories night after night.

steinbeck *n.* A well-groomed mustache like the one sported by the author John Steinbeck.

tolstoy *n.* A particularly large pile, usually of manuscript pages, from Leo Tolstoy, whose *Anna Karenina* and *War and Peace* run around 800 and 1,200 pages, respectively.

vonnegut *n.* A cigarette, after the author Kurt Vonnegut, noted smoker of Pall Malls, who was once quoted as saying that cigarettes were "a classy way to commit suicide."

woolf *v.* To move as rapidly as the speed of thought, from the author Virginia Woolf, who perfected the art of converting her own fast-moving consciousness into prose in such novels as *Mrs. Dalloway* and *The Waves*.

ACKNOWLEDGMENTS

My utmost thanks to Jerome Kramer for proposing a challenge, without which this book would not have been written. Thanks also to Cindy Spiegel and Marly Rusoff for their continued support. Thanks to Christopher Cartmill, Bill DeMerritt, David Engel, Barbara Hammond, Virginia Lowery, Hemmendy Nelson, and Andrew Oswald for participating in the first reading of *The Thieves of Manhattan*. And thanks for many and various reasons to Masako and Rich Aloia, Beth Blickers, Maria Braeckel, Jennifer Gilmore, Richard Green, Mary Herczog, Hana Landes, Bradley Langer, Esther Langer, Kazoo, Val and Claudia Paraskiv, Mihai Radelescu, Wendy Salinger, Trixie the cat, and the staff of the Hungarian Pastry Shop and Café. Thanks always to Beate Sissenich, and to Nora and Solveig Langer Sissenich, the latter of whom entered the world less than three hours after the final draft of this book was completed. And, finally, thanks to all the fake memoirists, fictional poets, literary forgers, and hoaxers who have provided such great inspiration.

ABOUT THE AUTHOR

ADAM LANGER is the author of the novels *Crossing California, The Washington Story,* and *Ellington Boulevard,* and the memoir *My Father's Bonus March.* He lives in New York City with his wife, Beate; his daughters, Nora and Solveig; and his dog, Kazoo. Depending on your definition, this is either his fourth novel or his second memoir.